SWORN TO THE SCOT

BOOKS BY EMMA PRINCE

Four Horsemen of the Highlands:

Ensnared by the Laird (Book 1)

Wager with a Warrior (Book 2)

Hoping for a Highlander (Book 3)

Sworn to the Scot (Book 4)

Highland Bodyguards Series:

The Lady's Protector (Book 1)

Heart's Thief (Book 2)

A Warrior's Pledge (Book 3)

Claimed by the Bounty Hunter (Book 4)

A Highland Betrothal (Novella, Book 4.5)

The Promise of a Highlander (Book 5)

The Bastard Laird's Bride (Book 6)

Surrender to the Scot (Book 7)

Her Wild Highlander (Book 8)

His Lass to Protect (Book 9)

The Laird's Yuletide Bride (Book 9.5)

Deceiving the Highlander (Book 10)

The Sinclair Brothers Trilogy:

Highlander's Ransom (Book 1)

Highlander's Redemption (Book 2)

Highlander's Return (Bonus Novella, Book 2.5)

Highlander's Reckoning (Book 3)

Viking Lore Series:

Enthralled (Viking Lore, Book 1)

Shieldmaiden's Revenge (Viking Lore, Book 2)

The Bride Prize (Viking Lore, Book 2.5)

Desire's Hostage (Viking Lore, Book 3)

Thor's Wolf (Viking Lore, Book 3.5)

Highland Christmas:

To Kiss a Governess (Highland Christmas, Book 1)

A Governess Under the Mistletoe (Highland Christmas, Book 2)

Other Books:

Highland Feud (Shaws and MacRobs, Book 1)

Wish upon a Winter Solstice (A Highland Holiday Novella)

Falling for the Highlander: A Time Travel Romance (Enchanted Falls, Book 1)

The Siren's Kiss (A Medieval Scottish Romance)

SWORN TO THE SCOT

FOUR HORSEMEN OF THE HIGHLANDS, BOOK 4

EMMA PRINCE

For Scott. Always.

CHAPTER 1

Late November, 1332
Scone, Scotland

Artair MacKinnon hadn't laid eyes on the large, spreading oak tree outside Scone Palace's walls since…well, since he'd been hanged from it two months past.

He reined his horse to a walk, giving the tree a wide berth. Yet he couldn't help but stare at it as he passed.

Winter-bare, the tree looked like a skeleton clawing at the darkening sky. The thick branch where he'd swung in his noose still lay on the ground next to the tree's base. The freak lightning strike that had saved his life had left the tree's core hollowed out and charred black as the Devil's own heart.

No one had bothered to fell the monstrous thing. *Good.* It was a reminder of Artair's near-failure—and of his unlikely second chance to extract vengeance against the Usurper.

He doubted he'd get a third.

And mayhap the mangled tree was a reminder to the Pretender King Balliol as well—of his failure to quash the loyalists who would give their lives to unseat him.

Aye, though Balliol was no longer in residence at Scone Palace, mayhap the tree haunted his dreams, as it did Artair's.

At last ripping his gaze from the charred oak, he turned his attention to the palace itself. A high wooden palisades loomed before him, with the singular abbey tower rising beyond its spiked top. Though it was only early evening, night had already begun to fall, and the front gate was closed.

With a barely suppressed groan, Artair dismounted. He patted the destrier's lathered neck, offering a word of praise. He'd pushed the animal—and himself—close to the breaking point this day. Yet his news could not wait.

"Ho!" a voice called somewhere high up on the other side of the palisades. "What is yer name and yer business here, man?"

"Artair MacKinnon, to see Archibald Douglas."

It was strange to give his name so freely when he'd been living as an outlaw these last two months. To announce himself here of all places, where he'd been the Pretender King's prisoner, made a knot of unease tighten in his gut.

There were a few murmurs and the shuffling of feet on the other side of the gate, but it remained shut. Balliol was not here, he reminded himself. Archibald

Douglas, Guardian of Scotland and loyalist ally, controlled Scone in the Usurper's absence.

He'd met with Douglas once before, though not here. He and Douglas had convened outside Arbroath, under cover of night. Despite only one face-to-face encounter, along with a handful of secret missives, Artair instinctively trusted the man. Still, that didn't mean Scone was safe—nor that Artair didn't risk his neck a second time in coming here.

Only now, as he stood waiting outside the palace walls, did he notice the cold. It was sharp as a blade, cutting through his thick cloak. The ride from Old Blair's Stone had passed in a blur. He'd registered neither the icy touch of encroaching winter nor his body's protests at the grueling pace.

Despite his fatigue, restlessness gnawed at him. He resisted the urge to pat the pouch on his belt. The missive from Tavish MacNeal was still there. And even if it weren't, he'd memorized its contents.

At last, the gates groaned open. Despite himself, he tensed, readying to be set upon by Balliol's supporters. But instead of armed soldiers, all that spilled forth from the gates was torchlight.

Artair squinted. A single figure stood haloed in the golden glow. *A woman.*

"Ye are Artair MacKinnon?" she demanded in a low, wary voice.

"Aye."

She hesitated for a long moment. Finally, she stepped aside and motioned him in.

There was no turning back now. Not that Artair

would. He'd waited two long, hellish months to take action against the Usurper. At last the time had come.

At the woman's curt word, the guards closed the gates behind him with a heavy thud. She motioned, and a stable lad ran forward through the palace courtyard to take Artair's horse.

"See that ye walk him until he is cool, and take yer time rubbing him down," he called out after the lad. The destrier had served him well despite how hard Artair had pushed.

Now that his eyes had adjusted to the torchlight filling the yard, Artair took in the woman before him.

It was instantly obvious she was no mere servant. She wore a crimson velvet surcoat over a creamy kirtle that peeked out along the outer gown's square neckline and at the edges of the long sleeves. Both garments had been expertly sewn to hug her slim curves, though her skirts flared at the bottom where extra material had been added—a pure luxury that was apparently the style among fine ladies who could afford it.

Her thick auburn hair was plaited back from her face and held in a delicate clasp studded with pearls. The rest of its length tumbled down her back in waves that shone like liquid fire in the torchlight.

When Artair shifted his gaze to take in her face, he realized she, too, assessed him with keen eyes. Though he couldn't make out their exact color in the flickering light, he had the uncanny impression that they were a rich gold.

She was shockingly beautiful. Even in the yellow glow

of the torches, her skin was pale and faultless as freshly fallen snow. Her features were delicately drawn, except her lips, which were full and the color of summer berries.

More than her bonny face, he was struck by her regal air. She held herself with a refined grace that spoke of wealth and power. Her slim neck was straight and her shoulders back, her hands clasped in perfect repose before her. Despite the fact that he towered over her, she managed to take his measure down the length of her pert nose.

He couldn't imagine what she made of him. He itched with sweat and dirt from a hard day of travel— not to mention the two months he'd lived as a fugitive. He knew his golden hair was unkempt and his jaw bristled. Beneath his cloak, his tunic and trews were serviceable but plain and well-worn.

What the hell was a woman like her doing at Scone Palace at a time like this? Despite the fact that Balliol had taken his army south a month past, it was a time of upheaval and unrest. This was no place for a gentle-bred lady.

Mayhap she was Balliol's mistress, left behind for some unknown reason. Aye, those lips were made for kissing. Or pouting. Mayhap that was how she garnered such fine clothing. He assumed she was unmarried. Except for the pearl-studded clasp, her hair was unbound and uncovered.

Without a word, she turned on her heels and set off across the yard. Apparently he was to follow. Muttering a curse, he fell in behind her. His gaze slid down the length of her cascading auburn hair to the gentle sway of her hips.

He jerked his gaze away. In another lifetime, he would have already flashed her one of his most winning smiles and thrown out a flirtatious comment or two by now, no matter whose mistress she was. But not anymore.

He took in the courtyard instead. He'd only been inside the palace gates once before. He'd been marched through this very yard on his way to be hanged. Then, there had been a hastily erected gallows filling the open space. The hairs on the back of his neck lifted at the echo of the loyalists' screams just before the ropes snapped taut.

"The Guardian wasnae expecting ye," the woman said over her shoulder in that low, velvety voice. Her words yanked him back from the dark memories.

"This couldnae wait," he said simply.

Did she know who he was? She knew his name, aye, but did she understand what it meant—that he was one of the four Highlanders who'd escaped Balliol's noose? And that he now sought the Guardian of Scotland to overthrow the Usurper and return the crown to the rightful King?

Nay, she couldn't. She was a woman, and a high-born one at that. But then again, why was she escorting him to Archibald Douglas herself, when she was clearly no servant?

Once again, the fine hairs at his nape stirred. Something wasn't adding up. He would have reached for his sword, but he had none at the moment.

Despite nerves drawn tighter than a bowstring, he followed her onward. Beneath Scone Abbey's tower, which still rose ahead, several structures had been added to form the palace.

In Robert the Bruce's time, the abbey and the sprawling palace had become the seat of Scotland's power—where Kings were crowned and parliaments convened. And now, where the Guardian of Scotland resided.

Without hesitation, the woman pulled open one of the massive double doors off to the left of the tower. He followed her inside, finding himself in a great feast-hall. As they crossed the space, he took in the hall's grandeur.

It was illuminated with two enormous hearths and dozens of wall sconces. The ceiling soared high, its wooden beams hung with pennants and coats of arms. The walls bore thick, colorful tapestries depicting Scotland's lore—great battles and mythical creatures and the legends of the land's origin.

Several servants moved about, some carrying wood for the fires and others wiping down the trestle tables in preparation for the evening meal.

The woman before him gestured to a passing maid, who hurried over. "Send bread and wine to the solar, Tilda. And warm water for our guest."

"Aye, milady." The maid bobbed a curtsy then hurried off to her task.

Not just a mistress, but a lady with free rein to order the servants about, then.

She strode toward the back of the great hall, where a handful of arched doorways led to a series of corridors. She chose one without hesitation and they wound their way deeper into the palace. Several doors branched from the passageway, but she continued on until they reached a nondescript one on the left.

Without knocking, she pushed her way inside. Whether it was a trap or not, Artair could do naught but follow her.

The chamber was modest, with a single fireplace and no window. A few wall sconces and tallow candles added to the cheery glow. Besides some shelves filled with ledgers and scrolls and a few rough-hewn chairs, the only other feature of the simple space was a large oak desk—behind which sat Archibald Douglas, Guardian of Scotland.

His graying head was bent over a piece of parchment, a quill pinched in his large hand. He scowled in concentration at the note before him and didn't even look up when they entered.

"Sybil, now is no' the time—"

"Artair MacKinnon is here," she interjected. Though her voice was calm and smooth as the surface of an unruffled loch, Douglas jerked to his feet so fast that his chair toppled to the ground with a crash.

"Christ, man! What the hell are ye doing at Scone?"

Suspicion whispered through him. Though he did indeed trust Douglas, he knew naught of the mystery woman beside him. How much could he say?

"Have I come at a bad time?" he drawled.

Douglas visibly reached for his composure. "Nay, nay. But I thought we agreed in Arbroath that we ought to continue through missives. That it was too dangerous to meet until—"

"Aye, until the time had come to make our move," Artair finished.

He gave the woman—*Sybil*, Douglas had called her —a pointed look. Whether she was a servant, Balliol's mistress, or indeed the Virgin Mary herself, Artair would say no more until she was gone.

"We need to speak. *Alone*."

Yet the wench did not budge. Instead, she shifted her gaze—her eyes truly were rich amber in color—to Douglas, waiting.

"Go on, man. Spit it out," Douglas said testily.

Artair ground his teeth together to keep from snapping. Why the hell wasn't Douglas sending the lass away?

"This isnae fit for the ears of innocents," he reiterated tightly, flicking his gaze over the finely-dressed lass. "Or outsiders."

"Luckily there arenae any of those here," she shot back calmly.

Douglas turned to the woman, but instead of chastising her or sending her away, he merely frowned. "Ye didnae introduce yerself to him? Well then, let me do the honors."

Unease coiled in the pit of Artair's stomach even before Douglas spoke.

"Artair MacKinnon, allow me to present Lady Sybil Douglas. My daughter."

CHAPTER 2

S ybil allowed herself to indulge in observing Artair MacKinnon's face as he took in her father's words.

Confusion, followed closely by surprise, flitted through his leaf-green eyes before he shuttered them. If she hadn't been watching closely, she would have missed the subtle reaction, for he schooled his ruggedly handsome features well.

Remotely, she wondered what he'd taken her for if not the Guardian of Scotland's daughter. Aye, most men wouldn't bring their wives and children—or at least not their daughters—into the heart of the vipers' den that was Scone Palace at a time like this. But her father knew her to be more than capable of handling herself here.

Artair MacKinnon, however, did not.

Most men underestimated her—underestimated all women, really. MacKinnon was said to be a strategist, a blade-sharp wit with a keen ability to read and anticipate others' thoughts and actions.

Her very existence had already caught him off-guard once. Secretly, she was eager to do so again, to test herself against him. Now she would find out what sort of man he truly was beyond the wild tales she'd heard.

When he shifted those sharp green eyes to her, she gave him her most gracious smile and tilted her head ever so slightly.

He bowed stiffly. "My lady," he murmured.

"Please sit, MacKinnon," her father said. "Sybil, have ye sent for—"

"Tilda will be on her way now," she answered smoothly before he'd even finished.

Her father gave her an approving nod, which made her chin lift with pride. Aye, let MacKinnon see just how much her father trusted and relied upon her. Mayhap that would erase the cool appraisal that still lingered in his gaze.

As her father righted his chair and sat, she lowered herself gracefully into one of the two chairs before the desk. MacKinnon hesitated before taking his own seat.

"Ye look like hell, man," her father continued in his usual blunt way. "What news?"

MacKinnon looked at her again, clearly warring over how much to say in front of her. She stared back boldly, a wordless challenge lifting one of her brows.

Yet as the silence stretched and their eyes remained locked, she fought to keep her gaze steady and her chin lifted. There was something…unnerving about him.

She couldn't agree with her father's assessment that he looked like hell. Aye, travel-weary and in need of a scrub and a shave, mayhap. But his rough appearance only heightened the force of his presence. His imposing size and pent strength, even sitting, gave her the impression of a lion caged in some royal menagerie.

His dark blond hair was windblown from hard riding. Despite the fatigue that must have been gnawing at him, he sat uneasily in his chair, as if he wished to stand and pace, pick something up. Or mayhap grab a sword and fight, though he was safe here, whether he believed it or not.

The intensity of his eyes, the coiled strength contained in his large, lean frame… He seemed hardly civilized, a stark contrast to the stories she'd heard of his keen wit and easy charm.

At last he spoke, turning back to her father.

"'Tis urgent, but I can wait until yer daughter leaves."

"That willnae be necessary," she replied, even though he'd addressed her father.

This time, he did not look at her. Instead, he studied her father, waiting.

Arrogant Highlander.

She was halted from making another retort by a knock on the door. She rose smoothly, opening it to find Tilda with a tray of everything she'd requested. With a quiet word of thanks to the maid, she took the tray and shut the door firmly.

"My daughter is in a…rather unusual position," her father was saying as she returned to the desk. "I have turned to her for counsel for several years now. She is already aware of our efforts against Balliol. Aught ye would say to me, ye can say to her."

MacKinnon stiffened in his chair. "I thought we agreed to play this close to the chest, Douglas. Yet ye've divulged information—which could have us all drawn and quartered as traitors, mind ye—to yer gentle-bred daughter?"

Sybil set the tray down on the desk, careful not to let her annoyance slosh the bowl of warm water.

"Ye forget—or mayhap ye never knew," she commented evenly as she retook her chair. "I have been involved in this as long as my father. 'Twas I who facilitated first contact between the Guardian and yer fellow comrade in arms, Laird Domnall MacAyre."

From the flash of surprise in his sharp eyes, she knew she'd caught him off-guard again. *Good.* She was all too happy to inform this proud man of the role she'd already played in the rebellion. It seemed he was just like the others—with little imagination for women's abilities outside their roles in bedsport and as political pawns.

To his credit, he waited for her to explain herself.

She casually arranged her skirts for a moment before speaking. "After MacAyre captured the traitor Andrew Murray, he needed a way to deliver the man to the Guardian without drawing Balliol's attention."

"Aye, I knew that much. MacAyre met with ye in secret to turn Murray over to ye," MacKinnon said, looking at her father.

"Which was coordinated through me," Sybil said. "Ailsa Murray—or rather, Ailsa MacAyre now—wrote to inquire about the latest fashions at court. A note of such little import drew no interest from anyone at all. Of course, the encrypted missive inside was a wee bit more significant."

MacKinnon leaned back in his chair, a new light filling his gaze as he assessed her. For some reason she felt the fluttering of wings in her stomach. She smoothed a hand down her velvet surcoat without thinking. Why should she care what he thought of her? She already knew her worth.

"I see. I wasnae aware that MacAyre had taken a wife, nor of the details of yer meeting," he said, glancing at her father once more. "He only mentioned that he felt he could trust ye after ye took custody of Murray. I am glad the traitor received his just deserts for his betrayal at Dupplin Moor."

The last was spoken in a low, hard voice that once again reminded Sybil of some barely-leashed animal.

"Aye," her father said softly. "Once Balliol departed Scone, Murray was easy enough to deal with. Parliament agreed to a swift execution. But of course that doesnae answer the question of the cause's fate."

"That is why I am here."

The air in the small solar grew heavy with anticipation. Yet intuition told Sybil that MacKinnon still wasn't ready to talk. A man who was used to keeping so many vital secrets would need to be coaxed into sharing them, even to a trusted confidant like her father.

Luckily, that was her forte.

And I'll show ye I can do two things at once without my wits becoming muddled. She plastered on a serene smile to cover any chance of the acerbic thought showing up on her face.

"Before we break bread, allow me to wash yer hands after yer travels." She lifted the cloth from the tray and dipped it into the steaming, lightly scented water, then offered her own hand and waited.

MacKinnon's dark gold brows crashed down. "Nay, that isnae—"

"Ye are my father's guest. As the ranking lady of Scone Palace, I insist."

"Verra well," he muttered, then extended one large hand and gently rested it face up in her palm.

Despite that it was November, his skin was bronzed from much time spent out of doors. His palm was heavily callused, likely from both riding and sword-work.

He wasn't just a strategist, she reminded herself. He was a warrior as well. He'd fought and killed at Dupplin Moor, and who knew how many other battles.

As she worked the wet cloth over his skin, he began to relax, letting the weight of his hand settle more fully into her own. It was heavy and nearly twice the size of hers. An unexpected blush stole up her neck and to her face. Fortunately, she could keep her head bent to her task to hide it.

"When last we spoke, ye said one of yer comrades was in the north attempting to drum up support for our cause," her father commented. Though he didn't normally have a knack for delicate maneuvering, his remark worked in getting MacKinnon talking.

"Aye, there is news on that front," he replied. His

voice seemed close. She darted a glance up to find that he'd leaned in toward her as she worked on his hand.

He cleared his throat before going on. "Gregor MacLeod has amassed an army of over one thousand loyalists ready to fight. Highlanders."

Though she'd lived her whole life in the Lowlands, she knew what that meant. Even among fellow Scots, Highland warriors were revered and feared as ruthless, unrelenting fighters. The thought of an army one thousand strong of such men nearly stole her breath.

Her father, too, was stunned speechless for a moment. "Bloody hell. Forgive me, but I wasnae expecting quite such a large force—and in such a short time."

Sybil released his hand and MacKinnon offered his other one for her ministrations.

"There is more," he said after a moment. "When Balliol left Scone a month past, ye told me he was headed for the Lowlands."

Her father grunted. "Aye, the bastard hoped to find a more favorable climate there. He spread his army across the Lowlands to keep the peace, or so he said."

"But no one knew where the Pretender was exactly?"

Her father's bushy salt-and pepper brows lowered. "Nay."

MacKinnon drew a breath. "I've just received word from Tavish MacNeal, who has been hiding out in the Lowlands since…"

Since the four of ye were hanged for traitors, Sybil finished in her head.

Balliol had meant to make examples of them. Each had been a leader in his own way among those loyal to the bairn-King David. But after the loyalists' defeat at the Battle of Dupplin Moor, they'd been captured and taken prisoner, destined for a traitor's death.

After Balliol had crowned himself King, his first act was to order the four Highlanders hanged outside Scone Palace's gates and left to rot there—a reminder to all those who would stand against him.

But by an act of God—or the Devil, some whispered —they had escaped. Word had spread nearly as fast as the lightning strike that had saved them. The Four Horsemen of the Apocalypse, they were called—four Highlanders who'd sworn to rain hell and vengeance on the Usurper King Balliol.

Domnall MacAyre. Gregor MacLeod. Tavish MacNeal. And Artair MacKinnon, whose hand now rested in her own. Only a select few—including Sybil and her father—knew the men's actual names, but it seemed all of Scotland had heard tales of the legendary Highlanders.

She glanced up to find his features hardened, his gaze distant as he, too, likely thought of that dark time.

"What news does MacNeal bring from the Lowlands?" her father said into the awkward silence.

MacKinnon blinked, his gaze flitting across her before settling on her father.

"Balliol is weak—weaker than any of us had guessed. His wee parade through the south has failed to garner the support he'd hoped for. The will of the people isnae with him."

"Even in the Lowlands?" Sybil murmured.

"Aye. Even in the smaller border towns, there is no appetite for an English-sympathizing King. His only true backing comes from Edward of England. What is more, Balliol spread his army too thin. He cannae set a watch on every wee village and hamlet in hopes of quashing all seeds of rebellion. MacNeal reports that Balliol has realized this and is consolidating his forces."

Sybil's gaze shot to her father's. "If we knew where he was headed—"

"We already do."

The cloth stilled in her hand. Her father, too, seemed to be holding his breath.

"He retreats to the southwest with the intent to stay there through the Yuletide season."

Her father sank back in his chair with a sharp exhale. "I'd bet my right eye he plans to take up residence at Annan Castle. 'Twas a gift to the Balliols from the Bruce family—back when the Balliols and Bruces were friendly."

Sybil exchanged a swift glance with her father before they both turned back to MacKinnon.

"The Balliols have used it as a family seat of sorts for decades now," her father finished.

MacKinnon nodded slowly. "If ye are correct, Balliol will be a sitting duck there. It is our best hope for a counterstrike."

The air squeezed from her lungs. *Heaven help us all.* Were they truly plotting an attack against the crowned King of Scotland?

Of course, she'd known this day would come—her

father's loyalties to Robert the Bruce and his heir had never wavered once. Nor had her own. She was a Douglas, through and through. When that blasted Edward Balliol had slithered back into Scotland with a parchment-thin claim to the throne, she knew which side she and her family would be on if a reckoning ever came.

Yet after the loyalists' defeat at Dupplin Moor, the only hope for a free Scotland had rested on the shoulders of the four Highlanders who were said to have sworn vengeance. When Domnall MacAyre had first made contact with her father—through her—Sybil had assumed it would take months, if not years, to mount a counteroffensive with any chance of success against Balliol.

"Yule is only a few sennights away," Sybil said into the taut silence. "Ye cannae mean to form a plan of attack and mobilize an army in the Highlands in so little time."

MacKinnon's hand tightened to a fist in her palm. "If I could, I wouldnae wait even that long." With visible effort, he unclenched his fist and withdrew it from her hold. "But nay, I am no' so foolish as to rush our efforts. This will likely be the only chance we get. If we fail..."

They all knew what would happen.

Another defeat would likely be the end of the loyalist cause. The rightful King David would be forced out forever. Balliol would proclaim himself a mere vassal of King Edward of England just to cling to his own power.

And then there would be no free Scotland to speak of.

Sybil set aside the cloth and reached for the flagon of wine on the tray. Once she poured three glasses and passed them around, they all took a fortifying gulp.

"What do ye propose, then?" she murmured.

MacKinnon once more weighed her with those emerald-green eyes before turning a grave stare on her father. "Are ye sure ye wish to bring yer daughter into this?"

"I am already involved, MacKinnon," she said even before her father could reply. "If ye are worried about my loyalties, dinnae. Ye trust him, and he trusts me. Isnae that enough?"

"I say again, this information could get us all killed," MacKinnon replied, his voice like granite. But then he tempered his tone, adding, "It isnae just a matter of trust. It is also a matter of what might be lost."

"As ye may have observed, my daughter is rather headstrong," her father commented dryly. "But she is as clever as any man who's advised me as Guardian. And she knows her role." He leveled her with a dark-eyed glare. "Most of the time. She willnae be stepping onto the battlefield, and as a gentle-bred lady, she is afforded a few more protections than ye or I, MacKinnon."

She scoffed quietly. That was an interesting way of putting it. Aye, she wasn't likely to be drawn and quartered in a public execution, as a man would be. But nor was she allowed to pick up a sword and defend herself. Yet life at court had taught her to wield other weapons more suited to her station and sex.

MacKinnon still didn't look convinced, but it seemed his impatience to set whatever scheme he'd formed in motion outweighed his hesitation over her presence.

"Verra well." He drew a breath. "If a loyalist attack is to have its best chance of success, we cannae go in blind. We need to know the lay of the land first. I intend to lead a scouting mission to Annan."

Her father's salt-and-pepper brows flew up, but as MacKinnon went on, he stroked his greying beard in consideration.

"We will gather all the information we can—Balliol's precise location, the surroundings, the true number of his force—then return to plan our counterstrike," MacKinnon said. "As time is of the essence, I mean to leave at first light tomorrow morn."

Sybil frowned.

"And if ye are discovered—or captured?"

MacKinnon gave her his full attention, and she had to will herself not to lean back in her chair. Aye, his stare was intense, but she knew her perspective was valuable.

"A group of Scottish warriors poking about Annan Castle will undoubtedly draw attention," she went on. "And if ye are taken, the entire cause could collapse. Balliol would know the loyalists were planning a move. Edward would send reinforcements. Any element of surprise would be lost."

"Then I suppose I will have to try my best no' to get caught," MacKinnon said tightly.

But she hardly noticed his barely-leashed ire, for her mind already raced ahead.

"I have a better idea," she said, even as her thoughts began to take shape.

It was a bold plan, but it just might work.

Setting her goblet of wine down resolutely on the desk, she fixed MacKinnon with a confident gaze. "I'm coming with ye."

CHAPTER 3

"Nay. Absolutely no'," Artair blurted even before Douglas could sputter a reply.

He didn't have the time or inclination to debate with Douglas on the wisdom of bringing the lass into the fold. She was the man's daughter. Artair couldn't control what he chose to divulge to her.

But to drag her along on what would undoubtedly be the most dangerous and important mission of his life?

No' a chance in hell.

Douglas choked on an inopportunely timed sip of wine. "Sybil, ye cannae mean to—"

"Hear me out, Father," she countered smoothly. "A scouting team must move in stealth and avoid detection at all costs. How many men would ye take, MacKinnon?"

"Only a handful—mayhap half a dozen," he said through clenched teeth. "I wish to move fast and light."

She nodded. "And if they all look like ye, the lot of

ye will stand out like wolves among sheep. Ye dinnae exactly blend in with the average Lowland villager."

"Is that a compliment, my lady?" he said before he could stop himself.

Though it shouldn't, satisfaction surged through him at the way her cheeks pinkened. Yet she refused to back down. "One wrong move—one nosy villager who sees ye passing through on yer way to Annan, or one castle guard who catches a glimpse of ye—and yer whole mission is shredded to ribbons. Along with yer hide, most likely."

"And how does hauling a gentle-bred noblewoman along the way help us go unnoticed?" he countered, straining for composure.

"That is just it—we wouldnae need to hide."

"What exactly are ye proposing, Sybil?" Douglas demanded.

She turned keen eyes on her father. "Instead of a scouting mission, we ought to make it look like a diplomatic visit."

Douglas blinked, considering that.

"We could travel in the open without fear of discovery," she continued. "And what is more, we wouldnae be limited to lurking about outside Balliol's base of operations. We could go straight inside."

She shifted her attention to Artair. "How valuable would it be to examine the castle's defenses from within its verra walls? Ye could find the exact chamber where Balliol sleeps, for heaven's sake."

He had to admit, the possibility was...more than

enticing. Hell, he could put Balliol under his very own blade.

Nay, he reminded himself, he couldn't be distracted by that tantalizing prospect. Killing Balliol wasn't the goal. His whole campaign to hold the crown needed to be dismantled. But to look the Usurper in the eye before cutting him down… *No' for myself. For Ewan.*

"She has a point, MacKinnon," Douglas said, drawing him out of his dark musings.

"It is too dangerous," he muttered, avoiding looking at the lass.

"Quite the opposite, I believe," she replied. "Sending me will disarm Balliol. He wouldnae suspect aught afoot if I were there. 'Twould be merely a friendly visit—hardly more than a social call from the daughter of the Guardian of Scotland."

Christ, would Douglas actually agree to this? The man was staring contemplatively at his daughter as if he were about to. Damn it all, Artair would not be so easily overruled.

"Balliol is no fool. A social call out of the blue would indeed draw his suspicion," he threw out.

"Aye, I agree," Douglas said with a frown. "A diplomatic convoy needs a purpose."

Too late, Artair realized that rather than disqualifying her plan, he'd only managed to give the lass an opportunity to put that clever mind to work fine-tuning it.

Sybil pursed her lips in thought. "I could bring a missive, mayhap, or some bit of news from court. A hint at parliament's position for or against him?" Her brows shot up. "I have it—a truce. We offer him a temporary truce."

Bloody hell. "Ye cannae merely…make up a truce," Artair snapped.

"As a matter of fact, as Guardian of Scotland, I can," Douglas said.

"What of parliament? Willnae they want a say?" Artair replied. He turned to Douglas, fighting to keep his cool. "We cannae wait for all the earls and bishops to come to an agreement—it would take months, if it happened at all. We need to act *now*. There may no' be another such window of opportunity again."

Douglas began stroking his beard again, considering Artair with perceptive dark eyes.

"We are all eager to see Balliol off the throne, man," he said evenly. "But we cannae let our impatience override prudence. Ye must admit there is merit to Sybil's plan."

Artair exhaled, forcing himself to lean back in his chair. "Aye," he muttered after a moment. "Having an excuse to step foot inside the castle would be of great help."

His gaze slid to her. A small smile played at the corners of her lush lips—and not one of the practiced, courtly smiles she had used with ease a few times already. Nay, this was one of barely checked triumph.

"As for whether or no' he'll lower his guard in the presence of yer daughter," Artair continued stiffly, "I cannae say."

"Most men tend to discount the fact that women

have eyes, ears, and working brains," she murmured in a voice dry as sand.

Douglas cleared his throat. "Regarding parliament —when Balliol departed a month past, he was aware there was some…disagreement about the legitimacy of his claim to the throne. The last he heard, I was speaking to each member individually before calling for a final decision."

"What is yer sense of the mood among them?" Artair asked.

"Besides a few vocal supporters—that arse the Bishop of Dunkeld must have been promised something," Douglas muttered before going on, "almost all stand with young David. As the son of Robert the Bruce, the line of succession is obvious."

"Many in parliament were placed there by the Bruce himself," Sybil added. "Some even fought alongside him against the English. The only issue is David's age."

The bairn-King was only eight summers old. As far as Artair knew, the lad was in hiding somewhere in France.

Not for the first time, Artair silently cursed the Bruce's death three years past. If only he'd managed to live until David had reached his majority. As it was, Scotland was vulnerable to the likes of Balliol—men of opportunity who sought to capitalize on what would likely be a decade of uncertainty until David came of age.

"They hold their tongues because of the danger in speaking out against Balliol if he manages to retain the throne," Douglas went on. "But they dinnae like the Usurper any more than we do."

It was heartening to hear that the will of those in parliament matched that of the Scottish people. What was more, if the loyalists could deal a heavy blow to Balliol's cause, it seemed that parliament could be encouraged to publicly rule against the Usurper and officially restore David.

"Would parliament truly accept ye offering a truce to Balliol?" Artair asked with a frown.

Douglas shook his head slowly. "As Guardian, I dinnae believe I even need their permission. 'Twould be more of a stay on any further conflict rather than a final decision. And in truth, parliament isnae ready to issue a public ruling. We could present the truce to Balliol—and parliament, for that matter—as merely a way to buy more time for a verdict."

"Ye said Balliol means to spend the Yuletide season at Annan, MacKinnon," Sybil interjected. "An offering of peace through Yule—or mayhap the rest of winter—would appear as a gesture of good faith. We could even make it seem as though he is gaining ground at Scone."

Artair grunted. The thought of stroking the Usurper's ego made him want to vomit. But he had to admit, this scheme they were hatching had its advantages.

If it worked.

"The offer of a truce is reason enough for a diplomatic convoy to travel to Annan," Sybil continued, her gaze holding her father. "And the Guardian sending his daughter makes it seem all the more amicable—a social call with a bit of political business on the side. He'll think he's winning, which will only lull him further into complacency."

Muttering a curse, Artair grabbed his forgotten goblet of wine and took a swig. It seemed the chit had everything sorted.

"I am still going," he ground out. "I willnae be cut out of my own mission."

"I understand yer...enthusiasm," Douglas said. "But willnae Balliol know yer face if ye stood right before him?"

"Nay, he never bothered to lay eyes on us before sentencing us to be hanged. He would recognize my name, but that is easy enough to conceal. I *insist* on being part of this."

Douglas muttered an oath, then nodded in agreement.

Sybil hesitated, mayhap disturbed at the reminder of his recent hanging. But then she gave him one of those honey-sweet smiles that made him clench his teeth.

"I'm sure I'll need a retinue to escort me. A few warriors accompanying the Guardian of Scotland's daughter would be suitable—for protection, of course. Mayhap ye could play the part of my bodyguard."

Artair barely managed to suppress another curse. How had his plans been so thoroughly contorted by this wee slip of a lass?

"I still intend to leave at first light tomorrow morn," he said, eyeing her.

She nodded briskly. "Then I shall have Beatie begin preparing my trunks straight away."

"Trunks? As in, more than one?"

Sybil opened her mouth for a retort, but Douglas smacked his hand on the desk and rose.

"It is settled, then. I'll begin drafting the truce. MacKinnon, ye are my guest for the evening. One of the servants can show ye to a chamber and help ye freshen up before the evening meal."

Artair stood and gave each of them a wooden bow. When he'd set off at a dead gallop from Old Blair's Stone to the palace, he'd only meant to inform Douglas of his plan. Now he was to be saddled with a gentle-bred lady whom he was coming to realize was more a spitfire than a shrinking violet.

Though it was far from ideal, he forced himself to focus on the advantages of this new scheme. Instead of skulking about, hoping for mere scraps of information, he'd be headed straight into the lion's den.

Bringing the lass would be an annoyance, naught more. And Balliol would be made to answer for his actions at last.

CHAPTER 4

By the time Sybil made her way to the great hall for the evening meal, she found Artair MacKinnon already seated beside her father on the raised dais.

She blinked. An hour of rest and refreshment had done him wonders.

His shoulder-length hair, which had been a wind-blown riot of dark gold waves before, was now pulled back into a tidy queue at the nape of his neck. He'd shaved away the bristle to reveal the sharp angles of his cheeks and jaw. And he'd changed into a fresh tunic of forest green, which made his eyes, a few shades lighter, seem to glow even from a distance.

Belatedly, she realized he was staring back at her across the hall. Smoothing her hands over her velvet surcoat, she plastered a serene smile on her face and glided toward the dais.

The trestle tables were filled with the palace's men-at-arms and some of the servants, who bowed their heads to her as she passed. As she got closer to the dais, lower vassals and their wives greeted her with equal respect. She acknowledged them with a tilt of her own head, and an occasional comment or question.

Since parliament was not currently convened, the dais was empty except for her father and MacKinnon, and the hall was rather subdued. There were no regally dressed earls or powerful bishops present this eve. Yet she knew most outsiders would still find it an intimidating place bearing a great deal of significance—not to mention the fact that there were always eyes and ears ready to observe one's every move.

Even before her father had become Guardian and brought her to Scone, she'd visited the palace dozens of times when he'd served in parliament. And the various Douglas holdings weren't exactly remote, rustic estates either. Nay, this was her world, one she had been born and bred into.

Which made the butterflies filling her stomach as she reached the high table nonsensical. 'Twas only because MacKinnon's unnervingly intense gaze was still fixed on her, she reasoned.

He rose smoothly from his chair and stepped around the end of the table, extending his hand to her. It seemed the man possessed at least a few manners.

Just as when she'd attended him in the solar, she couldn't help but notice how large and callused his hand was as she took it. He helped her up the steps and guided her around the table, but instead of seating her on the other side of her father, which was proper, he pulled out the chair next to his own.

Knowing that several sets of curious eyes followed

her, she did not correct his error. Or mayhap he had done it on purpose, so that he could speak to her father without her interference.

It had been obvious in the solar that he was none too pleased with how she'd inserted herself into his plans. Did he take her for no more than a feather-headed nobleman's daughter, even after her stroke of brilliance in turning his scouting mission into a diplomatic one?

Before she had the chance to speak to him, servants arrived with trays of steaming meat pies, roasted vegetable stew on trenchers, puddings, hard cheeses, and honey-glazed fruits, along with flagons of wine.

"Apologies for the simple fare," her father said to MacKinnon as he cut into the flaky crust of a lamb pie. "Despite what ye may have heard, we dinnae feast and cavort *every* night at the palace, eating and drinking away the bounties granted us here at court."

MacKinnon snorted softly. "This is far finer than aught I've had in quite some time. Ye will recall these past two months I have been living in hiding—and before that, in a war camp."

"The palace must seem verra grand, then," Sybil offered, reaching for some other polite topic.

He turned to her, one side of his mouth pulling up in something not quite mirth. "Indeed, especially considering I had only seen the dungeon before now."

Luckily no servants were near enough to overhear. Sybil looked away, silently cursing herself for the blunder. This was supposed to be her strong suit—playing hostess, entertaining guests with pleasant conversation— yet MacKinnon's large presence only a hand-span away was unsettling. Mayhap his surprisingly refined appearance had made her forget the truth.

He was a wanted man. A fugitive. And aye, she already knew he'd been held here in Scone's dungeon for a fortnight before he'd been hanged with the other captured loyalists.

What a strange study in contrasts he made. She'd heard rumors even before MacKinnon had made contact that the man was renowned as a tactician. He'd served directly under Robert the Bruce, then later in the loyalist army, to shape both battle tactics and political strategy.

Yet he was clearly a man of action as well—he bore the breadth and strength of a warrior, not to mention the calluses. An hour earlier, she could have mistaken him for a simple man-at-arms, so rugged was his appearance. But he carried himself with a lethal grace that made him suited to court as much as the battlefield.

They passed the rest of the meal largely in silence. When the trays were cleared and the servants were well out of earshot, MacKinnon leaned toward her father and the two began speaking quietly.

Sybil could only sit still, straining to hear with a placid expression on her face. To lean over and insert herself into their conversation would be a ridiculous breach of etiquette. To all those present, she was merely the Guardian's daughter, no more than an adornment to the charms of court. None knew just how fully her father had taken her into his confidence.

From what she could make out, they were discussing

the other three Highlanders—the Horsemen, as they were known in whispers—leading this secret rebellion.

Apparently they'd been communicating via missive at a clandestine location, but now that they were approaching a major offensive against Balliol, MacKinnon was entrusting her father with the task of communicating directly with the others.

"...Send them each missives alerting them to this new plan," MacKinnon was saying. "I'll tell them to be ready to move. I dinnae know how quickly after we scout Balliol's location we'll need to strike. I will ensure..."

She clenched her hands in her lap, her teeth locking behind her serene smile. Blast the man! He had no trouble taking her father into his confidence, despite the fact that it had been less than a month since they'd begun communicating about the cause. Yet she was to be left on the outside, in the dark.

It wasn't the first time she'd been treated thusly. In fact, by now she should be used to being seen as unimportant, an afterthought at best. But Artair MacKinnon was a strategist. Shouldn't he be able to see her value— to the cause, and to this mission—despite the fact that she was a woman, and a lady at that?

As the last of the trays and trenchers were cleared from the rest of the tables, a group of musicians gathered in the far corner of the great hall. Though not every night at the palace involved an elaborate feast and grand revelry, as her father had said, most nights they did have music. And dancing, when the mood struck.

It was just the opportunity she needed to wedge

herself back into MacKinnon's attention. And to remind him of why her involvement in this mission was just as important as his.

"Do ye dance, MacKinnon?" she asked, leaning over so that he and her father couldn't ignore her any longer.

Her father blinked, then lifted a bushy eyebrow at her. For his part, MacKinnon gazed at her coolly.

"No' normally after being in the saddle from sun up to sun down, nay," he commented, but his gaze lingered on her, moving slowly over her face. She had to fight to keep her features smooth even as warmth inched up her neck and into her cheeks. "But I suppose I could make an exception this eve," he said at last.

Once again, he rose and offered her his hand. She took it, and even deigned to tilt her head at him.

As proof that those in the great hall were always watching closely, the moment they stepped from the dais, the men-at-arms and servants began pushing the trestle tables and benches toward the hall's walls. Or mayhap they were eager for the entertainment themselves.

The lesser nobles, too, rose and hastened to join the large circle forming in the middle of the hall. Men and women arranged themselves in an alternating pattern, then took up their neighbors' hands. The pipe and flute lifted in a lively tune, to which the drum and lute joined, and the circle of dancers began to turn.

Out of the corner of her eye, Sybil noticed that MacKinnon followed every weaving step and kick. Apparently he did indeed dance plenty to be familiar with the carole dance. She, too, followed the steps, making sure to keep her kicks modest so that her skirts didn't ruffle too high.

After two more songs, some overeager man-at-arms called out to the musicians for a new song, one meant for pair dancing. No doubt the young man had his sights set on some serving lass or other, but it would actually suit Sybil's purpose even better than the would-be courter's.

The musicians shifted into a slower tune and there was an awkward rush as the circle broke apart and the dancers hastened to pair up.

Before she could even glance at him, MacKinnon's grip tightened on her hand and pulled her toward the back of the hall. For an instant, she feared he was fleeing before the dance even began, but then he halted, drawing her around in front of him.

He'd positioned them away from the hot fireplaces and the densely packed center, where other couples were picking up the steps and setting into the dance. Usually these pair dances were reserved for wedding feasts, for even with prescribed steps, it was considered rather too intimate for men and women to dance alone. Yet the privacy worked to Sybil's advantage. She had a thing or two to say to MacKinnon before they set out together in the morn.

But just as she opened her mouth, he spoke.

"Ye cannae truly mean to come with me to Annan, my lady. There is still time for ye to change yer mind."

She gaped at him, but before she could form a retort, he guided her into a turn that had them both arcing away from each other. By the time the steps brought her face to face with him again, she hardly managed to keep herself from glaring at him.

"Why on earth would I reconsider?" she demanded. "After all, it was *my* idea to form a diplomatic convoy."

"I'll answer yer question with another. Why would ye *want* to leave all this" —he jerked his chin to take in the entire great hall and all its finery— "for an arduous journey and a dangerous mission? Ye neednae give up the comforts and luxuries of the palace."

Though there was no overt insult in his words, she knew what he got at—that she was naught more than a spoiled lady who would crumple at the slightest inconvenience.

She fought for composure, but she could feel her eyes narrow at him as they turned slowly together. "Can only men love their country, then? Can only men want justice and peace and freedom for their people? Mayhap ye forget that while ye men are off fighting yer battles and wrestling for power, the rest of us bear the consequences."

"And are these the consequences ye must bear?" he quipped, dry as dust, once again nodding to their surroundings. "Living in the palace must be quite the burden for ye, then."

"I make no such complaint," she snapped. "I was born into this life, and know I am among the lucky few. But we all must play the roles we are given. With more privilege bestowed upon me, I have an obligation to use it for good."

"Aye, we all have our roles to play." To her surprise, his voice softened ever so slightly. "There is no reason ye must be more than ye are. Ye seem far more suited to a place like this."

Once again, the cut was subtle but unmistakable. He was underestimating her again, placing her within the same confines as the rest of society.

"Ye presume too much, MacKinnon," she said tightly as she passed around his shoulder. "Though we may operate on different planes, my life is pledged to the cause—to Scotland—just as much as yers is. My obligations as a nobleman's daughter might no' be the same as a soldier's, but I've been conscripted all the same by dint of birth."

There was more she could say. Yet she couldn't muster the will to speak of the future that awaited her.

MacKinnon must have sensed that she held something back, for he remained silent for a moment, letting the music wash over them. But it seemed he still wasn't satisfied enough to drop the topic.

"I could deliver the truce just as well as ye," he murmured, annoyance threading through his low voice.

"Och, ye could transport it, I'm sure. But when it comes to stepping inside Annan Castle… I am far more suited to the task."

They circled each other, their gazes locked.

"Oh? Why would that be?"

It seemed he needed a demonstration before he could be made to understand.

Just as he pulled her in to pass under his lifted arm, she stomped on his foot.

He gave a muffled grunt, but to his credit, he

completed the turn and maintained his grip on her hand.

"Look around, MacKinnon. Did anyone notice what I just did?"

Grudgingly, he glanced at the handful of dancing pairs nearest them. None had turned or let their gazes linger on them.

"My skirts hid my action," she said, giving him a saccharin smile. "Ye see, there are advantages to my approach. While ye men's maneuverings are out there for the world to see, women can hide theirs with a bit of fine brocade or silk, a smile, a word of flattery."

"Is that what ye plan on doing with Balliol?" he asked, his voice suddenly blade-sharp. "Flattery and smiles?"

"'Twould be better than whatever ye'd do in his presence," she retorted. "Ye claim ye could be stealthy in gathering information against him, but ye've acted like a bull under the brand since ye arrived."

He extended his hands and she took them, letting him draw her in close before pushing her away.

"Is that so?" he ground out.

"Aye. Ye are obviously too eager, too impatient. Yer haste to set off after Balliol blinded ye to the flaws and pitfalls of yer own strategy. Luckily, I saved yer ill-conceived plan before it could fail. Ye are welcome, by the way."

She should have bitten her tongue for such an unladylike comment, but her father had always encouraged her to speak her mind. In fact, he prized her clear perspective and unapologetic judgement.

That was why he'd turned to her for counsel over the years.

But it seemed MacKinnon didn't share her father's sentiments. He circled her again, and the fine hairs on her nape stirred. Suddenly she felt as though she was being stalked by a lion.

"I'd heard of ye, MacKinnon," she murmured as he came around to face her once again. "Even before ye made contact with my father. They say ye are a great strategist. Yet ye still willnae accept my plan—or mayhap my role in it."

They drew together in another turn, shoulder to shoulder, gazes fused.

"Is it because I'm a woman?" she demanded in a low voice. "Or because I am a high-born lady?"

He clucked his tongue, something in his hard features giving way ever so slightly. "I am sure ye are more than capable—at least in a place like Scone. Yer father obviously trusts ye. But I dinnae like the idea of dragging an innocent into this mess."

Though it was a small victory, she silently reveled in hearing him admit—albeit grudgingly—that he thought her more than capable. Still, she couldn't help but take issue with that last comment.

"Just because I havenae stepped onto a battlefield doesnae make me an innocent," she countered. "I can handle myself."

Though her father had done what he could to shield her from certain things, she'd seen more than she ought to have as a gentlewoman. More than MacKinnon would believe.

Something passed behind his eyes, darkening them for a moment. "Even on battlefields, there are always innocents who pay the ultimate price." He blinked, shuttering away the shadow she'd glimpsed. "Yer courage and convictions are noble, I'll give ye that, but I still dinnae think ye understand what ye are getting yerself into."

"Oh? Care to enlighten me?"

He watched her as they drew closer, their arms lifting in a mirrored arc.

"If Balliol truly has taken up residence at Annan Castle, the place will make Scone look like bairns' play. 'Twill be a vipers' den swarming with the English and others who support him, no' these simpering vassals here this eve."

She lifted her chin in that way that allowed her to stare imperiously down at him. "Where do ye suppose I grew up, a field of daisies? I am a Douglas. My uncle was James the Black Douglas, closest advisor to King Robert the Bruce. My father is the Guardian of Scotland. I was born and bred into this world, MacKinnon. I'm no' some wide-eyed, feather-headed fool."

To her satisfaction, he tipped his head in capitulation at that. But it seemed he still wasn't convinced.

"And there is the journey to Annan, as well," he said as he drew her under his arm again. "It may no' be an active battlefield, lass, but getting there will be no small feat. 'Twill be dangerous, no' to mention cold, grueling, and uncomfortable. A far cry from all this."

His gaze scanned the great hall again, taking in its finery.

She looked up at him as she brushed past. "Ye have managed to insult me several times over this eve," she said with hard-fought poise. "But despite what ye might think, I am no' some pampered princess, nor a spoiled housecat. I am perfectly capable of surviving without all the comforts of the palace."

This close, she could see his emerald eyes flash with surprise at her boldness, followed by a light that was dangerously close to mirth. "I suppose we will see about that, *princess*."

The last word was murmured so low as he released her for another wide arc that she wasn't entirely sure if she'd imagined it.

"Just remember," he said as they came together once more. "Ye may be the face of this mission, but *I* am in charge."

She opened her mouth for a riposte, but just then the music ended with a flourish.

"We have a long day ahead of us tomorrow," he said, stepping close to her side. "I'd suggest ye get yer rest while ye still can. Be ready at first light."

With that, he strode away, leaving her standing alone. He shared a few words of thanks with her father as he passed the dais, then disappeared through one of the corridors leading out of the great hall.

It seemed she'd won this battle, if not the war.

43

CHAPTER 5

A rtair checked the buckles on his horse's saddle for the dozenth time. As with all the others before, the inspection was unnecessary. But at least it prevented him from having to watch the palace servants load the wagons.

Wagons. Not one, but two of the bloody things.

In the gray light of the early winter dawn filling the palace courtyard, they packed canvas and poles for a tent, several trunks full of who knew how many gowns and household wares, and even a small table and a pair of wooden chairs.

As each item was loaded, Artair found himself muttering increasingly colorful curses.

This mission was supposed to be about speed, stealth, and agility. Aye, the loyalists weren't yet prepared for an open attack against Balliol. But scouting the Usurper's headquarters would make them so. And the sooner Artair completed the task, the sooner Balliol could be stripped of his stolen crown.

And made to pay for the damage he'd done.

He could admit that Douglas and Sybil were right about one thing—he was champing at the bit to see this through. He wasn't so blinded by his impatience that he didn't recognize the merits of Sybil's new plan. He'd agreed to it, after all. But to be slowed by a train of wagons he imagined were filled with dancing slippers and down pillows and jewel-encrusted chamber pots…

Hell, first light had already come and gone half an hour past. Even before they'd left Scone Palace, Lady Sybil Douglas was slowing him down.

The doors that led from the great hall to the yard opened then, and there she was.

Damn it all. Something dangerously close to desire clenched inside him. She was just as strikingly beautiful as she had been last eve, even beneath the dull gray sky and dressed in far simpler clothing.

To his relief, she wore a sensible wool gown in a rich shade of russet brown. The cloak she'd donned over it, however, was trimmed with fine fox fur that set off the auburn in her hair. She'd plaited the thick waves away from her face, then wrapped the braids around her head like a crown, making her appear regal even in her traveling garb.

And she claimed not to be some pampered princess. Artair rasped an oath as she glided toward the wagons to observe the final preparations.

Another woman scurried out of the hall after her, swinging a more modest wool cloak over her shoulders as she went. The woman had at least two decades on Sybil, her simple brown braid showing threads of gray. Yet as she moved to Sybil's side, the two fell into conversation, pointing at various items and instructing the servants as they finished loading.

Leaving his destrier, he strode to the two women.

"Ye are late," he snapped at Sybil without so much as a greeting.

She turned, sweeping him with eyes the color of amber amulets.

"Good morn to ye, MacKinnon. Allow me to introduce my lady's maid, Beatie. She'll be accompanying us to Annan."

Blast the lass's cool composure. She'd certainly embraced the power of honey to catch flies. He'd once been the same, but not anymore. Not since Dupplin Moor.

Artair glanced again at the maid next to her. Though plain of face, the woman had keen brown eyes that assessed him with just as much hauteur as her mistress.

"I wasnae aware ye were bringing a servant."

Sybil arched an eyebrow at him, taking on a patient tone as if speaking to the village idiot. "It would hardly be proper for me to travel in the company of men without a female companion."

Artair barely managed to bite down on another curse. Now he was to haul not one but two women across half of Scotland? What the hell was this mission turning into?

"MacKinnon here will be serving as my personal bodyguard," Sybil went on, turning to the maid. "Ye see, Beatie? There is no reason to fash over our safety on this trek."

So, the lass was leaning into her wee fabrication about his role in this supposed diplomatic journey. From the headstrong, almost competitive way she'd challenged him at every turn thus far, he wouldn't put it past her to derive more than a pinch of pleasure at the opportunity to put him in his place.

Aye, he was to act as a lowly guard, following at her heels—at least for appearance's sake. He would have to find a way to remind her just who was in charge here.

The maid muttered something about the Guardian's daughter and outlaws running rampant, but Artair gripped Sybil by the elbow and steered her away. When they were out of earshot of Beatie and the other servants, he turned on her.

"Is all that truly necessary?" he ground out, waving at the wagons.

She blinked, then lifted her mouth in a practiced smile. "Is there a problem, MacKinnon?"

"Aye," he muttered. "Ye are late, as I said. And this load of rubbish will only set us back further."

Cocking her head, she studied him. Though her features remained serene, something danced behind those gold eyes.

"I thought ye would be pleased at how well I am playing my part," she said in a soft, low voice. "Is this no' exactly what a diplomatic convoy which includes the Guardian of Scotland's daughter would look like?"

Damn it all, she had a point. Still, if he'd done things his way, he could have made it to Annan in four days of hard riding. As it was, they would be lucky to make it in a sennight—and only if the dry weather held.

"Nevertheless," he replied, fighting to match her unbothered air, "ye seem to be attempting to take the entire palace with ye. I did warn ye that this journey wouldnae be quite so…comfortable as what ye are used to."

She slipped her elbow from his grasp, somehow managing to turn the motion into a reassuring pat on his forearm. "Ye whine like a cat with its tail caught under a boot. 'Tis only a few basic necessities."

"Whatever ye say, *princess*," he muttered as she turned away.

Her head snapped around and she gave him a narrow-eyed stare. Apparently, however, she thought better of forming a rejoinder on that blade-sharp tongue of hers and instead glided back to Beatie's side.

Just then, Douglas emerged from the great hall, his weathered features set in a grim frown.

Sybil instantly moved to him, looping her arm through his and murmuring something to him even before Artair could join them. From her tone, he gathered that Sybil sought to reassure her father.

"I know, I know, lass," Douglas said, patting her hand. "But a father is allowed to fuss over his only daughter."

It seemed that in addition to trust, there was genuine affection between the two of them. Something painful twisted in Artair's chest, a memory flitting unbidden through his mind.

Ewan saying goodbye to his young sweetheart before they'd ridden south from MacKinnon lands.

The lass's tears, and Ewan's promises to return by the first frost.

He swallowed hard, shoving the memory back into a dark corner.

Feeling as though he was intruding on a private moment, he clasped his hands behind his back and pointedly turned his gaze away. A groom was leading two mares out into the yard, presumably for Sybil and her maid. The horses looked rather dainty compared to his destrier. The animals would hardly cover more ground in a day than the wagons.

Though he tried to keep it leashed as long as possible, his impatience finally got the better of him. He cleared his throat pointedly, turning back to Sybil and Douglas. To his surprise, Sybil's amber eyes were sheened with tears. Douglas coughed and blinked as if he, too, battled his emotions.

Artair suddenly felt like an arse for being in such a hurry. A few more moments of farewell would make no difference to their mission. Especially if…

Once again, the lurking fear rushed to the surface. *Especially if these are their final moments together.*

Aye, bringing Sybil along to deliver a mock truce was the better move. It would lull Balliol into a false sense of security, just as she'd argued. And it would get Artair inside the castle, giving the loyalists a far greater advantage in planning their attack.

But bloody hell and damnation, it was too risky by his measure. He'd made the mistake of bringing an innocent into this cursed fight once before. If something happened to Sybil under his watch...

"I have the missives for the other Horsemen," he said, fixing his gaze on Douglas.

The man nodded curtly, his serious scowl returning. "I'll see them sent this verra morn."

Artair pulled the three packets of folded, waxed parchment from the pouch on his belt and handed them over. It was a risk to communicate directly with the others. Missives could be intercepted. Messengers could be followed—or killed. But if they were to succeed, some risk was unavoidable.

And this wasn't Douglas's first time dealing with such sensitive information. A lifetime spent defending Scotland's interests against England, serving under Robert the Bruce, and angling in parliament had positioned him perfectly to be Guardian in such uncertain times.

Douglas tucked the three missives into a pocket inside his doublet, removing his own folded packet.

Unlike Artair's, this one bore a large red wax seal on the outside with the Guardian's signet pressed into it. "Let us hope Balliol takes the bait," Douglas said, extending the truce.

To Artair's annoyance, Sybil reached for it. He moved faster, snatching it up first.

"I think I'd better hold onto this," he said.

Her russet brows lowered. "Only until we reach Annan. Remember, *I* will be the one to deliver it to Balliol."

"But until that time," he replied through clenched

teeth. "*I* am in charge of this mission. And I insist that ye adhere to my instructions. For yer safety, of course."

She pressed her lips together, but it was obvious from the light in her eyes that she still didn't consider the matter settled.

"Speaking of safety," Artair said, turning back to Douglas. "Have ye selected the guards who will accompany us?"

"Aye. In fact, they are already waiting outside the postern gate. Trusted men, each and every one of them."

Sybil looked between the two of them. Inwardly, Artair smiled. She hadn't been a part of this discussion, which clearly irked her. As it had naught to do with her role as a faux ambassador, however, Artair hadn't seen a need to inform her of what he and her father had decided before she'd arrived for the evening meal last night.

"How many men are we taking?" she asked, pointedly focusing on her father.

"A dozen," Artair answered.

She turned a frown on him. "That seems a bit much. We dinnae want to look like a war band. This is meant to appear like a friendly visit. Mayhap eight would be better."

"As yer bodyguard," Artair said, emphasizing the word with sardonic weight, "I believe we need all twelve."

"I thought ye wanted to keep the party small."

"That was before I agreed to transport a gentle-bred noblewoman across half of Scotland," he countered.

Reaching for composure, he added, "Even for a social call, the Guardian would naturally wish for his daughter's protection. No one will bat an eye at a few extra guards."

Without the wagons, they would indeed look like a war party. Artair had instructed that the warriors Douglas selected be armed to the teeth. He wasn't going to take any chances with Sybil in his care. As it was, the wagons would draw the attention of opportunistic bandits and reivers. All the more reason for the additional reinforcements.

Artair himself had raided the palace's armory earlier that morn. The reassuring weight of a sword on his hip already provided some comfort. Though Highlanders rarely wore armor, he'd opted for a padded gambeson over his tunic to give him both the freedom to draw his sword easily and an extra layer of protection against the threats they might face.

The lass was about to speak again, no doubt to continue this debate, but thankfully Douglas cut her off.

"Sybil." The man pinned her with a firm frown. "Put that bullheaded brain of yers to good use. MacKinnon is right—about the men, and about ye obeying him when it comes to matters of safety."

"Aye, Father," she muttered.

"Ye each have a role to play in this," he went on, spearing them both with dark eyes. "Neither will be enough on its own. Dinnae get crosswise of each other, understand? And dinnae forget that this is bigger than all of us. Scotland herself is counting on ye."

Artair gave the man a curt nod. He didn't need the

reminder of all that was at stake. Hopefully the head-strong lass heeded his words, though.

Sybil took her father's hand and gave it a long squeeze, then turned with one final murmured farewell and moved toward her waiting mare. Artair fell in behind her, but Douglas's low voice stopped him.

"One last word, MacKinnon."

The man's dark eyes followed his daughter even as he spoke to Artair.

"I dinnae take my next words lightly. I am entrusting my daughter's life to ye, man."

Apprehension clenched like a fist in his gut at the reminder. "Aye, I know. And I vow I will do aught in my power to keep her safe. But... Are ye sure ye wish to do this, Douglas? It isnae too late to alter course and—"

"Nay, nay. It is a sound plan." Douglas rubbed his gray-streaked beard, one corner of his mouth tugging up. "One just bold enough to work."

Artair watched Sybil mount her gray mare with assistance from the groom. She carefully arranged her skirts once she was settled in the saddle, letting the fine wool fall modestly over her riding boots. Even though the animal was suited to her size, she looked small atop the horse, slim and delicate-boned. Far too fragile for what they were about to undertake.

It was as if Douglas read Artair's thoughts. "I can see why ye'd think me a fool to let her go," he commented, his gaze still following his daughter. "Believe me, I have spent the night asking myself if it is so. But we all must play our parts for the cause, even Sybil. I truly believe she can succeed in this mad scheme. She has a good head on her shoulders. And she is stronger than she looks. Even still…"

Artair eyed Douglas, uneasily waiting for him to finish.

The man turned to him, pinning him with a sharp black gaze. "A warning, MacKinnon. I saw the two of ye dancing last eve. My daughter's beauty and charm have a way of making men believe she is within their reach. Of course, I dinnae expect a man like ye to be easily swayed. But if she doesnae return to me unharmed—and untouched—ye will answer for it."

Good Lord, was Douglas implying… Had Artair just been threatened over the lass's virtue?

"There is naught to fash over on that front," he said evenly.

He'd once been called a charmer himself, though after Dupplin Moor, he felt as though his polished exterior had been ground down into naught but sharp edges and hard determination.

Aye, the lass was undeniably bonny. The reminder of their dance made his palms tingle at the memory of the feel of her, soft and real. But he wouldn't be distracted from his mission. Indeed, he was more likely to strangle the lass for her impertinence than seduce her.

Yet it seemed Douglas was not through. "Allow me to be crystal clear," the older man continued. "Sybil has another role to play beyond this mission, one that is nigh as important to Scotland's future. She is promised in marriage to a powerful ally of the cause."

Surprise—and an unexplainable surge of displeasure—washed through him. "She is engaged?"

"All but. The arrangement was made long ago between our families. Now that she is of age, the engagement was to be made official this past summer, with a wedding come spring. But with that bloody bastard Balliol throwing aught into chaos…"

Douglas rolled his shoulders back from his barrel chest before continuing. "Once we are rid of him, the marriage can move forward. The union would unquestionably strengthen the stability of the country, providing a bridge between my regent Guardianship and David's eventual reign, when he comes into his majority."

Artair would have scoffed at that rather inflated proclamation if he didn't know Douglas to be a level-headed, plain-speaking man. But what marriage arrangement could possibly provide such a significant alliance?

"Who is the man?" he demanded.

"Alexander Bruce."

Artair's jaw slackened as the name sank in.

Bloody fecking hell.

Aye, that would do it.

Alexander Bruce, Earl of Carrick, was the son of Edward Bruce, Robert the Bruce's younger brother. Many years ago, there had been rumors about Alexander's legitimacy, but his father Edward had recognized him as his heir, thus securing the Bruces' continued retention of the Carrick title and lands.

Bastard or nay, that made Alexander the nephew of King Robert the Bruce himself, and first cousin to young David II.

Which meant Sybil would be cousin-by-marriage to the King of Scotland—assuming Balliol could be ousted and David restored.

Douglas hadn't been exaggerating. A union between the Douglases and the Bruces, the two most powerful loyalist families in all of Scotland, would be unquestionably significant. The Guardian's daughter and the King's cousin joined together made a formidable proclamation about the future of the nation—Scotland would be ruled by Scots, free of English tyranny.

And Sybil would be at the center of it all.

Something she'd said last eve rose in his memory. About a noblewoman's obligations, and being conscripted as surely as any soldier.

My life is pledged to the cause—to Scotland—just as much as yers is.

He hadn't understood then, but now her words made sense. As the daughter of a man as powerful and connected as Douglas, her role was clear—marry for the benefit of the family. Or in this case, for the whole of Scotland. Her life—and her body—were to be sacrificed for the greater good, no different than a soldier.

Bloody hell, Artair had been needling her about being a pampered princess, and the frivolities of life as a lady at court. What was more, he'd questioned her involvement in this mission—and in the cause. If it was possible, she was even more entangled in the loyalist cause than he was.

He silently cursed himself for a blockheaded fool and an arse. His only defense was that his thoughts had been clear as mud since learning that the time was finally ripe to move against Balliol. Nay, that wasn't true. He'd been practically useless since Dupplin Moor.

Even at his sharpest, however, he'd wager Lady Sybil Douglas would continue to confound him. Her pretty smiles and easy manners hid blade-sharp wits and a stubborn streak to match his own. And though she did indeed lead a life of feasts and balls, brocades and silks, she also carried the burden of grave responsibility.

As a new thought hit him, Artair didn't bother trying to muffle his next curse. This knowledge of her almost-engagement and the important role she must play only confirmed what he already believed—that it was too dangerous to bring her on this journey.

His gaze swiveled to where she waited atop her mare. "If she is injured, or worse—"

Douglas must have followed the line of his thinking, for he interjected, "That is why she needs yer protection. Though I trust in her ability to handle Balliol, I wouldnae let her go with anyone but a man like ye."

Artair began to protest, but Douglas overrode him. "I know ye can fight, for ye survived in the Bruce's army all these years. But ye are also known to be clever. Ye see things others dinnae." He huffed a faint laugh, one bushy brow lifting. "No' to mention ye are one lucky bastard to have survived Balliol's noose."

It felt as though a fist clenched around Artair's heart at that. Nay, he wasn't lucky. Quite the opposite, considering what had happened at Dupplin Moor.

"Ye more than anyone understand the import of this mission," Douglas said, sobering. "The verra existence of the loyalist cause rides on it. As does the stability of

Scotland's future. This plan is our best hope. Sybil can get ye into Annan. But I say again—ye *will* return her to me unharmed, and untouched. Understand, MacKinnon?"

Bloody rotting hell. Acting as her bodyguard was only supposed to be a ruse to get him inside Annan Castle. But it seemed there was no escaping it—once again, he would be charged with keeping an innocent safe from harm through this shitestorm Balliol had created.

He could not fail in this. Not again.

"Aye," he replied gravely.

At last, Douglas's grim features eased slightly. He clapped Artair on the shoulder. "I have every confidence in ye, MacKinnon. Safe travels, and I'll do what I can from Scone to aid ye."

With a final nod and murmured thanks, Artair strode to his waiting destrier, his thoughts a gnarled tangle. Though he appreciated the Guardian's support, there was little the man could do besides deliver the three missives. Even the other Horsemen would be forced to wait for word from Artair before they could plan their next move.

The entire loyalist cause hung in the balance. As did Sybil's life. And for the time being, at least, Artair was on his own.

CHAPTER 6

By the time darkness began to fall and MacKinnon called a halt to their procession, Sybil was gritting her teeth against the discomfort radiating through her body.

If they had taken the smoother, wider road leading out of Scone toward Stirling, it would have no doubt been an easier trek. But MacKinnon had insisted that they take a lesser used route, one he said would skirt both Stirling and Glasgow. She could only imagine how the drivers of the two wagons had fared, given the bumpy, pocked path.

Her mare had performed admirably, though it was only the first day. She, on the other hand...

Although she was used to nigh-daily rides on a wooded path behind the palace, she couldn't remember a time she'd spent the entire day in the saddle. Thank goodness they were nearing the winter solstice, for they'd had just under eight hours of daylight. If this had been the height of summer, she had no doubt Artair MacK-innon would have pushed them twice as long.

As it was, her back ached, her legs trembled, and her rump...heaven help her, she wasn't sure she had one anymore, so numb had it become.

MacKinnon had led them to a wee glade just off the road, where the trees and underbrush were thick enough that they wouldn't be visible from the path. He barked orders to the dozen guards, setting some to work straightaway on making camp while others were to take first watch. The men jumped to their tasks, eager to follow MacKinnon's orders.

Earlier, she'd watched as he'd briefed the guards just outside Scone Palace's walls. Though he'd been rather grim-faced, he took command effortlessly, positioning the men around the wagons—and around her and Beatie.

His firm, decisive leadership was rather... compelling. Aye, he was clearly used to such a position. He still bore the taut, restless energy of a caged lion, but at least now he seemed to have something to direct it toward.

She, however, felt suddenly out of her element. Beatie had scurried off the moment they'd halted to relieve her bladder. But Sybil had stayed in the saddle, unsure of what to do.

She watched as the men swarmed with activity, unloading the wagons and making a perimeter around the glade. Surely it wasn't appropriate for her to join in. But would remaining atop her horse while they worked make her seem like the spoiled princess MacKinnon thought her?

This wasn't Scone, she reminded herself. Aye, she was a lady, but outside the palace, away from the ever-watchful, judging eyes of the nobles and politicians, she could bend the conventions of station and gender at least a wee bit.

And deep down, she wanted to prove to MacKinnon that she wasn't some delicate flower who would wilt the second she was plucked from the comforts of the palace.

With that decided, she gripped the pommel to prepare to dismount—and realized she faced a far more pressing conundrum than any issue of propriety.

Her legs were like pudding, and with her strength fading along with the last of the gray evening light, she was about to slide face-first out of the saddle and onto the ground.

Just as she began to slip sideways, large, strong hands clamped around her waist.

Without her even seeing him move, MacKinnon had managed to dismount and make it to her before she could embarrass herself. Somehow, he was able to turn the beginning of her tumble into a fluid lift, hoisting her free of her horse and slowly lowering her safely to the ground.

"Thank—*mmph*." When her boots met earth, she barely managed to muffle an unladylike curse. Her hands clamped around his arms to keep from crumpling into a heap of woolen skirts and indignity at his feet.

So much for putting on a show of strength.

Thankfully, his hands remained on her waist, steadying her.

"Regretting yer decision yet, my lady?" His low, deep voice gave naught away, but when she looked up into his bright green eyes, she saw a hint of dry mirth in them.

"Nay, of course no'," she bit out.

His incisive gaze swept her. To her embarrassment, she was sure he could easily read just how exhausted she was. "Mayhap I should have called a halt sooner," he commented evenly.

Despite the fact that her knees quaked beneath her skirts, she drew herself up as best she could—without releasing her hold on his arms.

"Or mayhap we ought to have taken the main road. It would have been a smoother ride, no' to mention we could have covered more ground. Werenae *ye* the one who wanted to make haste?"

Of course, even if they had, it wouldn't have changed the fact that she wasn't prepared to ride for a full day. Still, his amusement at her suffering vexed her.

"And risk becoming easy prey for bandits? Nay, no' with all this shi—*ahem*, rubbish to make us a target," he said, lifting his chin toward the wagons.

His voice dropped further. It practically vibrated through her hands and into her arms where she clung to him. "I warned ye this trek wouldnae be easy, *princess*. Mayhap now ye see just how soft yer life at the palace was—and how much different the world outside its walls is."

"And mayhap ye think ye understand me better than ye do," she retorted.

He cocked a brow at her. "Good. Ye still have some fighting spirit in ye. I was worried ye wouldnae last the day."

She opened her mouth for a rejoinder, but as his comment sank in, all she could do was huff indignantly. He'd been baiting her? His arrogant mirth at her discomfort, his criticism, and that damned princess moniker—all just to see if he could get a rise out of her?

Impossible, irksome man!

Before she could form the words to put him in his place, his features drew serious. "Despite what ye might think, my purpose isnae to torture ye, Lady Sybil. I didnae choose the route nor set the pace to punish ye or prove a point. Ye will just have to trust that I act with what is best for both this mission and yer safety in mind."

"Trust is earned, MacKinnon."

Now the mirth was back in his eyes, flickering like green fire. "Dinnae I get any favorable marks for no' letting ye fall on yer arse just now?"

Damn the arrogant Highlander!

Drawing herself up to her full height—which only brought the top of her head to his shoulder—she lifted her chin and donned her most composed air.

"I believe I will check on how my tent progresses."

It took effort, but she pried her hands from his arms and forced herself to stand fully on her wobbling legs. MacKinnon stepped back, sketching a half-bow and extending a hand as if clearing her way.

"As ye wish, princess," he murmured as she hobbled away.

Damn him twice over for that ridiculous epithet! The man seemed determined to vex her.

But how in heaven was he able to worm his way under her skin so completely? She prided herself on her ability to remain composed and calm even amidst the swirling gossip, power struggles, and backstabbing of Scottish court. What was it about the blasted Highlander who could so easily ruffle her feathers?

To her relief, much progress had already been made in setting up camp. Her tent had been erected and the men were carrying in several of the trunks. Beatie, who had returned from her hasty visit to a nearby shrub, stood directing them next to one of the wagons.

The maid pointed to various trunks, indicating which ones should be unloaded and which could remain on the wagons for the night. Some contained fine gowns she wouldn't need until they arrived at Annan, while things like her cot, bedding, and wash basin all needed to be brought into the tent.

Catching sight of Sybil, Beatie paused in her orders and hobbled over to her side.

"Are ye well, milady?" Beatie asked, keeping her voice low.

"I've been better," Sybil admitted. Now that the numbness was ebbing from her lower half, an insistent ache that ran all the way into her bones was taking its place.

"Even if I never sat a horse again, I think I will be

sore just looking at a saddle," the older woman muttered.

That brought a weary chuckle out of her. Though Beatie was normally tough as old leather, she was even less used to riding than Sybil.

"What was that about with MacKinnon?" Beatie asked.

Sybil glanced sideways at the maid. Beatie had been with her since she'd been a wee lass. The older woman had both a deep well of tenderness for her, but also an ability to see right through her practiced manners to the truth. If she'd been born into a different station, Beatie would have made an excellent castellan or even lady of the keep, for her keen brown eyes missed naught.

"He helped me down from my horse," she replied evenly. That *was* the truth, after all.

"Then why were ye blushing?"

Beatie truly did see all—even in the fading light.

To her embarrassment, new heat rose to her face. Had she been blushing while she and MacKinnon had spoken? Argued, more like.

Sybil waved her hand airily. "That man is a constant thorn, is he no'? He seems to take a great deal of pleasure in getting a rise out of me."

Aye, it was annoyance that had made her skin warm when he'd caught her, and when his hands had lingered around her waist.

Beatie was still eyeing her. "Be careful with that one, milady," she murmured. "Ye two clash like steel on steel. But remember, such clashes make sparks—one of which can start a fire."

"Dinnae be ridiculous, Beatie," Sybil replied. "I can hardly stand the man's presence without wanting to strangle him. Now I'd best go direct things inside before my wash basin gets mistaken for a chamber pot."

She wasn't running away from Beatie's too-perceptive gaze, Sybil told herself firmly as she did her best not to hobble to the tent.

The canvas flaps had been pulled back so that the men carrying various items could move in and out more easily. Four poles tethered each corner, and a larger pole held up the center so that even a man as tall as MacKinnon wouldn't have to stoop inside.

Someone had already unfolded her cot and pushed it to the far side. The chairs and small table sat opposite, with the trunks Beatie had indicated placed directly on the ground.

Thanking the guards as they deposited the last few items, Sybil closed the flaps behind them and set about arranging things. First she drew out a few candles from one of the trunks and lit them with the flint stones she'd packed alongside them. That gave her enough light to begin rummaging about.

In short order, she'd found her down-filled coverlet and pillow and made a cozy nest on her cot. Beatie bustled in and together they laid out a wash basin, pitcher, and bar of Sybil's favorite finely milled soap on the little table. While Beatie made up her own pallet on the ground near Sybil's cot, Sybil laid out a clean shift for later that eve.

But she couldn't retire for the night just yet. There hadn't been time that morn to formally greet each of the guards who'd accompanied them, for MacKinnon had wanted to head out the moment after he'd briefed them. Sybil intended to remedy that now. MacKinnon could call her a princess all he wanted—at least she had good manners.

When she emerged from the tent, she saw that they'd already started a fire a half-dozen paces away. Two of the guards were poking through the provisions they'd brought. Before she'd retired for the evening last night, Sybil had instructed the palace cook to gather plenty of non-perishable food for their journey, and make a few extra items for the first couple of days. Besides all her personal items, the wagons MacKinnon scorned so much also held great quantities of dried meats, fruit, bread, hard wheels of cheese, a few dozen fresh hand pies, and even a cask of weak ale for their party.

As some of the pies were passed around, Sybil moved from one man to another, greeting each and learning their names.

"I am pleased to meet ye, Nevin, and thank ye for yer escort," she said warmly to the last of the men gathered around the fire.

Like several of the others, he beamed at her then ducked his chin a bit sheepishly. "Of course, milady. 'Tis my honor, milady."

She tilted her head graciously, inwardly pleased to find that while the men all snapped to attention under MacKinnon's gruff orders, they seemed just as eager to serve her.

'Twas far easier to catch flies with honey than vinegar, her mother had always taught her.

"Tell me, Nevin, where will ye and yer men sleep this night?"

"Right here, milady, under the stars."

"Willnae ye be dreadfully cold?"

"No' if Dermid here does his job." Nevin nodded at the youngest guard in the retinue, a lad who appeared to be a year or two younger than Sybil but with a serious set to his smooth features. "He drew the short straw and is charged with keeping the fire burning all night," Nevin added with a grin.

Dermid's scowl deepened, but Sybil didn't miss the way the young man's eyes darted to her and then away, his face reddening. Like the others, he was a bit flustered by her attention. Still, by ingratiating herself to them, she knew she was earning their loyalty.

A firm hand closed around her elbow and drew her back from the fire.

"Are ye done turning my men into pudding-headed fools, Lady Sybil?" came MacKinnon's low voice behind her.

She turned to find him looming over her, his features cast in light and shadow from the flames. Had he been watching her?

Sybil narrowed her eyes on him but kept a smile on her lips.

"Not at all, MacKinnon," she commented lightly. "I was merely introducing myself. Since we are to travel together for a sennight, and another on the return to Scone, it would be rude to go on as strangers, dinnae ye think? Which reminds me, I'll still have to meet the guards currently on watch."

"Ye'll have to wait until morn for that," he murmured. "Allow me to escort ye to yer tent. I believe yer maid already secured yer supper."

He guided her away from the fire and toward the shadowy outline of her tent. As they left the circle of light, the night chill sharpened. Thank goodness for the down coverlet waiting on her cot.

Just then, she noticed that MacKinnon carried a bedroll under his other arm.

"Ye will sleep with the others, aye?" she asked, somewhat uncertain why he was carrying the bedroll away from the fire.

"Nay. I'll be on the far side of yer tent."

Right next to her cot, she realized, with only a thin wall of canvas between them. For some reason, that made her stomach flutter strangely.

"Why?"

He halted before the front of the tent, releasing her elbow at last. In the darkness, his features were inscrutable.

"Playing the part of yer bodyguard may be just a ruse for Balliol's benefit, but I dinnae take yer protection lightly, Lady Sybil," he said, his voice surprisingly soft.

She blinked, words failing her for once. What a confounding man. Not for the first time, she puzzled over the study in contrasts he presented. One moment he was needling her, the next contradicting her, and now he turned noble?

"I see," she managed lamely. "Well then, goodnight, MacKinnon."

She slipped into the tent without waiting for a reply, fearing he might detect just how flustered he made her.

Inside, Beatie was arranging a few more things in the weak light of the candles. The maid had indeed fetched two pies for them. The wash bowl had already been filled with water, waiting.

Sybil moved to her cot, sinking down on the edge for a moment. Outside, she heard a few faint footsteps and the rustle of MacKinnon's bedroll.

Gracious, he was likely less than an arm-span from her now. It would be bitterly cold on the ground, away from the fire, with only a few blankets to ward off the late November chill.

"Is all well, milady?" Beatie was watching her again, waiting for her to wash her hands and sit to eat.

"Aye, of course," she said, her voice just a touch strained with the lie. She rose and went to the wash bowl, pushing all thoughts of Artair MacKinnon from her mind.

Or at least attempting to.

CHAPTER 7

The rains finally arrived just before dawn.

Luckily—or unluckily, depending on how he looked at it—Artair had already been awake. The nightmares had stayed away, thank God, but his sleep had been broken.

He was used to the cold and sleeping on the ground. He was not, however, used to lying a few feet from a beautiful noblewoman who'd fallen into his arms just hours before.

Though she'd clearly struggled with the day's ride, and had likely never slept out of doors—even in a tent —somehow seeing her outside the sumptuous luxury of Scone Palace only increased her allure. Like a polished gem dropped among plain pebbles, her refined loveliness stood out even more starkly here.

She's naught but trouble, he'd told himself over and over during the night. Too bonny, too headstrong, too…the Guardian of Scotland's daughter.

And too all-but-engaged to Alexander Bruce, Earl of Carrick.

He'd thought Douglas's warning about leaving the lass untouched had been ridiculous just yesterday. Artair had no intention of dallying with a lass who was sworn to another.

And even if she weren't promised to Bruce, she wasn't for him. Not only was she far above him in station, but they belonged to different worlds. Aye, he'd moved in circles that included nobles, generals, and even the King. Yet for all that, he was more comfortable in a war camp than a palace.

Even still, there was an undeniable pull within him toward her.

He'd only been half-truthful about teasing her to test her spirits yesterday. Indeed, he'd noticed her flagging and was concerned about her remaining strength. In the short time he'd known her, he'd learned that it only took a few prods and a well-placed insult or two to stoke her to a blaze. Keeping her dander up—even if it meant taking the brunt of her fiery ire—would help her get through these next grueling days of travel.

Still, in the secret recesses of his mind, he could admit that his intentions in riling her weren't entirely… noble. It was perversely satisfying to ruffle her feathers, which she normally kept so perfectly smooth.

Yet he could not let himself contemplate why he enjoyed seeing fire flash in her amber eyes so much. Nor why his palms itched at the memory of touching her. Nor why he found his gaze following her every move as if tugged by an invisible thread.

He was acting the fool, just like the guards last night when she'd approached them one by one. They'd gazed at her like they were sunstruck, hardly able to find their tongues. And these were grown men who'd been hand-selected by Douglas for their skill and reliability.

Aye, she was radiant and charming and mouth-wateringly bonny. It was no crime to enjoy her beauty with his eyes alone. But he needed to keep his wits. He had no intention of becoming distracted from his purpose, he reminded himself grimly.

She's naught but trouble, he repeated for the thousandth time. *Another man's trouble.*

As the rain grew steadier, he rose, folding his bedroll, and made a quick sweep of their camp.

The watch had already turned over in the middle of the night. Those who'd been on first watch were now hunkered down, some snoring softly, around the low fire, which Dermid had diligently fed on the hour. The soft patter of rain made several of them stir. *Good.* No man worth his salt as a warrior should be able to sleep too soundly.

All their horses were accounted for as well. They'd been hobbled under the trees a stone's throw away, with one man exclusively assigned to watch them. The wagons, too, were untouched. Fortunately, they'd been covered with oiled canvas to protect the rest of Sybil's things and their provisions.

As the guards woke and began rising, Artair eyed Sybil's tent. Was she one of those noble ladies who liked to lounge in bed until practically midday? She had risen by dawn yesterday, but mayhap that had been a rarity spurred by his insistence on an early departure.

To his relief, just as he was about to approach, the tent flaps drew back. Beatie emerged, grumbling about the cold and damp as she hunched into her cloak.

Sybil was close behind, squinting against the gray sky as she came to the opening.

This morn she'd donned another stout wool gown, this one in a deep forest green that set off her hair. The dark red locks were once again plaited around her head like a crown, which she hastily covered with her cloak's hood against the rain. Though she was as poised as ever, he didn't miss the tightness around her mouth, nor how stiff her walk was as she stepped from the tent.

Aye, she'd be smarting this morn. Mayhap she'd slept as poorly as he had, too. He'd been a wee bit hard on her last night, teasing and pointing out her discomfort. Of course she wouldn't be used to traveling thusly, nor sleeping on a cot. Though she'd certainly been given more leeway than any nobleman's daughter he'd ever met, she was gentle-bred nonetheless.

Still, he had to give her credit. She hadn't murmured a peep of complaint yet, and had even managed to charm the men last eve. Mayhap it was only her pride that forced her to hold her tongue. Or mayhap Douglas had been right and the lass was tougher than she looked.

Either way, Artair felt a subtle softening toward her as she picked her way rigidly across the rapidly dampening ground toward him.

"Good morn, MacKinnon. The interior of the tent

is all packed and ready to be loaded. We will await yer word on a time of departure."

He blinked. She truly was making an effort to adapt to their conditions. And there was no thinly veiled annoyance in her tone, nor her usual attempts to subtly take the lead from him. Mayhap she was finally accepting that he was in charge—of this portion of their mission, at least.

And mayhap, just mayhap, she felt a similar softening toward him.

"We will leave just as soon as yer tent can be dismantled and packed," he replied. "Ye'd best see to breaking yer fast while ye have the chance."

She gave him a curt nod and turned toward the fire, where Beatie stood warming her hands.

With a few quick orders, the men set about hauling out the trunks and furniture they'd unloaded last night, filling the wagons once more. A sharp whistle brought the additional guards scattered on watch back to camp. Someone had dug out a packet of day-old bannocks from their provisions, and to Artair's surprise, Sybil herself saw to the task of passing them around, ensuring each man got something to eat.

Faster than he'd imagined, they were packed and ready to depart. Without thought, he moved to Sybil's side to help her mount. He held the stirrup steady as she lifted her boot, but her foot only made it halfway. Muttering something, she used her hand to try to hoist her leg higher. No doubt she was far too sore to manage the maneuver, so without asking, Artair gripped her around the waist and hoisted her up.

She gave a little squawk, yanking her skirts down around her knees as she settled in the saddle. Yet instead of a tongue-lashing for his rather overfamiliar action, she gave him a tip of the head.

"Thank ye, MacKinnon."

Tamping down a surprised grin, he gave her a curt nod in return.

One of the other guards had already helped Beatie, who grumbled and groaned like a rusted portcullis being forced to rise, but eventually made it into her own saddle.

Mounting, Artair took the lead, the others falling into a ring around the women and wagons. Mayhap this journey wouldn't be as bad as he'd feared after all.

A MERE HOUR LATER, Artair was already cursing his earlier optimism.

The rain pounded on, quickly turning everything into nigh-freezing mush. Icy water soaked his cloak and seeped against the back of his neck and shoulders.

Despite his own discomfort, his thoughts kept tugging toward Sybil. The fine kidskin riding gloves she wore would be soaked through by now. Likely so was her cloak. Today's ride would make her soreness even worse, with some relief likely only coming a day or two before they reached Annan.

The overgrown path narrowed further, forcing the party to ride two by two. He fell back, letting Nevin and Bartram take the lead. He found himself riding next to

Sybil, with Beatie and Uilliam behind, followed by the wagons and the rest of the men.

Out of the corner of his eye, he noticed she looked rather pale. Her gloved hands gripped the reins with a bit too much force.

Curse him to hell. Though her silence was admirable, he wasn't the beast she likely thought him. He had no desire to run her into the ground just to prove his point about her being unprepared for this kind of trek.

"Shall we stop, my lady?" he murmured, low enough to protect her pride from the others' hearing.

She jerked her gaze to him. "Is something amiss?"

Despite himself, he lifted a wry brow at her. "Ye tell me."

She exhaled, visibly working to smooth her features and relax her grip. "I promised my father I wouldnae question yer decisions regarding my safety on this journey. Barring a matter of security, I willnae be the reason we are delayed. Nor do I require ye to change the course of yer plans just for my comfort."

"That is a pretty speech, and a noble intention, to be sure. But ye keeling over in the saddle will delay us just as surely as a rest here and there. No' to mention yer father will have my hide if ye hurt yerself—even with yer own stubbornness."

"I can keep going," she insisted.

Under his continued gaze, her rigidly held back slowly sagged, as if melting under the pounding rain.

"At least a little while longer," she amended, darting a glance at him. He made sure to keep his features sober so that she didn't think he taunted her for showing any sign of weakness.

"Verra well. We will look for a dry spot to stop for the midday meal," he said evenly.

In the meantime, the best he could do was distract her from the miserable conditions. He contemplated teasing her again, in the hope of raising her ire enough to divert her attention. Yet some instinct told him not to. Her pride was likely tender enough at the moment, along with her backside.

"I have been wondering since I met ye, Lady Sybil," he began, picking his words carefully to ensure he caused no offense. "How did ye come to give yer father counsel on matters of politics and diplomacy?"

She studied him around the edge of her hood. Just as he suspected, her sharp amber eyes looked for signs that he was challenging her over her role. To his surprise, he found that he was genuinely curious of her answer. As Douglas had said, it was a most unusual arrangement.

He waited, letting her see his earnest interest.

"My father is a man of action by nature," she said at last, her russet brows unknitting slightly. "As the second-born son, he was expected to fight, even in a family as politically connected as the Douglases. But once his fighting days were behind him, it was only natural that he be thrust into leadership, given his clan and experience."

The Douglases were indeed well connected. Archibald's elder brother, James, had been Robert the Bruce's closest confidant, advisor, and right-hand man throughout his reign. Hell, after the Bruce's death, James had been tasked with carrying the King's heart to the Holy Land. He'd died completing the task, and it was said that even as he was cut down, he flung the Bruce's heart at his enemies, ensuring they both achieved a noble end in battle.

It seemed proximity to power and political influence practically ran in Sybil's blood.

"Off the battlefield, many of the finer details, the more delicate matters and subtle maneuverings required for parliament and the Guardianship, well...they arenae my father's strong suit," she said, her voice tinged with fondness. "For gentle-bred ladies, however, those skills— how to please, how to charm, how to navigate around those in power without making enemies—are *all* we are supposed to know."

Artair considered that. Most of the powerful men he'd worked with—generals, Lairds, and even the Bruce, toward the end of his reign—consulted their wives in private, and would heed their insights if they held merit. He'd never heard of a father doing so with a daughter, but it seemed the impetus was much the same.

In fact, it was the same reason such men brought Artair into the fold—to help them see things from a new angle, to strategize with fresh perspective.

"Ye said before that ye were raised in this world of intrigue. Do all Douglases begin their political careers in the cradle, then?" he asked.

She huffed a faint chuckle. "I wasnae quite a bairn, but aye, I suppose I started early. Besides my elder brother, John, my parents werenae blessed with any other living children."

Her gaze turned soft and distant as she went on. "John went to foster in France before I was five summers old. Then it was just the three of us. Though my father never made me feel lesser, I got it in my head that he would've liked to have another son, one to keep close by while John was away. So I set my mind to doing whatever I could to be of use to him, even though I was only a lass."

He pictured her as a bairn, small and adorable, but with the same force of will, the same stubbornness and blade-sharp wit she possessed now. As he imagined her applying those traits to the challenge of becoming the perfect offspring to her powerful, connected father, he couldn't help but smile.

"He allowed me to study with the same tutor who'd trained John before he'd left to foster," she continued. "So I got an education in not only needlework and decorum, but also in reading and writing, history, and arithmetic."

"Most unusual," he murmured.

Hell, she probably had more formal education than Artair. He'd learned much through hard-earned experience, first with his clan and then as part of the Bruce's army, which had morphed into the loyalist cause after the King's passing. He'd gleaned what he'd needed to as he went, but he'd never had a tutor.

"Indeed," she acknowledged. "And it only grew more so. After my uncle's death, my father took his place as head of the clan—and gained his seat in parliament.

He always allowed my mother and me to accompany him to Scone when parliament was called into session. I found I had a knack for understanding the unspoken and navigating the murky waters of court society. But it wasnae until a few years past, just after the Bruce's death and the tumult that followed, that he began turning to me for counsel."

"What sort of counsel did ye provide him?" he prompted.

"Well…it began with a deadlock in parliament," she replied, clearly pleased at his continued interest. "My father had squared off with the Earl of Moray over a bit of legislation. They'd gathered their supporters on their respective sides and both refused to budge. So I befriended Moray's wife, Isabelle, who was only a handful of years older than I, and who was rather shy and struggling under the pressures of court."

Another smile flitted across her face, her current discomfort apparently forgotten for the moment.

"We decided to throw a grand masquerade," she continued, "which for all intents and purposes was to help her feel more at ease among the noble crowd, and to speak with more comfort behind the protection of a mask. But the *true* goal was to allow the stalemated members of parliament to talk freely with one another. No one could tell who belonged to which side, and soon they began to find common ground. Within a sennight, the impasse had been resolved and they were on to their next battle."

Artair couldn't help but be impressed. "Clever," he said, lifting his brows at her. "I will admit, I have never gotten out of a political standoff by throwing a party before, but I will have to tuck the idea away just in case the need arises in the future."

She gave an unladylike snort, her gold eyes lighting with pleasure and mirth.

"Do. I highly recommend it."

To his surprise, he found himself sobering, his next words filled with sincerity.

"I can see why yer father keeps ye in his confidence. Douglas has been a success as Guardian, especially given this turbulent time. And ye are part of that success."

Abruptly, her open, easy features turned wary. "Ye dinnae think it strange or inappropriate that I have a say in such important matters, given that I am a woman?"

He frowned. "Nay, of course no'. Only a great fool would refuse to accept good ideas, whatever quarter they come from."

"I had the impression back at Scone that ye werenae particularly thrilled to adopt my modifications to yer mission," she said, her voice low. "Nor to have me join ye."

He cleared his throat. He didn't wish to offend her, nor shatter the delicate trust they'd been building. But the fact was, though her method of approaching Balliol was indeed better than his, he still thought her presence in the midst of this dangerous mission was a mistake. There had already been too many innocents lost to this bloody cause.

Skirting the truth was likely the best course of action. "If I gave ye that impression, it is only because I have been a wee bit…impatient to see this task done. I was so focused on getting to Balliol that I may have missed the forest for the trees."

"I noticed." She lifted a russet brow at him. "Yer proposed plan wasnae exactly the most strategically savvy or well thought-out."

"Aye, well, being hanged can have that effect on a man's ability to reason," he murmured.

The truth was, it hadn't been the hanging that had so thoroughly shattered Artair's world. He'd once been calculating, shrewd to the point that it had been wondered more than once if he could read his enemy's thoughts, so capable had he been at anticipating them.

And he'd once had the patience for charm, to use his talent of reading others to subtly guide them into his course of action—just as Sybil did.

All that changed on the night Balliol's army attacked the loyalists at Dupplin Moor. The night he'd held Ewan as his lifeblood had drained away…

"I saw ye, ye know," she said quietly. Like a rope thrown to a drowning man, her voice drew him out of the dark sea of memories.

He twisted in his saddle to look more fully at her. "When?"

"The day ye were hanged." She spoke so softly now that he could barely hear her over the rush of rainfall. "I saw ye and the others."

"What?" The word was spoken sharper than he intended, but shock prevented him from caring. "Ye were at Scone then?"

Sybil opened her mouth to answer, but behind them, Uilliam cleared his throat loudly.

Artair shot daggers with his eyes at the guard for the interruption. "What is it, man?"

Uilliam nudged his horse closer to Artair's, though the narrow road did not allow them to ride abreast.

"Er, Beatie requests a stop, sir." Uilliam, who was a stalwart, quiet fellow from what Artair had gleaned thus far, blushed like a maiden on her wedding night. "She says she will embarrass herself if we ride another moment."

Artair rotated to eye the maid. She rode with her shoulders bunched against the rain, her face set in a scowl. He sighed. He would have liked to cover more ground before calling a halt in another hour or so for the midday meal. The older woman certainly had a touchy bladder.

Raising two fingers to his lips, he let out a sharp whistle, then pointed into the trees to indicate where they should get off the road.

The caravan trundled through the bracken and wet underbrush toward a copse of massive pine trees, whose needled boughs would provide at least a little shelter from the rain.

The moment she reined her horse to a stop, Beatie awkwardly dismounted and shuffled toward a nearby rock outcropping, behind which she would be out of their line of sight.

Artair swung out of the saddle, his mind swirling with what Sybil had just said. She'd seen him hanged? How? There had been no audience other than Balliol's men, who'd led them from the dungeon to the tree and fitted the nooses around their necks. Even Balliol himself hadn't deigned to lay eyes on the men he'd sentenced to death.

He moved to her, reaching for her without thought. She let him lift her from the saddle without comment, though she did wince as he eased her to the ground.

"What do ye mean, ye saw me?" he demanded again, unable to suppress his need to know. At least he managed to keep his voice low enough that he doubted the others could hear.

Just then a shriek pierced the air, followed by a low groan.

"Beatie!" Sybil cried, her head snapping toward the outcropping where the maid had gone to relieve herself.

To their credit, the guards' hands all instantly went to their sword hilts, their gazes darting in every direction in case of some unseen attack. Artair, too, found his palm closed around his hilt, though other than the maid's yelp, there was no indication they were being waylaid.

Sybil started off toward the rocks, but Artair caught her arm, halting her.

"Stay here," he told her, fully unsheathing his sword. "I'll check on Beatie."

"But—"

"In matters of yer safety, I am in charge, remember?" he snapped.

Without waiting for her reply, he stalked toward the outcropping. As he went, the others closed ranks around Sybil.

Cautiously, he edged around the damp rocks, on high alert for an attack. Beatie moaned again just as Artair came upon her. She was half-reclined on the rocks, propped on one elbow.

"Are ye well?" he asked, sweeping the surrounding trees with his gaze.

She squinted up at him through the rain. "I slipped is all," she said, yet her voice wobbled with strain and she still hadn't risen. "'Tis nau—ow!" She attempted to sit upright onto her rump, but quickly sagged back down.

Artair eyed the maid. From the way she was gingerly leaning to one side, he had a sinking suspicion her slip had caused more than a sore rump.

"Bartram! Fingal!" Artair barked.

The two men soon appeared, worry creasing their brows and swords in hand. "Help Beatie back to the others," Artair ordered, resheathing his blade.

It seemed they were safe from attack—but not from bad luck.

CHAPTER 8

Sybil rushed forward as Beatie came into view. The maid limped toward the wagons, leaning heavily on Bartram and Fingal. At every step, she groaned and winced.

"Beatie! What happened?"

"Dinnae fash, milady," Beatie said through clenched teeth. "I am fine."

Sybil darted a glance at Artair, who trailed behind. From the grim set of his mouth, she suddenly doubted Beatie's words.

With the two guards practically carrying Beatie by the elbows, there was naught to do but fall in next to Artair and follow as they made their way back to where the others waited.

"What happened?" she repeated when they came to a halt beneath the pine boughs.

"The rocks were wet," Beatie said, shifting on her feet as if she couldn't find a comfortable way to stand. "As I was…*ahem*, preparing to return, I slipped."

"Let me guess—ye landed hard on yer ar—rather, yer behind," Artair supplied.

Her lips pressing together, Beatie gave a curt nod.

"From the amount of pain ye're in, ye've likely cracked yer tailbone."

"Nay, I'm just a wee bit sore, that's all," Beatie retorted, but another wince betrayed her.

"Give me the truth, Beatie," Artair said sternly. "The pain is radiating from yer tailbone, aye?"

The maid scowled fiercely, but again nodded sharply.

"Ye cannae walk without it shooting down yer legs and up yer back." He waited for her confirmation, then added, "Sitting will be a torment, to say naught of riding."

Sybil looked from Beatie to Artair. "What do we do?"

"Mayhap…mayhap I could ride in one of the wagons," Beatie offered, though from the way her face went pale, just the thought of jostling about on the wagon's wooden bed was its own form of torture.

"We are at least five days from Annan," Artair said in a low voice, his gaze holding Sybil's. "Longer if we slow our pace further."

Her stomach twisted with apprehension as the reality of their predicament began sinking in. An injured tailbone certainly wouldn't kill Beatie. But it could throw their entire mission in jeopardy.

She took in Beatie's pinched features, Artair's grim ones, and the uncertain looks on the faces of the guards. Calling on her deepest reserves of composure, Sybil straightened her spine and leveled her chin. Now was not the time to fret and fuss—at least not outwardly. They needed to make some hard decisions, and falling apart would help no one.

"MacKinnon, may I have a word with ye?" she asked evenly.

At his grunt, they moved away from the others. He guided them to the far side of another nearby pine, so that they were still somewhat sheltered from the rain, but well out of earshot.

Once they were alone, she let her shoulders slump. "*Damn and blast.*"

At her muttered curse, his brows shot up. "I didnae think ye capable of speaking in such an improper way," he commented, eyeing her.

"Aye, well, when I find myself in a blasted thornbush of a situation like this, I make an exception."

Artair snorted, but then sobered. "She cannae ride. And even in one of the wagons, she willnae make it to Annan. Every moment would be hell for her."

"But nor can we stay here," she added, a question lurking behind her words.

He shook his head slowly. "'Twould take weeks or mayhap even months for her to recover enough to be able to sit a horse."

"There is only one course of action then." She drew a steeling breath. "We must send her back to Scone."

"I have considered the same solution," he said, "but if she cannae ride—"

"We'll have to transport her in one of the wagons. Aye, it will still be a day and a half's journey to Scone—

mayhap longer for her comfort. But that is a far better alternative than her bouncing about for at least five more days."

"I thought ye needed both wagons."

"If we shift a few things around, we can still make do. I'll have to send some of my trunks back" —she tsked softly— "which will mean re-wearing a few gowns."

"Och, the indignity," he murmured dryly.

"It will reflect poorly on me at Annan," she retorted, her voice turning tart. She took another calming breath and went on. "But no matter. I suppose we could also send back my table and chairs, and obviously Beatie's pallet and trunk."

He considered that for a moment. "The remaining wagon may still be a bit overburdened, but we will eat down our provisions as we go, which should help," he offered slowly.

"Then ye agree this is the best course of action?"

He fixed her with a penetrating green gaze, ducking his chin so that he assessed her under his brows. "No' quite yet. I am no' convinced I shouldnae send ye back with Beatie."

"What?"

He lifted his hands in supplication. "Just hear me out. Dinnae pretend this has been easy for ye thus far."

She began to protest, but he went on. "There is no shame in it, lass. The fact is, ye arenae used to such conditions. This could be yer last chance to reconsider the wisdom in making this trek."

"I thought this was settled," she bit out. "I am the

key to the appearance of diplomacy, MacKinnon. *I* get ye inside Annan Castle."

"This isnae about that. Ye saw the state Beatie is in," he countered, his voice dropping. "Any number of things —accidents, attacks, who bloody knows what—could befall ye as well."

Sybil had been about to gird herself for another battle of wills with him, but the unexpected edge of worry to his voice caught her off-guard. In attempting to send her away, he was trying to protect her, though she didn't quite understand why.

"Ye arenae actually my bodyguard, MacKinnon," she murmured, her brow creasing as she studied him.

"Aye, I know that," he replied testily. "But I promised yer father I wouldnae let any harm befall ye. The fact is, I am no' sure I can keep that promise." He exhaled, looking off into the trees. "I shouldnae have agreed to bring another innocent into this mess."

Sybil blinked. There was much to ponder in the word "another." It was clear from the way a muscle in his jaw worked as he stared into the distance that there was a good deal he wasn't saying. But that was a ball of yarn to be unraveled some other time. The day was slipping away as they stood here debating.

"Sending Beatie back to Scone is our best option, and ye know it," she said quietly. "Ye need me in Annan. And time is of the essence. As ye have already pointed out, we may no' get a better opportunity to infiltrate Balliol's base of operations."

Muttering something, he returned his gaze to her. "And what about propriety? Ye said at Scone it would be preposterous for the Guardian of Scotland's daughter to travel without a female companion."

That was indeed a problem—one without a good solution. "We could wait for Beatie to reach Scone and for another lady's maid to be sent, but that would take at least four days."

At his grumbling curse, she added, "My sentiments exactly."

"Are ye sure ye want to agree to this?" Artair asked, frowning at her. "Ye'd be traveling alone with a dozen men—no companion, no lady's maid, naught."

"I cannae see a better path forward. Can ye?"

He scrubbed a hand over his jaw and exhaled another oath, which she took as a nay. Yet still he did not look convinced.

She studied his features as a clear war waged across them. "What other objection can ye have?"

He did not speak for a moment, but at last gave a sharp exhale. "And the fact that ye are promised in marriage to Alexander Bruce?" he murmured. "How will this appear to him?"

Surprise hit her like a blast of freezing wind. "My father told ye?"

"Aye. Before we left Scone."

An unexpected surge of displeasure quickly replaced her surprise. What did Alexander Bruce have to do with aught? Why had her father divulged her impending engagement to MacKinnon, and why was MacKinnon throwing it in her face now?

Reason wrestled with that impetuous reaction in her mind. It made no sense to feel annoyed. Her father had likely wanted to ensure MacKinnon understood Sybil's importance to the cause before they set out. And MacKinnon now raised a valid concern—the appearance of impropriety could harm the marriage alliance.

He must have read her thoughts on her face, for he added, "If continuing on endangers yer union—and therefore the loyalist cause—that is reason enough to turn back."

"Nay," she said too quickly. Blast it all. Where was her normal composure? Being reminded of her looming marriage with Alexander Bruce—by MacKinnon, no less—had flustered her, was all.

"There is no need to abandon course," she said, striving for a level tone. "Aye, traveling without Beatie... isnae ideal, but it willnae thwart the planned union."

"Why no'?" he demanded.

"As the Guardian's daughter, there are certain expectations, but also a fair bit of leeway. No one would dare question my honor—no' without facing the wrath of my father and all his allies. And Alexander Bruce wouldnae rock the boat. The Bruces want this marriage alliance just as much as the Douglases do."

Except this Douglas. The thought managed to flit through her mind before she could block it.

"Besides, we cannae prevent every fluke accident or bit of bad luck we encounter on the road," she said instead. "When we arrive at Annan, we can tell Balliol the truth about Beatie's injury, but say we didnae wish to delay the offer of a truce. The importance of our business warrants a wee...bend in propriety."

Yet MacKinnon continued to glower, unconvinced.

In an attempt to brighten both their moods, she shot him a half-grin. "If ye are worried about me being able to handle myself without assistance, I suppose ye could serve as my lady's maid as well as my bodyguard."

Though she meant the comment to be a light-hearted jest, her cajoling smile slipped as his gaze collided with hers. His eyes were dark with something she couldn't quite name, but which made her cheeks heat abruptly.

"Nay, I doubt ye'd find me of any use in that regard," he ground out. "Still…" He cleared his throat. "I cannae see any better alternative."

She had to swallow before she could find her tongue again. "It is decided, then. Beatie will return to Scone in one of the wagons. And we will continue on to Annan."

"We'll have to send at least two of the guards with her—one to drive the wagon, and another to watch the rear."

"Then we have managed to find a compromise," she said, once again aiming for a cheerful tone. "Ye wanted a dozen-man escort, I wanted only eight, and now we will have ten."

"Dinnae try to charm me over to yer side, princess," he muttered. "Ye'll only be disappointed."

She opened her mouth to respond, but he'd already strode past her toward their waiting party. She hurried after him, her face warming once again despite the bite of chill in the damp air.

CHAPTER 9

The rest of the day's ride was a dreary slog. Once they'd rearranged the wagons and gotten Beatie safely, if not exactly comfortably, secured in the back, the maid, along with two guards, trundled off toward Scone.

The remainder of the party continued on largely in silence. Because of the time they'd lost over Beatie's injury, Artair pushed them onward until the overcast sky had turned nearly charcoal with the encroaching nightfall.

Blessedly, the rains stopped just as they quit the road to make camp for the night.

As their party came to a halt in a wee clearing between the trees, Artair watched her for signs of strain. She hadn't made a peep since they'd bidden farewell to Beatie. Though he would have liked to continue their earlier conversation—he still needed answers about her comment that she'd seen his hanging—he'd taken the lead of their caravan to guide them through several crossroads.

Though she'd put on a calm, confident façade over the decision to send her lady's maid back to Scone, he was beginning to see cracks in her composure. And it was more than just fatigue. She'd seemed a bit...unsettled ever since he'd mentioned her upcoming engagement.

It was none of his business, nor his problem. Still, his mind gnawed on questions he had no right to ask. Why had a little worry line formed between her copper brows when he'd spoken Alexander Bruce's name? And why was she so quick to dismiss his concerns about the risk to her reputation—and the alliance her union was slated to forge—in traveling without a companion?

It was obvious by the time he dismounted and moved to her side that she was far too weary to answer such questions, however. As he lifted her from her mare's back and set her on her feet, she didn't even attempt to lift her chin or stand up straight. Instead, she leaned into his hold on her waist, her amber gaze unfocused with fatigue.

"Once yer tent is up, ye will retire for the evening," he ordered, all teasing gone from his low murmur. "The men dinnae require aught of ye. I'll see ye get some supper, as well."

She glanced up at him and nodded. The fact that she didn't argue or contradict him was only more evidence of her exhaustion.

The men worked swiftly against the rapidly falling

darkness. In only a handful of minutes, they had the remaining wagon unloaded and Sybil's tent erected. Even as they were still carrying in her trunks, she ducked inside.

Despite the damp conditions, Dermid had managed to coax a weak fire into existence a few paces away. Artair had gathered from one of the other men that as the youngest member of the contingent, Dermid would keep conveniently drawing the shortest straw for fire watch, as it required continuous wakings throughout the night. He made a mental note to relieve the lad so that he could get at least a few hours' sleep strung together.

By the time Artair had swept the camp's perimeter and assigned first watch, the others were already hunkering down around the fire with their supper—tonight, it was simply bread, dried meat, hard cheese, and a few small green crabapples from the fall harvest.

Gathering portions of each, along with a waterskin, Artair moved to the tent. He cleared his throat outside the door flap.

"Lady Sybil?"

"Enter."

When he ducked inside, he found the space lit with the soft, warm glow of a few candles. The tent only contained a cot and half a dozen trunks, on which the candles sat.

Sybil herself perched on one of the wooden chests. All her remaining furnishings had been sent back with Beatie. She'd draped her dripping cloak over another trunk, but she still wore her forest-green gown.

Though he'd been swift to criticize all the items she'd insisted on bringing as rubbish, it now seemed preposterous to make a gentle-bred lady sit on a trunk to eat a supper of stale bread and cheese. He might have pointed out that this was why he'd thought it best she remain in Scone, but from the way her shoulders sagged beneath her undoubtedly damp gown, he thought better of it.

He crossed the tent and bent to place the provisions on the wooden chest beside her.

"Thank ye," she said genuinely, looking up at him as he did. He froze, riveted. In the golden light of the candles, her eyes were like liquid honey. They almost seemed to glow with a light of their own.

Suddenly he was acutely aware of just how alone they were. The guards sat a mere dozen paces away, yet they could see naught that happened on the other side of the tent's canvas walls. Nor would the others hear their words if they kept their voices down. No one would know if they were to—

Bloody hell, where had that thought—which he wouldn't even let himself finish—come from? She was practically engaged to someone else. Not to mention high-born. Even within the confines of his own mind, Artair was treading into dangerous waters when it came to the lass.

He straightened abruptly, ripping his gaze from Sybil to the tent's door flap.

"I should—"

"Nay, willnae ye stay and dine with me?" She gave

him a self-conscious smile. "It is rather lonely without Beatie to talk to."

Aye, it would be, given that she was surrounded by men of a different station. Though she'd shown warmth toward the others, they knew not to be so familiar with her as to strike up a conversation or sit down next to her.

Such rules had always seemed ridiculous to Artair, but now he had to admit their purpose was sound. They were meant to keep people out of trouble.

The kind of trouble he was courting now.

"I am no' sure that would be…appropriate," he offered, sounding rather like a clot-heid to his own ears.

She waved her hand as if brushing away a midge. "Ye arenae besmirching my honor simply by keeping me company for a single meal."

How funny she should mention besmirching her honor, for Artair had been skating dangerously close of late, at least in the privacy of his own mind.

He hesitated. Should he bring up her engagement again as reason to keep his distance? If her earlier reaction was any indication, it would certainly shut down further conversation this eve.

Which was probably for the best. He had no business lingering in her tent like this.

Yet despite the soundness of that route, his own niggling curiosity got the better of him. He needed to know what she'd meant about seeing him hang.

"Verra well," he said reluctantly, casting one more look at the tent flap before turning back to her.

He cautiously lowered himself onto the trunk opposite her, but instead of peppering her with questions straight away, he sat in silence while she set into the food. The lass needed her strength, for they were still at least five days from Annan.

But it seemed she had a few questions of her own.

"Ye have heard the tale of how I got my start as my father's advisor," she said, tearing off a hunk of bread and extending it toward him. "What of ye? How did ye come to be a strategist in the loyalist cause?"

He took the offered bread but hesitated before answering. It was an innocent enough question. But telling it would mean staying even longer than he intended. Nevertheless, he felt his defenses lowering in the warm, quiet glow surrounding them.

"It started with cows."

Sybil blinked at him. "Cows?"

"Och, aye, everything in the Highlands starts with cows."

"Go on," she said, eyeing him skeptically.

"The MacKinnons and MacDonalds have been neighbors as long as either clan has existed—which means they've had a feud just as long, too," he began. "To hear the elders tell it, some years the feud was over a broken marriage contract, some years over some slight to one Laird or the other's honor, and so on. But there was always trouble with the cows."

"Dinnae tell me a MacKinnon heifer broke her marriage contract with a MacDonald bull, thus staining his honor," she commented.

He barely managed to suppress a grin. Though he

knew she needled him on purpose, he couldn't help but rise to the tease. He cocked an eyebrow at her.

"Nay, *princess*. I suppose ye think we Highland savages couldnae have complex problems like ye soft nobles who play wee games with each other at court. But our problems are just as nuanced. The only difference is when we disagree, we spar with swords instead of words."

She held up her hands in mock surrender, and he was gratified to see mirth shimmering behind her honey eyes. "'Twas only a jest. My apologies, MacKinnon."

"Artair," he blurted. "Call me Artair—if ye wish," he amended. He had no right to give her orders. Despite the position he'd earned within the cause over the years, by society's standards he was little more than a glorified foot soldier, and she the daughter of arguably the second most powerful man in Scotland at the moment.

Yet here they sat, alone, breaking bread and talking like a married couple.

Which they were not, he reminded himself swiftly. And never would be.

Surprise flickered across her features before she could smooth them. Mayhap it was just a trick of the warm candlelight, but Artair thought he detected a blush pinkening her cheeks.

"Verra well...Artair. And ye may call me Sybil—when we are alone," she murmured.

He couldn't help himself. "As opposed to princess?" he shot back, softening the tease with a disarming grin.

Now he was sure she was blushing. For an instant, he felt like his old self. The smile, the tease, the overfamiliarity which had so often won over his opponents—and concealed his calculating wit underneath.

But this time he had no ulterior motive, no elaborate strategy to deploy against her. He simply…liked to watch her blush.

He wiped the smile from his face and cleared his throat. What the hell was he doing? He was already treading on thin ice just sitting here with her. And not because Douglas had warned him away from his daughter, nor because of her impending engagement.

The lass was tempting, to be sure—temping enough to distract him from his purpose. Artair didn't need Douglas's threats or an almost-arranged marriage to remind him of the need to stay focused.

"About the cows," he said stiffly.

She looked down, busying herself with the food. "Aye, do go on."

"There was an ongoing dispute about where exactly the border between the two clans' lands lay," he continued. "The problem was, it crossed through a glen with exceptional grazing. Each clan drove their cattle to the glen in the spring, but whenever one clan decided that a cow had crossed the border—which, mind ye, seemed to move at the most convenient times—they claimed the cow as their own."

Sybil chewed thoughtfully on a wedge of hard cheese as she listened. "I can see why that would lead to neighborly…tensions."

Artair snorted as he tore off a bite of the bread she'd shared with him. "We came close to all-out warfare," he commented with a shake of his head. "Dozens of cattle were being stolen nigh on every damn night, and several scuffles led to bloodshed."

"Where were ye in all of this?"

He smiled faintly at the memory. "I was a young lad when this business with the cattle thieving was brewing. Newly seventeen, and I fancied myself a seasoned warrior already." He cleared his throat, glancing at her. "I may have been involved in a few of those wee scuffles."

She gave an unladylike snort. "*May have.* Ye men and yer need to bash each other in as the solution to every problem."

He surprised himself by barking out a laugh. "Ye arenae wrong—except that ye havenae heard the whole story yet."

"Go on, then."

"It was obvious where the situation was headed— more 'bashing in,' as ye say. But one night when I was… ahem…lightening the MacDonalds' stock of cattle, I ran into a few MacDonald lads. They gave me this."

He tilted his head so she could see the scar under his left ear. "I nearly lost the whole ear—no' to mention a few inches lower and the dirk would have opened my neck wide enough to drain me in a handful of heart-beats. After the MacKinnon healer stitched me up, I went to my Laird."

Her hand, holding a hunk of bread, stilled halfway to her mouth as she waited, clearly engrossed in the story.

"When he saw my sliced head, and learned of the escalation of violence between the clans, he was ready to attack outright," Artair went on. "In truth, I think he was spoiling for any wee reason, for the feud had been simmering so long that it seemed only natural to bring it to a boil. But I had hatched a different solution."

"Oh?"

"We needed a third herd."

Sybil blinked. "A third…?"

A smile tugged at the corner of his mouth. All this talk of cows was well beyond a typical noblewoman's purview, yet Sybil still sought to grasp the situation. "Each clan had its own herd of cattle, but we needed a third, one that would be pastured in the disputed borderland between the two."

"Wouldnae each clan simply steal from the border herd, then?"

"Aye, which was why we needed a few more rules in place. The clans would each contribute an equal number of cows, as well as herdsmen to tend them. Both Lairds grumbled at the thought of losing both cattle and men, but the cost of all-out war would have been far greater. And all the benefits—milk, calves, meat, and hides—had to be split evenly so that both clans felt inclined to make the whole arrangement work."

"Ye got no' only yer Laird but the MacDonald Laird to agree to that?"

"It took six months' worth of missives, followed by two months of meetings—and enough ale and whisky to fill a small loch—but aye. The fact was, neither Laird truly wanted a bloody, drawn-out battle. Neither wanted to appear weak, but both understood the suffering a war would cause. And besides a few hot-headed lads, the clans didnae want to fight and kill each other, either."

"How verra clever," she murmured.

She studied him with those glowing, intelligent eyes, and damn him to hell, but a wave of warmth rose in him that lapped at the icy resolve that had taken up residence in his chest ever since Dupplin Moor.

Hadn't he just told himself to remain focused? Then again, what was the harm in letting himself enjoy Sybil's nearness? Staying outside with the guards wouldn't get them to Annan any faster. And sharing a smile and a tale or two with Sybil wouldn't thwart his determination to take down Balliol. Naught could do that.

"How did ye go from cows to the loyalist cause, then?" she asked, handing him a piece of dried venison.

Artair accepted the meat, lifting one shoulder in a shrug. "No' long after the matter with the cows was settled, the MacKinnons backed Robert the Bruce at the Battle of Bannockburn."

At seventeen, riding off to war in support of the King and his cause for Scottish freedom had seemed like the grandest adventure. It was the same feeling Ewan had so desperately longed for—the desire to test his mettle, to prove his worth. To fight for something bigger and nobler than himself.

It all seemed so pointless now.

Artair swallowed hard against the sudden acrid tightness in his throat.

"I would have fought as a foot soldier, but my Laird, who took up arms right alongside the rest of us, kept me close," he continued. "He brought me along for meetings among the other Lairds supporting the Bruce. I drank in all they knew of battle tactics and lent what few insights I could. They seemed to think I had a natural aptitude for combat strategy. After Bannockburn, I rose quickly in the ranks."

"They say ye have an uncanny gift," she commented quietly. "That ye seem to know yer opponent's move before they do."

"*Who* says?" He'd already gathered that she'd heard tell of him before they'd met—which caught him off-guard, considering he didn't even know Douglas had a daughter, let alone one who advised him on matters of political import.

She gave him a sideways glance. "My father spoke of ye, as did others in parliament. They claimed ye planned the strategy that won us the Battle of Stanhope Park."

"No' just me, but aye, I was part of it—along with Tavish MacNeal, who truly does have a gift. He can read terrain like the back of his hand, and can tell ye the weather before the sky itself knows."

"One of yer fellow Horsemen," she murmured, looking askance at him.

"Aye," he admitted.

It was strange, being able to speak openly with her like this. He'd been sleeping in hay lofts and hiding out in untraveled woods since escaping Balliol's noose. He hadn't even used his own name for two months, except when he'd first made contact with Douglas.

Now here he was, speaking of the secret band of men who planned to take down the Pretender King with a gentle-bred noblewoman. And not just any noble-woman—the Guardian of Scotland's own daughter, who knew practically as much about the cause as he did.

A war waged inside him between needing to protect her from the ugly business of revolution and longing to draw her even deeper.

He picked up the waterskin and took a swig, attempting to wash away his unease.

"Whatever the gossips say, I dinnae have some preternatural ability to read the minds of my enemies," he said, aiming for a bemused tone to lighten their conversation. "I just learned early on that most men are only motivated by two things."

"Which are?"

He felt her curious gaze on him and couldn't help but meet it. "Pride and power."

She cocked her head at him. "Only those? What of men who hunger for coin? Or sleep with other men's wives? What motivates them?"

Curse him, but he was enjoying this—batting ideas about with Sybil. Mayhap more than he should. Yet he couldn't muster the will to stop.

"What would such men do with all their riches?" he countered. "More often than no', it is to buy position—for either the sake of pride, or to have power over others. And why would a man wish to take a tumble with another's wife? Besides the obvious," he amended.

To his amusement, Sybil blinked and flushed again at his crude insinuation. For all that she claimed to be well-versed in the harsh realities of court, she was still obviously inexperienced. He would expect no less of a lady, even one with Sybil's unusual upbringing. Still, Artair found a strange pleasure in knowing she was innocent to the coarser facts of life.

"Men at war are no different," he continued. "Besides the rare few who fight for true justice, most either seek glory for their name, or the authority to rule. It is easy to anticipate what those on the other side of the battlefield will do when ye know that."

"And what of women?" she prodded, her eyes narrowing ever so slightly. "Do we fit neatly into yer two wee categories?"

A sharp chuckle rose in his throat. "God, nay. Ye lot are far too confusing for me to ever understand."

A self-satisfied smirk curled one corner of her mouth, but then she shook her head. "I still think ye are too harsh on yer own kind. Dinnae men have room for more in their hearts? What of love? My father loves me, and he loved my mother, God keep her soul. So does my brother."

Once again, a memory of Ewan rose unbidden. His grinning, boyish face beneath the golden mop of hair, so like Artair's. And those same youthful features twisting in pain and fear in his last moments on earth.

And then he thought of Balliol, who'd brought war and chaos to Scotland all because of his longing for a crown. He hadn't cared who was hurt along the path to stealing the throne.

"I can only speak to what I've seen with my own eyes, lass," he murmured.

"Then which motivates *ye*?" she demanded. "Pride or power?"

All the mirth and enjoyment at their banter extinguished in him like a snuffed candle. He dropped his gaze to the ground between them. "Neither."

"But something drives ye," she said, her voice filled with confusion at his sudden sobering. "Of course, we all want to be rid of Balliol. He's brought naught but disorder and uncertainty to Scotland—no' to mention opened the door to Edward of England to put his boot on our necks again. But back at Scone ye were slavering like a rabid dog to set out for Annan."

She paused, clearly choosing her words carefully. "Are ye one of those few men driven by justice instead?"

Aye, part of him rankled at the wrongness of it all. The Balliol family's claim to the Scottish throne had always been weak. After the Bruce had stepped up as King, he'd made Scotland what it was now—free and united. The Bruce's son David was clearly the rightful heir to the throne. Balliol couldn't be allowed to storm into the country with an English-backed army and simply take the crown by force.

But in the dark recesses of his mind, he could admit the truth. The fire that burned inside him wasn't fueled by noble motives. When the Usurper was removed, Scotland would be better for it. Yet what he truly hungered for was retribution.

"Nay, I cannae claim to be such a man." Involuntarily, his hands clenched into fists. "What I seek is vengeance."

His voice cracked like a whip through the tent. The hush that followed practically rang with the echo of his words.

"For...for Dupplin Moor?" she ventured carefully. "And yer hanging?"

If those were his reasons, he'd call it pride.

Aye, he'd run the memories of his failure at Dupplin Moor through his mind countless times. He blamed himself for the loyalists' shocking defeat. He'd counted on their far greater numbers, plus their superior position over Balliol's army, not seeing how vulnerable they were to a stealth attack.

He knew he was not the only one to hold himself responsible. In the bowels of Scone Palace, when he and the other three Horsemen had awaited their deaths, they'd each confessed their responsibility for the loss. But Artair's role was especially galling, given that the strategy he'd developed at Stanhope Park was the same that Balliol's army had used against him.

Mayhap if it hadn't been for Ewan, Artair would be trying to salvage his pride over the stunning defeat. But he didn't care about his own failure anymore, nor in reclaiming his self-respect. None of that mattered. Not with Ewan's blood on his hands. And on Balliol's.

He met Sybil's searching gaze and almost told her all of it. But she was as innocent as Ewan had been in all this. He would not drag her into the horrible truth with him. So he left her question unanswered, letting her infer what she would.

"Ye said before that ye saw me hanged," he redirected. "How?"

She instantly stilled, a shadow passing behind her luminous eyes.

"Are ye sure ye wish to speak of that time?"

He hadn't meant to stay this long in her tent. Hell, the men outside were probably beginning to wonder. But he needed answers. Lady Sybil Douglas was an enigma he couldn't seem to leave alone.

"Aye. Tell me."

CHAPTER 10

S ybil folded her hands in her lap, the remains of
their meal forgotten on the trunk beside her.

Though she might appear serene and composed on
the outside, inside she was a riot of questions and
confusion.

All that Artair had said left the air raw within the
tent. Yet despite how much he'd shared, some intuition
told her there was even more lurking beneath the
surface. Something about the way his emerald-green
eyes had darkened when he'd spoken of revenge made
gooseflesh race up her spine.

Every time she thought she had a handle on him, it
seemed there was more she did not understand about
Artair MacKinnon.

She could not imagine why he'd want to speak of his
hanging, but since he'd insisted, she would oblige him.

"My father was already Guardian then," she began.
"We'd moved to Scone months before Dupplin Moor.
Word had it a conflict was brewing, that Balliol was

gathering an army in England, but no one thought he'd dare defy the Treaty of Northampton."

Artair nodded. Of course he would know that the treaty, which had held these past four years, stipulated that no army would cross the border between Scotland and England. But Balliol had found a work-around. He'd sailed his army from England into the Firth of Forth, thus skirting the border while still landing on Scottish soil.

"After Dupplin Moor..." her brows pinched. "We were so sure of a loyalist victory that we hadnae planned for Balliol to storm Scone. There wasnae time to leave without being swept up in the chaos."

Artair muttered an oath. Though she sat before him unharmed, clearly the possibility of what could have befallen her rankled him. That realization sat like a fanned ember in her belly, glowing and warm. He had no reason to be so protective of her. For heaven's sake, they hadn't even met then.

"He and his army came straight to the palace after the battle," she went on before she could unravel the meaning behind her tangled reactions to him. She paused in thought. "I suppose ye arrived at the same time—with the other prisoners."

"Aye," he ground out. "Though we were dragged to the dungeon before his 'coronation.'"

She nodded. "I didnae witness it either. My father locked me away in one of the chambers in the Abbey tower."

It had been at first a frightening, and then a very lonely time. Beatie had come to her multiple times a day with food and news of what went on in the palace, but otherwise, she had little contact with anyone, and never actually left the tower until Balliol had departed a month later.

Of course, she understood her father's insistence that she stay hidden for what was essentially a coup. The palace had been swarming with Balliol's English soldiers, who, like their leader, acted as if they owned the place.

"It wasnae clear if there would be violence over Balliol claiming the crown without the approval of parliament or the Guardian," she added. "Luckily no blood was shed."

"Except during the executions."

Sybil had to swallow against the bile rising in the back of her throat. "Aye," she whispered. "Though I couldnae leave my chamber, my window looked down on the courtyard. I saw Balliol's men building the gallows, and…and when they brought their loyalist prisoners out…"

As the memories rushed back, her throat closed, cutting off the rest. The horrible noises the men made as they were pushed from their blocks one by one still haunted her dreams.

Artair's large, warm hand suddenly covered hers where they sat clenched in her lap.

"Ye shouldnae have had to see that." Though the words came out low, his voice was drawn taut as a drum head.

"It shouldnae have happened," she countered softly.

"The fact that I saw it matters little compared to those men's lives."

"Still." He leaned forward so that he caught her downcast gaze. "I am glad yer father locked ye away, but ye shouldnae have been subjected to that sight."

She'd never seen violence like that. Obviously she'd never stepped foot on a battlefield. But she'd seen plenty of men fight. Before her brother had left for France, he would grapple with surprising ferocity with his friends. And she'd witnessed more than a few scuffles between men who bore genuine animosity toward each other over some slight or other, the heat of the moment making them brutal.

But the hangings…it had been so cold, so calculated. The prisoners were defenseless. The battle had already been won. To kill men with their hands bound behind their backs seemed both cowardly and evil.

"I saw the four of ye being led through the court-yard," she went on, her gaze dropping once more to where his big hand rested over her own much smaller ones. "I thought ye were meant for the gallows, but when Balliol's guards marched ye through the gates, I noticed the ropes hanging from the oak tree outside."

His fingers clenched ever so slightly before they relaxed on her.

"I didnae know which one was ye—nor who any of ye were at the time," she breathed. "But I couldnae look away. It seemed ye must have been different from the others. Yet none of ye so much as flinched as the nooses went around yer necks."

She pulled in a breath to steady herself. "And then

115

the lightning struck. I was blinded for a moment, for I'd been staring right at ye all when the tree was hit. The next thing I saw, the four of ye were struggling free and taking off to the south."

Although she shouldn't, she took a surprising amount of comfort from their continued contact. It was a miracle he and the others had survived. Though she'd seen them escape with her own eyes, his hand, warm and solid, soothed the still-raw memories of what she'd witnessed.

"The whispers began almost immediately," she said, "about the four men who'd escaped Balliol's noose—Highlanders, all, of some import to the loyalist cause to have been singled out as ye were. But then as the sennights went by, there were rumors that the four of ye had vowed vengeance on Balliol. They called ye the Four Horsemen."

Artair scoffed quietly. "We gave ourselves the name, along with our mission." Slowly, reluctantly, he withdrew his hand from hers. Without his warmth, she suddenly felt the cold dampness seeping into her bones, and the discomforts and fatigue of the day.

"As soon as Balliol departed Scone for the Lowlands with his army, I was finally able to leave the Abbey tower. My father and I knew we had to find a way to rid Scotland of him. No' long after that, Domnall MacAyre reached out—through Ailsa—and we learned that the rumors of the Four Horsemen were true. He and I both knew ye were Scotland's best hope." She lifted one shoulder. "Does that satisfy yer curiosity?"

He exhaled slowly through his teeth, leaning back.

"It ought to," he murmured. "But nay. Ye continue to confound me, lass. But I willnae keep ye any longer." He swept her with perceptive eyes. "Ye need yer rest. And ye ought to get out of that wet gown before ye catch a chill."

"Och, that." Despite the cold wintery night, a wave of heat washed over her. "I tried. But the laces run down the back, and they are wet and swollen, so I wasnae able…"

He blinked, then breathed a curse. "Dinnae tell me ye cannae undress yerself." Suddenly he jerked to his feet, taking a step back as if she'd sprouted a second head. "I warned ye I wouldnae play the part of yer lady's maid."

Despite the tense conversation earlier and the serious scowl on his face, she just barely managed to suppress a laugh. "I am no' conscripting ye permanently," she replied. "But would ye mind aiding me? I beg of ye. I cannae sleep in a wet gown."

When he continued to glower at her suspiciously, she added, "I promise I willnae wear any more gowns with such complicating lacing again until we reach Annan and I can be served by a new lady's maid."

Yet still, he did not move. His gaze flicked to the tent door as if he expected her father to come barreling in at any moment.

"I am no' asking ye to undress me," she prodded. "Just, please, a wee bit of help." To show him, she stood and turned around. She pulled her hair over one shoulder to expose the laces.

"See? The rain seeped through my cloak and the laces are waterlogged. Simply—"

He didn't even touch her—only the material of the soaked laces. Yet the instant she felt the contact, all mirth died in her and she froze.

She hadn't let herself consider how intimate an act this was. She was in a bind and needed assistance, naught more. Or mayhap she'd been lying to herself so that she wouldn't have to face the gnawing need to be closer to him.

Either way, she now stood like a hare in a wolf's sights, acutely aware of every tall, broad inch of him behind her.

His large form cast a shadow onto her, blocking the flickering candlelight. He loomed over her, close enough that she imagined she could almost feel warmth radiating from his lean, powerful body.

His breath feathered over the exposed skin at the back of her neck as he bent to study the laces. Gooseflesh rose unbidden across her flesh as she held her own breath.

"My fingers are too large for this," he murmured, but he began tugging lightly nevertheless.

She swallowed hard, fixing her eyes on the blank wall of the tent. Good lord, what would Beatie make of this? The maid had warned Sybil about clashes leading to sparks.

But she genuinely didn't know what she would have done about the laces without his help. She couldn't ask any of the other men. She might have been able to cut them, but more likely than not she would have sliced herself instead, given the odd angling that would have been required.

Still, this suddenly seemed far more dangerous than wielding a dagger at her own back.

She'd told him the truth about the fact that any perceived impropriety in her traveling without a lady's maid would be overlooked by Alexander Bruce and the rest of his family. No one wanted to threaten the marriage that would bring together the two most powerful loyalist families in Scotland.

Nay, that was not where the danger lay.

It lay in her own madly hammering heart. In her fluttering stomach. In the heat that washed her skin and settled low in her core.

She was drawn to Artair MacKinnon. Drawn in a way that she should not be. She had a duty to her father, to the cause, to all of Scotland to wed Alexander Bruce. She was to play her part, marry for the betterment of all.

Yet it was the man standing behind her, his breath fanning her exposed neck, his fingers working the laces of her gown, who dominated her thoughts and filled her with longing for what could not be.

The only sound in the tent was his breathing, which was rather serrated as he continued tugging at the laces. Did he feel it too? This impossible yearning that drew them together yet kept them apart?

He gave another swift jerk on the ties and the top of her gown loosened, the wet material sagging away from her shoulders. She hastily clasped it to her chest before it could peel away from her chemise.

With the laces now free of their swollen knots, she ducked a glance over her shoulder.

"Thank—"

The tent's canvas door flapped closed, cutting off her quick glimpse of Artair's retreating back.

He'd already gone.

Leaving her alone with her swirling thoughts and her flaming cheeks.

CHAPTER 11

"I need a bath."

Those were Sybil's first words upon emerging from her tent on an overcast, frosty morn four days later.

Artair's head snapped up from the fire, his gaze landing on her. Would he ever get used to the sight of her, like a punch to the gut every time?

Her copper locks were halfway plaited back from her face and wound into their usual crown and pinned with her favored clasp, the rest of the russet waves falling down her back. Cold touched her cheeks and nose, pinkening her pale cream skin. Despite the gray light of morn, her eyes seemed to glow with determination as she stared back at him. She looked like a fairy queen amidst the deep greens and chestnut browns of the surrounding woods.

He blinked. Belatedly, he realized that the other guards, who sat around their small fire next to him, were not gaping at her like moon-eyed dolts. They seemed to have adjusted to having Sybil in their midst these last several days.

Artair, on the other hand, was more addlepated with each passing day.

Get ahold of yerself, man.

He cleared his throat in an attempt to clear his wits. "A bath?"

"Aye. I cannae present myself to Balliol like this." She swept a hand over herself.

He had no idea what she referred to, however. She looked as radiant as ever, as he'd just noted against his will.

He did observe that she'd donned the same loam-colored wool riding gown as she'd worn the day before. Though the gown was finely made and hugged her slim curves to perfection, he doubted she'd want to be presented to a King—even one who'd unjustly usurped the title—in it.

Over the last four days, they'd skirted past Stirling and Glasgow and crossed into the Lowlands. Though they'd been forced to travel out in the open through moorlands and gently rolling hills, Artair had managed to keep them mostly isolated by choosing smaller roads and avoiding even modest towns.

The rains had stayed at bay, which, combined with the cold, had kept even the most rustic roads they traveled firm and solid. And thank God, for that had allowed them to make good time—far better than he'd expected, given the fact that they traveled with a lady and a wagon.

Six days after departing Scone, they were only an

hour or two's ride from Annan now. If they'd pushed, they might have even made it last eve, but neither Sybil nor Artair had wished to ride after nightfall, nor arrive at the castle so late.

They'd made camp several miles from Lochmaben. Artair had spent time in both the town and the castle while serving in the Bruce's army. He knew this landscape well enough to guide them to a wood that had once been part of the vast hunting grounds the Bruce had enjoyed whenever he was in residence at Lochmaben Castle, but was now little-used.

Though the intent had been to allow them all to rest and collect themselves before making the final push to Annan, Artair had barely slept last night. Now he felt pulled tauter than an overstrung longbow.

Of course, the closer they drew to Annan, the more impatient Artair grew to be inside the castle's walls. But that was not the only reason he was grateful that this trek was nearly done. He doubted he could stand to be in such close proximity to Sybil without doing something... unwise.

Damn it all. She was waiting for a response from him.

"'Tis cold as Lucifer's tooth out, my lady," he said, aware that the guards followed their conversation even though they kept their gazes on the low flames.

"Which is unfortunate, but unavoidable." From her crisp tone, he knew this would be a battle he could not win. She'd already made up her mind. Still, he had to put up a fight.

"We were going to depart just as soon as we could break camp."

"I'll be quick, I promise." She huffed a little chuckle. "The cold will ensure my haste."

"In an hour or two, ye can take a bath in the comfort of Annan Castle without—"

"MacKinnon, a word, if ye please."

He straightened stiffly from his crouch and approached. He came to a halt a few feet away from her tent, however. There was no way in hell he was going back inside. Not after what had happened last time— and what had almost happened.

Sybil glanced over his shoulder, dropping into a low whisper. "Making a good first impression is vital to my chance at success in lulling Balliol into a false sense of security. If he sees aught other than a pampered lady on a social call, his suspicions will be stirred. Arriving at Annan looking like a bedraggled hag who's been dragged across half of Scotland at a breakneck pace makes us seem desperate. And untrustworthy."

He exhaled through his teeth. She was right, damn it. "Does it help if I say ye dinnae look like a bedraggled hag?"

One of her russet brows inched up. "Thank ye kindly, but nay."

He hadn't meant to compliment her, nor to notice her effortless beauty in the first place, but it seemed that he was as witless as pudding in her presence.

"Ye cannae leave camp alone."

Aye, there was the true reason he was arguing against a bath. The best place to take her was to the small loch they'd passed just before they'd trundled off the road to make camp last eve. But it wasn't safe to let her go by herself. And he wouldn't even consider letting one of the other men accompany her.

Which meant that he had to go with her. And watch over her. While she undressed. And washed.

Bloody hell and damnation.

From the deepening pink on her cheeks—which was not due to the cold this time—she had arrived at the same conclusion.

She lifted her chin, visibly straining for a serene expression. "As this is a matter of safety, I shall defer to yer judgement."

Before he could mutter an oath, she'd ducked back inside the tent, presumably to gather the necessary items to wash.

She'd made it seem as if she were ceding to him in agreeing to let him come, yet she'd easily won the battle for a bath in the first place. But he didn't care about their wee power struggle at the moment.

Nay, all he could think was—what new torture had he just agreed to?

Ever since that night he'd stepped foot in her tent, he'd been trying to avoid her. Which was impossible, given their small party and their traveling conditions.

He had to touch her when helping her up or down from her mare's back, but beyond that, he'd vowed not to lay a finger on her. A vow which he'd managed to keep thus far—barely. When her hands clenched in discomfort on her reins as they rode, he'd nearly covered them with his own to ease the tension. And when she'd shivered in front of the fire one morn as they'd broken their fast, he'd ached to draw her close.

He'd also promised himself not to be alone with her again. Naught good could come of it. When she'd asked him to help with her laces, he'd nearly destroyed everything. Even now, the memory was so vivid it was almost painful.

Gooseflesh had prickled over her pale, exposed skin as he'd come to stand behind her. It likely ran beneath her gown and chemise from the cold. Would she have the same reaction to his touch? He would have liked to chase each ripple with a dragging fingertip, mapping every silky inch of her.

With her auburn locks swept over one shoulder, he'd found his gaze riveted on the spot where her neck met her shoulder. He'd nearly bent down and kissed her there, inhaled the sweet scent of her, which had teased him even from where he stood.

His fingers had trembled as he'd fumbled with the waterlogged laces. Suddenly this was all too real. It was one thing to let his mind roam over her lush lips, her soft curves, her dancing eyes like warm honey. It was quite another to be undressing her, alone in the privacy of her tent. It had taken all of his willpower to resist the urge to peel her gown away, spin her into his arms, and take her with the need that thundered in his blood.

Her own short, shallow breaths, which made her rib cage flutter just below where his hands had worked, told him she was not immune to the situation, either.

But even if she were willing—a possibility he shouldn't even let himself consider—it made no difference. She was not his to take—nor to want. She was sworn to another. And knowing her commitment to the cause, and her role to play in it, naught could ever come to pass between them.

Tearing himself from his dark musings, he turned and gave a few quiet orders to the men around the fire. They could break camp and ready themselves to depart while Sybil saw to her ablutions.

As the others rose to see to their tasks, Sybil emerged once more from the tent. She carried a stack of linen toweling, a bar of soap with dried flowers pressed into it, and an armload of rich wine-red brocade, which he assumed was the fresh gown she wished to appear in when they arrived at Annan.

"This way," he said gruffly, trudging off into the woods without waiting to see if she would follow.

From the faint sounds of her footfalls behind him, he knew she stayed close, yet neither of them seemed inclined to make small talk. As perceptive as she was, no doubt she read the tension rolling off of him in thick waves. Yet the fact that she did not attempt to make the situation more pleasant revealed her own tension as well.

After only a few minutes' walk, they reached the wee loch he'd noted before. It was so small as to be more of a pond, and probably bore some name that only the locals knew.

"Be quick about it," he said, nodding toward the water and then turning his back on the pond.

"Ye…ye are just going to stand there?" she murmured uncertainly behind him.

"What would ye have me do, help ye scrub between yer toes?"

She made a sound that was a bit too strained to be

called a laugh. "Nay, of course no', but ye could at least go back into the tree line."

He crossed his arms over his chest. With a sigh, he forced his tone to soften. "I willnae look, lass. Believe me, I would prefer to be anywhere else right now. But ye are far safer with me near."

If only that were completely true. Aye, she'd be safer from bandits and brigands, but at the moment his own desire for her seemed the biggest threat.

Though he'd just promised her not to look, he knew she was still fully clothed, so he dared a glance over his shoulder to assess her face.

Uncertainty warred on her bonny features—and likely modesty as well, for she'd flushed up to her auburn hairline again. But she must have decided being clean was worth the risk of embarrassment, for she turned and set her bundle on one of the large boulders that lined the loch.

Artair snapped his head around, pinning his gaze on the trees ahead of him. The rustle of fabric cut through the thundering of blood in his ears. Would she leave on a chemise, or bare herself completely while she washed? He silently cursed himself for letting the question bubble up in his mind.

At her hiss of breath, he knew she'd waded into the water. It would be bitterly cold to the point of being dangerous this time of year.

"Dinnae go past yer knees," he ordered without turning. "Otherwise ye willnae be able to get warm again before we reach Annan."

"But how will I wash my hair?"

He sighed through clenched teeth. "Must ye?"

"It smells of smoke and horses," she retorted.

He didn't have the strength at the moment for this battle. He was barely managing to maintain control over himself as it was.

"Fine," he ground out. "Finish yer washing first and dress yerself. Ye cannae be standing about in this chill. Then ye'll have to lie on one of those rocks along the waterline and dip yer head in."

Faint splashing sounds told him she hastened to do as he'd bid. He looked heavenward, praying she was nearly done.

"Have I done something to offend ye, Artair?"

The combination of her soft voice and the use of his given name nearly made his knees buckle.

"Ye seem rather…cross with me," she offered when he didn't answer right away.

He released the breath he hadn't realized he'd been holding. Bloody hell, he was being an arse. It wasn't her fault that her nearness was slowly turning him into a witless, lusting beast. Turning cold toward her was an act of self-preservation. But before he'd nearly lost control of himself, they'd been building a delicate trust between them.

"Nay," he muttered. "Ye havenae given me any offense, and I'm no' cross with ye." Cross with himself, aye, and this blasted situation, but not her. "Ye havenae done aught wrong. I am simply…eager to get to Annan."

"As am I. When we arrive, I think we ought to—oh!"

At her exclamation and the splash that followed,

instinct took over before he could stop himself. His head jerked around, looking for a threat.

But all that filled his vision was her.

She stood in profile to him, in the midst of hastily bending to retrieve her bar of soap, which she'd apparently dropped.

Even before she could register his movement, he'd snapped his gaze away, facing the trees once more. But the sight of her would likely be burned into his mind for the rest of his life.

She did indeed wear her chemise, though the whisper-thin linen did almost naught to conceal her. She'd likely been impelled by deeply ingrained modesty to keep it on, given that she stood in broad—albeit overcast—daylight and out in the open. Yet she could have no understanding of just how erotic she appeared with the soaking garment plastered to her every curve and delicate swell.

The wet linen hugged the contour of her breast, the shadow of her pink nipple beaded to a tight pearl against the cold. Her hair fell in a riot of fiery waves down her back, ending just before the luscious swell of her pert arse. The chemise clung to her lithe legs until her knees, where it floated like a delicate cloud in the water.

Bloody fecking hell and damnation. The sound of his blood hammered in his ears—and surged lower.

At the sound of scrabbling pebbles, he knew she'd stepped from the water. Now she would be peeling that wet chemise from her skin, abandoning what little cover it had provided, before toweling dry.

He could hear her teeth chattering as she worked to dress herself once more. *Think of shoveling dung*, he ordered himself. Or jumping into the ice-cold loch behind him.

Nay, that brought him back to Sybil, naked in the water.

Mayhap he ought to be focusing on her almost-fiancé.

"What do ye know of Alexander Bruce?" he blurted before he could think better of it.

The rustling of fabric behind him abruptly stopped. God, he hoped she was already in her gown, for he was a hair's breadth from turning around again.

"Why would ye bring him up?" she said, her voice unusually brittle.

"Just making conversation," he offered. *And trying to keep myself in check.* "I havenae met the man myself, but I heard he was at Dupplin Moor."

He didn't add the reason he had never encountered the earl despite being at the same battle. Many of the nobles had stayed in a more luxurious camp a furlong away from where the army encampment had been erected along the river. That was why almost all of the nobles had survived the fight, despite the devastating slaughter of so many loyalist soldiers. They'd had time to react to the surprise attack and escape, unlike those on the front line.

Artair could have camped with the elites if he'd chosen to. Despite his common birth, he'd earned a spot among the highest echelons thanks to his role as strategist in the cause. But Ewan had been among the soldiers, and Artair had wanted to look after him.

The cruel irony—that he hadn't protected Ewan at all, but instead placed him directly in the path of the slaughter—burned like a coal in his throat all over again. He swallowed hard, shoving down the pain along with the memory.

"Then I know little more of him than ye," she commented tightly.

He felt his brows lower. Aye, he'd been rather clumsy in bringing up her almost-betrothed, but her reaction was odd.

Come to think of it, she'd responded similarly when he'd made it known that Douglas had told him of the arrangement before leaving Scone. She'd brushed off his concerns over the propriety of her traveling on without Beatie, given she was promised in a politically significant union.

He should have left the matter alone, for her tone clearly invited no further discussion on the topic, but his need to know got the better of him.

"'Tis interesting," he said, aiming for a casual tone. "Both times ye have spoken of him, ye have turned rather…prickly. Is there a reason for that?"

"Nay, it is just—och. 'Tis naught but—ach—"

"What on earth are ye doing?" he demanded.

"Trying to do as ye said and wash my hair," she snapped.

Though he was tempted to look, he would not make the same mistake as he had before. "Are ye decent?"

"Aye, but I cannae get the angles right to—oh!"

He spun around just in time to see her teetering precariously on the edge of one of the boulders that sat halfway into the loch. She'd been in a crouch, trying to bend over far enough to dip her hair into the water, but she must have leaned too far. She windmilled her arms, but he saw in an instant she was about to tumble head-first into the icy loch.

Without thinking, he darted toward her. He wouldn't reach her in time. Just as she began to fall, he caught the hem of her wine-red brocade gown. To halt the momentum carrying her forward, he gave the hem a hard yank.

With alarm surging through him, he belatedly realized he'd pulled too hard. He changed her course, all right. Instead of going tumbling into the loch, she was jerked backward.

Directly into his arms.

CHAPTER 12

One moment Sybil had been about to spill head-first into the pond. The next she was plowing into Artair's hard chest.

The air rushed from her lungs at the impact. He grunted, but he absorbed the blow, somehow managing to keep them both from tumbling backward. His arms closed around her, capturing her in the cage of their strength.

Heaven help her, what was wrong with her? Never had she been so clumsy as she had become suddenly. First her soap had slipped from her grasp and then she'd nearly toppled—fully clothed—into the water.

Even though she fought not to listen, the truth whispered to her.

She'd tried to maintain her composure, but disrobing with Artair standing only a few paces away had been like gulping a whole jug of wine. She'd felt hot all over despite the icy water. She was bungling even the most basic tasks. And her head felt muddled with a confusing swirl of longing.

Though he'd given her his back, she'd never felt so exposed before, so raw and vulnerable. And yet a mad part of her had wanted him to look at her. To move closer. To touch her bare body where she burned with need.

It was a feeling she'd never experienced before. This was desire. And she should not have it. At least not for Artair MacKinnon.

She blinked up at him. He gazed down at her, his eyes vivid as cut emeralds. His dark gold brows were drawn together, his mouth turned down slightly.

"All right?"

"A-aye." She had to cough to clear the breathiness from her voice. "I was just trying to…"

"Aye," he murmured, saving her from having to fumble to the end of that sentence.

"Thank ye."

Belatedly, she realized that her hands had twisted in his tunic for purchase. He didn't wear the padded gambeson he normally donned while they rode, which meant she could feel the hard contours of his chest right beneath the material she gripped.

Why on earth was she still holding on to him? She was no longer in danger of falling into the water, thanks to him. Yet there they stood, rooted, their gazes locked.

Release him, ye lack-witted lass! But her hands refused to comply.

Then again, he gripped her just as surely. In fact, as

the moment stretched, his powerful arms flexed ever so slightly, tightening even more.

His eyes turned stormy. A muscle jumped wildly in his jaw, which was dusted with several days' worth of stubble. Slowly, his gaze traveled over her face, settling on her lips. She swallowed hard. Were they about to…

And then they were. Artair ducked his chin, his lips brushing hers. Though his arms held her in a nigh crushing embrace, his mouth was shockingly soft, almost hesitant, as if he expected her to twist her face away and jerk back.

Which was exactly what she *should* have done.

But instead, she met the kiss, pushing back with the same feather-light pressure. At her acquiescence, a deep groan rumbled through his chest. She nearly pulled back, fearing she'd done something wrong, but suddenly they were kissing in earnest.

More like *he* was kissing *her*. Ravishing her. Devouring her.

One of his big hands rose to the back of her head, his fingers sinking into her hair. That sent shivers racing over her from her scalp outward. A gasp parted her lips. At the same moment, he angled her head to more fully fuse their mouths together. His tongue flicked inside, shocking and thrilling in its velvet heat.

This was so much more than she'd imagined a kiss could be. For the last several nights, she'd lain awake in her tent, staring at the canvas ceiling above her cot, wondering what it would feel like to kiss Artair.

She knew it was silly, but some small, irrational part of her feared he would hear her improper thoughts through the thin wall of canvas separating them where they lay.

And now, she was in the midst of those same improper thoughts, except they were real. And they were much more intimate and intense than anything her mind could have conjured. Her body hummed with a mounting need she'd never known before.

For all her claims of worldliness and experience, she was an innocent, foolish lass, for he was taking her into a realm of sensation she never knew existed.

His tongue delved deeper, finding her own and mating slowly with it. His fingers squeezed tighter in her hair, demanding her surrender.

So she did.

She melted into him, releasing the tension in her neck and dropping the full weight of her head into his hand. She leaned into him, trusting his rock-like strength to support them both. Now she pressed against every hard plane and angle of his lean, powerful body.

Uncaring that she was relinquishing control, she opened further under his demanding mouth. Heat blossomed in her, and a restless need for more—more sensation, more contact, more pleasure.

This is madness, a distant voice warned. Aye, a delicious madness she could lose herself in forever.

She had never done something so rash before. She'd never indulged in dalliances or stolen kisses behind tapestries or in shadowy alcoves, as so many of the other ladies at court had. Even before her father had become Guardian, she'd always known she was meant to serve some larger purpose.

As a woman, the benefit she brought to her family was in her virtue—and her marriageability. And being the dutiful daughter she was, she'd held herself apart from the flirtations and liaisons so common at court.

In fact, she'd only been kissed once before.

The first time had involved naught more than a chaste pressing of closed lips with Alexander Bruce three years past. It had taken place in front of her father, not to mention a dozen others, when the understanding regarding their future union had originally been formed. She'd only met Alexander moments before, and the whole affair had been miserably embarrassing and awkward.

This time was so different than the first that they couldn't both be labeled with the same word. Now that she knew what kissing could feel like, it only further lowered the memory of the dry meeting of lips with Alexander Bruce.

As if merely thinking Alexander's name conjured him in Artair's mind as well, the spell abruptly and forcefully shattered around them.

Artair jerked back, releasing her and stepping away so quickly that she swayed and stumbled. She caught herself before she lost her balance and made a fool of herself yet again, but it took a long moment before her brain could catch up to what had just happened.

She dared a glance at him. He stood a pace away, panting hard. His eyes, like liquid fire, swept her.

What must he see? She raised a trembling hand to her lips, which still tingled at the memory of their kiss. They were damp and likely swollen. Her hair fell in disheveled waves around her shoulders, tangled from his fingers. And though she willed it down, the heat of a fierce blush rushed to her face.

He raked a hand through his own tousled hair. "That was... *Christ.*" He released a shaky breath. "I shouldnae have done that."

Something in her that had only just blossomed withered with equal swiftness. Of course, he was right. *They* shouldn't have done that, for though he'd initiated their kiss, she'd been the one to abandon all reason and give herself over to it so completely.

"I..." What could she say? That although it was wrong, she'd do it again in a heartbeat? That she ached to close the distance between them even now? That she felt foolish and small and unwanted, even though she knew from the heat that still simmered in his eyes that he felt the same burn inside as she did?

"That cannae happen again. It willnae," he ground out.

"Aye," she breathed, unable to do aught but concede to the truth he spoke. *Never again.* She had her duty, and he had his. Her path took her to Alexander Bruce—not Artair MacKinnon. No matter how badly she wanted it to be otherwise.

"'Twas...a moment of weakness, naught more," he continued. "One we'd do well to forget."

She couldn't tell if he already believed what he said or if he was trying to convince himself. Either way, she knew she might be able to carry on as if their kiss hadn't happened, but she would *never* forget it. Nay, it would be seared into her memory until the day she died.

"Then let us speak of it no more," she managed. In truth, she could not bear to hear him utter one more word of regret over what had been one of the most vivid, stirring, powerful moments of her life.

He watched her for another long moment before nodding warily. "Aye, that would be best."

Despite her brittle nerves and the lump rising to her throat, she forced her features smooth. *Change the subject*, a desperate voice inside pleaded. *Do something*. Aught other than standing here staring at him like a lost puppy.

She dragged in a fortifying breath. "I'll just...finish washing my hair."

She hadn't exactly *started* washing her hair before she'd nearly dunked herself into the loch and then gone falling into Artair's arms. Nevertheless, to salvage what was left of her pride, she spun on her heels and returned to the edge of the water.

There was no way in hell she was going to undress and attempt to wade back in. So she was left with the only other option—climbing onto one of the boulders and leaning far enough over to dip her head in.

Which had worked so brilliantly last time.

Still, feeling his eyes following her every move, her wits were too muddled to come up with a better solution.

She scrambled up onto the rock she'd perched upon before. It was a low, relatively flat boulder that sat halfway in the water. Leaning her head over from a crouch had nearly led to disaster, so she wouldn't be attempting that again.

She lowered onto one hip and tried tilting sideways.

The lower few inches of her hair slid over her shoulder and dangled in the water, but a good foot of air still separated her head from the loch. Biting down an oath, she strained and twisted, but to no avail.

Behind her, Artair muttered a curse and sighed.

"Let me help ye, then."

"Nay, that willnae be—"

"I insist. 'Tis far preferable than having ye drench yerself, as ye nearly did last time."

Even without turning, she sensed his approach. Heat yet again threatened to wash her face.

"Ye dinnae need to—"

"Lie back." His low voice was shockingly close.

Arguing would only make this humiliatingly awkward situation more so. With a tight swallow, she obeyed, rolling from her side to her back. She yanked at her heavy skirts as she went in an attempt to untangle them from around her legs.

As she turned toward him, he caught her arm, helping her ease back. Though she refused to meet his eyes, his gaze was as palpable on her face as a caress as he lowered himself into a crouch over her.

Now she stared up at the overcast sky, her head dangling off the side of the boulder. The water gently pulled at her hair where it drifted down. Her neck went stiff to keep her head up, but suddenly his warm hand slipped to the base of her skull, supporting its weight.

Just as it had when he'd kissed her.

She hastily shoved that thought away, but it was impossible not to think of the kiss in this position. He loomed over her where she sprawled on her back, his hand tangled in her hair, his warmth and strength held a mere hand-span above her.

In some ways, even without their lips fused, this was more intimate than the kiss had been. And mayhap just as inappropriate.

"All right?" he murmured, staring down at her.

"A-aye," she practically choked.

Blessedly, he did not point out that she sounded far from all right. Instead, he leaned down toward the water and scooped up a handful, lifting it to pour over her hair.

She pressed her lips together against a gasp. The icy water made her skin prickle with sensation as it soaked to her scalp.

"Ye still havenae answered my question."

Involuntarily, her gaze flicked to his face. He wasn't looking at her now, his gaze trained on the water he continued to cup and pour over her head.

"What question?"

"About why ye turn cagey at the mention of yer fiancé."

"He is no' my fiancé." *Blast.* She'd spoken too quickly, proving his point.

He knew it too, for he spared her a quick glance, one dark gold brow lifting deliberately.

In truth, she should be welcoming the topic of Alexander Bruce and her impending union. 'Twas far safer than speaking of other things…like the wit-melting kiss they'd just shared. Aye, let them speak of her almost-fiancé.

She released an uneven breath.

"As I said, I hardly know him," she began. "In fact, I've only met him once."

"And ye didnae like him?" It was subtle, but his voice now had a hint of an edge to it. She looked up to find his jaw had tightened slightly.

"He did naught to give offense," she clarified. Was Artair…concerned for her? Not for the first time, his protectiveness, misplaced though it was, made something tighten low in her belly. "It is just…"

"What? Is he a warty old toad, then?" he commented dryly. "Or does his head only come up to that nose ye point skyward so often?"

Despite the tension that radiated through her, she gusted a laugh. "Nay, he is perfectly acceptable in those regards."

Now that her hair was soaked through, he reached behind him, producing the bar of soap she'd set on the rock. Without removing his hand from the back of her head, he worked the soap against her hair, producing a lather. The sweet, familiar scent of her favored soap— honey and cream, with a hint of the dried wildflowers that had been pressed into it—wafted to her, soothing her raw nerves somewhat.

"What is it, then?" he asked, his tone surprisingly gentle.

She hesitated, but when he set the soap aside and began massaging it into her scalp with his fingers, any hope of maintaining a semblance of self-possession evaporated. She felt incredibly vulnerable lying beneath Artair, his fingers entwined in her hair and his low, soft voice washing over her. She couldn't help but tell him the truth.

"My upbringing was so…unusual," she murmured. "My father has given me leeway that no other nobleman's daughter would normally have. Or nobleman's wife, for that matter."

His hands stilled for a moment as he absorbed her words. "Ye think he is the type of man who willnae allow ye to help in matters of politics. That he willnae listen to ye."

"That is just it—I dinnae know him well enough to know what kind of man he is. Mayhap he will be as openminded as my father. But far more likely, he will think as most other men do—that wives, even high-born ones, are for getting heirs and naught more."

She let her eyes slide closed as he continued to work in silence.

"The only thing high-born wives can do that lowborn ones cannae is provide powerful alliances," she added quietly. "Which is exactly what this arrangement is. A political union. Naught else. If all goes well and the loyalists oust Balliol, I'm sure we will be wed by spring."

The sting of emotion behind her eyelids surprised her. She had never spoken so plainly about her impending marriage before. She'd never questioned it. And she'd even believed that she was happy to be part of such a union—not for herself, exactly, but for the good it would do for her family, and for Scotland.

Never had she let herself consider an alternative. *Love. Happiness.*

Choice.

It was not her place to want such things. Yet journeying with Artair this past sennight, she'd let herself imagine…

"He would be a fool to keep ye behind closed doors. To see ye as naught more than a means to an alliance." His voice, though quiet, held that hard edge again, as if he were trying to leash his frustration. "Ye are so much more than that."

She opened her eyes to find him staring intently at her. His gaze was like green fire, lapping at her, burning her up inside.

Oh God. Were they going to kiss again? They couldn't, for she was no longer sure she would be able to stop once they started.

Abruptly, he ripped his eyes away, breathing an oath. He reached past her head to lift a handful of water from the loch again, rinsing away the suds from her hair. Though she was prepared, the cold still shocked her.

Good. She needed the clarity it brought. It seemed even the topic of her soon-to-be-marriage was no longer enough to keep her thoughts in line. If anyone were to find out about their kiss…or worse, the longing that even now gnawed away at her insides…

"Done," he said woodenly after pouring one last handful of water over her hair.

"Thank ye," she murmured, carefully avoiding looking at him.

She squeezed the water from her tresses, then he took her elbow to help her sit upright. Even before she could reach for it, he passed her the large square of linen she'd brought for drying.

She rubbed her wet hair as best she could, but there wouldn't be time to sit by a fire and let it dry completely. It wasn't ideal to arrive at Annan with damp hair, let along ride for an hour through the cold, but she would have to make do.

"What I wouldnae give to have Beatie now," she muttered, beginning to weave a simple braid with the damp locks.

"I could take a crack at it," Artair offered, looking dubiously at the rapidly forming braid. "I thought ye were jesting when ye said I could serve as yer lady's maid, but damn if I havenae done practically everything else besides that at this point."

She had to fight a sudden laugh. Of course he was teasing, but Sybil looked heavenward, drawing out a long-suffering sigh. "Och, if ye were my lady's maid, I'd send ye to the laundress straightaway. With those callused, ham-fisted hands, ye'd make a much more suitable washer woman."

He cocked a brow at her, that coy smile that made her heart race tugging at the corner of his mouth. "Is that so, *princess*? I didnae realize my skills were so inadequate. Next time, methinks I should let ye fall into the loch."

Aye, this was better. He could tease her all he wanted, for raising her ire kept her from thinking about how good his mouth and hands had felt when he'd—

"I did not know we were in the presence of royalty, lads."

The strange male voice came from the tree line behind Artair.

Panic spiked through her gut as she scrambled to stand. Even before she could suck in a breath, Artair had risen to his feet and spun, pulling his sword from its sheath on his hip in the same motion. Though he blocked her with his body, she could see five men emerge from the trees, swords drawn as they closed in slowly.

"Allow us to introduce ourselves, Your Highness."

CHAPTER 13

Artair cursed himself a thousand times over as his gaze darted between the men closing in on them. He hadn't heard them approach. He'd been so focused on Sybil, flirting and fawning over her like a moon-eyed whelp, that he'd been caught completely unawares.

And now, thanks to his failure, her life was in danger.

"Drop yer weapons and name yerselves," he barked.

The men glanced between each other, a chuckle rippling through them.

"I think you have that backwards, man," the apparent leader said, his mouth curling into a smile that did not reach his eyes.

In the shock of their sudden appearance, Artair had only taken in the most essential information. Five men. Each with swords. All a dozen paces away, but moving in. Yet now that his brain was starting to catch up, he began noticing more.

The men wore the blood-red tabards of Edward

Balliol's army. And the one who'd spoken bore an English accent.

These were no common bandits or reivers. Yet given the fact that they served the Usurper—as hired men from England, no less—Artair wasn't sure if that made them more or less dangerous.

He took a half-step back, not in retreat, but to more fully block Sybil with his larger frame. She was likely only a pace away from the boulder's edge. One more large step and they'd back right into the loch. He didn't know if she could swim or not, but either way, her heavy brocade skirts would likely pull her under.

Nay, the only way out was through the five men closing in on them. The odds weren't exactly on his side, but he'd faced worse before.

His grip tightened on his sword's pommel. He sucked in a fortifying breath, his gaze locking on the first man he would take down.

"*How dare ye?*" Sybil's voice cracked like a whip behind him.

"Dinnae—" he hissed, but before he could get another word out, she carried on.

"Do ye understand what ye have just done?" she snapped.

Artair refused to turn his gaze away from their attackers to glance over his shoulder at her, but from the volume of her voice, he could only assume she spoke to the men before him.

They were so startled by her shrill demand that they actually froze in their advance for a moment. Before they could recover themselves, she continued.

"Ye have just raised yer weapons against the Guardian of Scotland's daughter."

Bloody rash woman. It was obvious that she was high-born. Even without the fine gown, her delicate beauty, faultless skin, and regal bearing marked her as noble. Yet throwing about that she was the Guardian's daughter might only encourage these ruffians to seek a ransom for her—after they'd used her as their plaything.

The sickening thought made Artair's lips curl back from his teeth in a wordless snarl.

For their part, Balliol's soldiers glanced uneasily between Artair and each other. He couldn't be sure if they were more thrown off-kilter by Sybil's words or the feral light that surely filled his eyes now.

"And what is more," she continued sharply, "ye are impeding official business involving King Balliol, the man I assume ye serve judging by yer tabards. The King will be most displeased to hear that his men accosted the Guardian's daughter—and on her way to see him with important news, no less."

Through the haze of battle lust that had taken over his mind, a realization slowly came to him. There was a scheme behind her cutting words and imperious tone.

It was reckless. And mad. But she was trying to... disgrace their would-be attackers into backing down. Put them in their place—which was apparently well below her—with her well-polished demeanor. And she was playing the part of an uppity noblewoman perfectly.

"Which one of ye will answer to King Balliol for this?" she demanded. "Whose idea was it, attacking the party carrying vital communications between the

Guardian and the King? And who will be hanged first for accosting the Guardian's daughter and her bodyguard?"

The leader blinked, clearly stunned by Sybil's fiery diatribe. "Balliol is...expecting you?" he asked cautiously.

"Of course he is, ye clot-heid!" she snapped.

That was a bold-faced lie, one which Artair dearly hoped they would not pay for later. Then again, they could deal with those consequences as they came. Right now, it was far more important to find a way out of this that left them both alive and unharmed.

"We came across more men not far from here," the leader continued, subtly angling to try to catch a glimpse of Sybil behind Artair. Artair shifted, keeping himself directly in front of her. "Are they part of your party?"

She huffed an annoyed breath, sounding for all the world like she was running out of patience for such ridiculous questions. "Aye. I left them to wash up before my audience with the King later this verra morn. My bodyguard came along to keep me from being waylaid by bandits."

The pointed emphasis she placed on the last word was clearly directed at Balliol's men. Another glance passed between them, this time carrying the strong waft of uncertainty.

Sybil must have sensed it, too, for she struck again at their weakening defenses.

"What is yer name, soldier?" she demanded of the leader.

Seemingly without thought, his back stiffened like

that of a naughty lad being reprimanded by his mother. "Lieutenant Erwin Harcourt, mistress."

"That is *Lady* Sybil Douglas to ye," she snipped back.

The man's mouth compressed, but he gave what little of Sybil he could see around Artair the barest incline of his head. "Aye, milady."

Good God. Was Sybil's mad scheme…working? If Artair had known what she was about before she'd begun berating the soldiers, he wouldn't have let her attempt it in a thousand years. But judging from the way the men's swords had lowered a few inches, the tide was rapidly turning in their favor.

"Now that I know yer name, I'll be sure to report it to King Balliol," she went on in that high-handed tone. "It remains to be seen what I will tell him, however. I could either explain how ye ambushed me, swords drawn like barbarians. Or…"

The men waited, and Artair doubted if any of them drew a breath. Christ, they were eating right out of her hand now.

"*Or* I could tell him how ye and yer men provided an escort to me and my traveling party, ensuring that we arrived at Annan Castle safely," she finished. "After all, all manner of miscreants seem to be on the loose in these parts."

If he hadn't been drawn tauter than a bowstring and ready to strike at the men's slightest provocation, Artair would have laughed at the added insult she'd thrown in at the end.

Despite his men's crumbling resolve, the lieutenant

apparently had to make one last stand. He narrowed his eyes. "How do we know you're telling the truth?"

Sybil muttered something about incompetent idiots just loud enough for the soldiers to hear. "When we get to Annan Castle and the guards take me directly to see King Balliol, I suppose then ye'll know," she said slowly, as if speaking to a dimwitted pet hound.

She paused dramatically as if considering. "Or I suppose ye could ride there yerself and ask the King if he wishes to receive the Guardian of Scotland's daughter, who comes bearing news straight from court. Then when he skins ye alive for yer impertinence and ill-treatment of me, ye'll know for certain."

They all stood frozen for a long moment. Artair waited, never letting his guard down. He would fight to the death if he had to in order to protect Sybil.

At last, the lieutenant flinched first. He exhaled sharply, then lowered his sword. With a quick motion to the others, so did the rest of the soldiers.

"We would be happy to provide you and your travel party with escort to Annan, milady," Harcourt said stiffly.

A small hand landed gently on Artair's arm. "Ye can put away yer weapon, MacK—Maxwell."

The catch was so swift that he was sure none of the soldiers noticed her slip.

Despite the nigh-disastrous situation they were in, she'd astutely thought better of using his real name. The MacKinnon name would clearly mark him as a Highlander, which would draw further suspicion from the soldiers, as the Highlands had been openly hostile to Balliol's claim to the throne.

What was more, if word of the Horsemen's names had spread within Balliol's ranks, the rather nondescript Lowland surname she'd selected for him would more than likely save his neck from another noose.

Eyeing the soldiers for another drawn-out moment, Artair at last relented, resheathing his blade. She glided around him, chin lifted so that she could look down her upturned nose at the lot of them.

"Come along then, Maxwell," she said airily as she stepped down from the boulder and set off toward where they'd made camp the night before.

Unless he wanted to give the soldiers a chance to change their minds and surround her, he had to scramble to gather her discarded bathing supplies and hasten after her. For appearances' sake, he was now little more than a servant with a sword. Luckily, the soldiers made no move, instead falling in behind her as she led the way.

When they reached the section of woods where he'd left the other guards, he nearly reached for his sword again. The men had indeed broken camp, but the wagon and horses had been wrangled into a small circle, along with the Douglas guards themselves. They were surrounded by at least a score more mounted soldiers, swords drawn and pointed at them.

To the guards' credit, several sported rapidly swelling eyes and Nevin was clutching a bloodied arm. Yet they must have been swiftly overpowered by the far larger number of soldiers. Blessedly, all ten men were accounted for. Thank God Balliol's soldiers had stopped to interrogate Sybil instead of slaughtering the lot of them straightaway.

"Lower your weapons," Lieutenant Harcourt barked at them. The soldiers blinked in surprise but slowly did as they were told.

Nevin's wide eyes landed on Artair. He opened his mouth to shout something, but before he could speak, Sybil piped up.

"Maxwell, go check on yer men. Make sure none has been injured." She cast a withering look at the lieutenant as if to say, *ye'll answer for it if anyone is*.

A surreptitious look passed between several of the guards, yet they were wise enough not to gainsay their mistress in front of Balliol's soldiers.

Artair strode past the circle of soldiers to the guards. He hastily shoved Sybil's things—her discarded traveling gown, the linen drying clothes, and the bar of soap—into the back of the wagon before turning to his men.

"All is well?" he asked, passing a swift, assessing look over each one. Luckily Nevin's arm seemed to have only received a flesh wound. The others nodded soberly.

"We tried to send Dermid to warn ye, but they surrounded us too quickly," Uilliam said in a low voice.

Artair glanced at the lad. He bore a rapidly worsening black eye and a split lip, but was still in one piece.

"All is well with ye, MacK—Maxwell?" Nevin murmured.

Artair nodded slowly, lifting his brows a hair's breadth to indicate that the men should continue to play along with the new name. "Aye. These lads have kindly offered to escort us to Annan Castle."

He gestured with his chin at the soldiers, who were now dispersing under Harcourt's orders.

As he watched them rein their mounts into a looser ring around their little party, a question gnawed at him. What the hell were so many of Balliol's men doing here, on lands that belonged to the Bruce family? Even though they were a mere hour's ride from Balliol's current base of operations, these woods should have been safe.

Though Tavish MacNeal's missive had indicated that Balliol was on the retreat, consolidating all his forces for the Yuletide season, mayhap the Usurper still had a few regiments crawling like rats throughout the Lowlands.

"And Lady Sybil?" Bartram prompted, drawing Artair from his thoughts. "She is unharmed?"

Involuntarily, Artair's gaze found her. She stood like a queen among peasants a short distance away, her features placid besides a touch of annoyance, which only furthered the impression of her superiority. She didn't spare him a glance, nor check on the men herself, which was exactly how a lady of her stature should behave.

"Aye," he answered, unable to look away from her. "In fact, she is the reason we are all still alive."

He'd thought she couldn't possibly surprise him any more than she already had, but he was wrong yet again.

Thanks to her swift thinking—and the skills he'd been so quick to discount as frivolous back at Scone—she'd not only saved many a life that morn, but also salvaged the entire mission from what was nearly its utter ruination. Not only that, but she'd smoothed the way for them to walk straight up to Annan Castle's gates.

All he could do was marvel for a moment before ripping his gaze away.

In short order, the Douglas guards had mounted and waited with obvious discomfort in the midst of Balliol's soldiers. Artair would have helped Sybil mount, but Harcourt had already given her assistance.

Without caring about crossing the lieutenant, Artair reined himself alongside her, wedging between the two of them. He was supposed to be her bodyguard, after all, which gave him every right to stay close. Harcourt scowled at Artair, but then nudged his horse to the front of their riding party.

With a whistle and a barked order from Harcourt, they were off for Annan.

CHAPTER 14

I t was a tense ride to Annan—at least for Sybil, who clung to her cool air of authority even as nerves chewed away at her insides.

Yet as Annan Castle came into view before them, her anxiety ratcheted impossibly higher. She could only imagine what Artair felt at the moment. He rode stiff-backed and stony-faced, though that suited his role of a bodyguard who was still rather sour for having been caught unawares.

Still, as they approached the castle, she noticed that his sharp gaze scanned deliberately over the scene before them. He could easily have claimed to be looking for threats, but she knew that he was tucking away every detail, missing naught.

Approaching from the north as they were, the River Annan curled slowly through the winter-brown land-scape to their right. On the near-side bank, a motte-and-bailey style castle sat perched above the water, looking down on the little village below it.

A great mound of earth had been dug up along the river and piled into a motte that appeared to be nearly fifty feet high. The flattened top of the motte bore a stone tower keep ringed with a curtain wall.

At the base of the mound sat the bailey, which contained several smaller structures to support life in the tower. Like the keep, it was protected by a curtain wall, as well as a deep ditch that drew water from the river to make a moat.

The castle had been built by the Bruce family some two hundred years before. The keep would have originally been made of wood, but somewhere along the line it had been replaced with stone, which would weather the years far better. Still, the castle showed signs of age and wear. The backside of the motte, which faced the river, had been partially eroded, likely from a flood. That was a weakness in the keep's defenses—one she was sure Artair wouldn't miss.

Mayhap its lack of modern fortifications was why the Bruces had gifted the keep to the Balliols a few generations ago, before the wars of independence that had set the two families against each other in a quest for the Scottish throne. It would no longer withstand a major attack, especially not from a modern siege weapon like a trebuchet, yet its proximity to both the English border and the Solway Firth, into which the River Annan drained just a few miles away, made it a strategically significant estate nonetheless.

Their party skirted between the smattering of buildings and cottages that formed the village to their left and the castle's outer wall. When they reached the front of the castle, the drawbridge spanning the moat was lowered, but the bailey's wooden gates were closed. Several red-coated guards stood watching their approach, and Sybil spotted more dotting the inner walk along the top of the battlements.

Lieutenant Harcourt peeled away from the others, leading his mount across the bridge and to the gate. He spoke with the guards for a moment, gesturing back toward Sybil and her party. She held her breath, praying they wouldn't be turned away. If her lie about being expected were to unravel, the whole mission would implode.

The moment stretched as one of the guards slipped inside the gates. After a long wait, the man reappeared and gave Harcourt a nod. As Harcourt rode back toward her, she lifted her chin, forcing an almost bored look onto her face.

"Are we to be permitted entrance, Lieutenant, or must I continue to wait in the cold?"

"You are welcome to Annan Castle, my lady," Harcourt said stiffly.

But before she could release the breath she'd been holding, he turned his gaze to the rest of her retinue. "Your men, however, are not permitted through the gates. King's orders. No fighting men allowed in the castle who have not sworn fealty to him."

She exchanged a quick glance with Artair. His brows were lowered, but he gave her the slightest incline of his head.

"Verra well," she said on an exasperated sigh. "But at least see that my trunks are delivered."

Artair spoke quietly to the others, directing them to make camp outside the village and await word from their lady. The men grudgingly reined around, eyeing their escort as they went. When Artair did not budge, however, Harcourt gave him a scowl.

"That includes you—what was your name again, man?"

"Maxwell," Artair said, holding the lieutenant's glare. "And I dinnae leave my lady's side."

He managed to soften his Highland burr somewhat, yet his flat tone clearly irked the lieutenant. Just as the man narrowed his eyes and opened his mouth, Sybil sighed again.

"Must we have yet another delay, Lieutenant? Aye, Maxwell must accompany me. My father ordered him to follow me like a hound, and Maxwell cannae verra well disobey the Guardian of Scotland, can he?"

Harcourt glared at Artair for several heartbeats before muttering something under his breath. "Fine. But you'll leave your sword at the gates."

Artair gave the man a curt nod. Still frowning, Harcourt motioned for the two of them to follow him over the drawbridge. The horses' hooves clopped hollowly across the wood, echoing the pounding of her own heart. The gates creaked open ahead and they crossed into the bailey. They were in the belly of the beast now.

The enclosed bailey was filled with soldiers in blood-red tabards milling about. A few paused in their tasks, eyeing the newcomers speculatively. Artair dismounted and unbuckled his sword belt, handing it to one of the guards, then helped Sybil down. A lad approached and took their horses' reins, leading them away.

Though she feigned only a casual perusal of her surroundings, Sybil surreptitiously made out the stables, a smithy, and what appeared to be an armory, as well as several storerooms as they were led across the bailey yard.

At the back of the bailey, they crossed through another guarded gate, which opened at the base of the motte. Sybil glanced up—and up. Several dozen steps had been cut into the man-made hill upon which the tower keep sat. There was no way to reach the keep except to start climbing.

By the time they reached the top, she was winded and hot despite the sharp winter air. They were met with yet another gate and more guards waiting for them. Once through, they at last reached the base of the tower.

Sybil craned her neck to take it in. Its grey stones matched the overcast sky. At five storeys tall, it was rather modest in size, but well-fortified. Even from here she could see more guards patrolling the battlements overhead. Pennants bearing Balliol's new crest—a lion rampant on a crimson field—snapped in the breeze that lifted from the river below.

They crossed to the wooden double doors at the base of the tower. The doors were immediately opened thanks to Harcourt's presence, but Sybil couldn't help the dubious feeling growing within her.

There were at least four guarded gates to pass through just to step foot in the keep, where Balliol must reside. And the entire castle was crawling with Balliol's soldiers—more than a thousand of them, if she had to guess. How on earth would the loyalist army manage to launch a stealth attack under those conditions?

There was no time to worry about that at the moment, though, for they were striding through the double doors and into the keep's great hall. Blessedly, Harcourt remained outside. It seemed he hadn't been invited to an audience with the Pretender King.

Then again, neither had she. Which meant she needed to get everything exactly right in the next few moments. One small slipup would cost dearly. Drawing a steadying breath, she straightened her shoulders and glided forward.

The great hall was dim, lit only by a single massive hearth and a few scattered wall sconces. Overhead, the ceiling soared, flickering with shadows. The stone floors and walls were bare of rushes and tapestries, making her delicate footsteps, and those of Artair right beside her, echo loudly.

Ahead, her gaze landed on the raised dais, where a long wooden table stretched out—behind which sat a solitary man on a gilded throne.

Balliol.

Sybil forced her feet to continue, her strides slow and even. She'd spent her whole life surrounded by powerful men. She was made for this moment—for this mission.

As she approached, she glanced covertly around. The hall was vacant except for a few servants lingering in the corners. Balliol was eating the midday meal, apparently unbothered by the spare, empty hall he sat in. He paused, a piece of what looked like roasted pheasant lifted on the tip of his eating knife, and watched them advance.

When she was a handful of paces from the base of the raised dais, she halted, then sank into an elegant curtsy. Beside her, Artair bent in a bow.

Out of the corner of her eye, she noticed his hands were clenched so tight that his knuckles had turned white. What must this be costing him, bowing to the Usurper who'd slaughtered his compatriots and attempted to hang him as a traitor?

"Lady Sybil Douglas." Balliol's voice reverberated through the great hall. His accent was an odd hodgepodge of Scottish, English, and French, as he'd been raised and spent large chunks of his life in all three countries.

She kept her head ducked, waiting for permission to rise.

"I was not expecting to receive you here at Annan," he continued evenly.

Thank goodness Lieutenant Harcourt wasn't present to hear that.

"'Twas a shame I did not have the privilege of meeting the Guardian's only daughter at Scone."

Still she remained lowered in her curtsy. Without being able to read the man's face, she couldn't tell if he was toying with her or not. He seemed to be contemplating the same thing, for he fell silent for a long moment.

"Rise," he said at last. "And tell me—to what do I owe the pleasure of your arrival?"

She would have gusted a breath of relief at crossing over the first invisible hurdle, but she was far from safe just yet.

Lifting herself gracefully, she tilted her head and gave him a modest smile. "Och, the pleasure is all mine, Yer Majesty. I, too, was sorely disappointed to have been away at one of the Douglas estates during yer coronation."

When ye stole the crown, more like. When her father had locked her away in Scone Abbey's tower, they'd agreed that for her safety, he would pretend that she wasn't even near Scone. It seems the ruse had worked, at least as far as Balliol knew.

Now that she was upright, she got her first good look at the Pretender King.

He was somewhere between his middling and older years, his forehead lined and his jawline going soft. She guessed his hair had once been rather orange, but now it was quite faded and slashed with gray. His manicured mustache, however, still held a surprising amount of red.

His brown eyes studied her down his nose. Though he looked rather pampered, sitting on his gilded throne in an ermine-trimmed robe of deep royal purple, she knew he had to be keen and resilient to have survived this long in the center of a decades-long political struggle for control over Scotland.

"Do not tell me you came all this way—in the winter, no less—just for a social call." His voice was flat and his eyes sharp as they flicked over her.

Behind her practiced smile and serene façade, her thoughts raced ahead. Balliol had no problem cutting straight to the point—and he was already dangerously close to seeing right through their ruse.

Regardless of the cordiality he'd shown initially, they both understood the complex dynamic between Balliol and her father. As Guardian, Archibald Douglas was sworn to serve young David—from whom Balliol had just stolen the throne. Yet ultimately her father had to follow the will of parliament, which could be swayed to accept Balliol's claim of succession.

So despite being at the heart of the loyalist cause to oust Balliol and restore David, her father could not proclaim himself Balliol's enemy— at least publicly. That tension had played out at Scone during Balliol's confirmation, with a taut civility hanging over the palace until Balliol had departed. Now, Balliol seemed willing to treat Sybil as a lady and a guest, but they both knew she walked a very narrow path between her loyalty to her father, and to her new King.

Aye, Balliol was no fool. Mayhap it was because he'd spent his life cast aside, trailing after England's Kings in hopes of receiving scraps, that he would not easily be played with naught more than flattery and a pretty face.

Which meant Sybil's every move now had to be perfect. Artair and her life, not to mention the entire loyalist cause, depended upon it.

She had expected a more elaborate dance with Balliol, slowly charming her way into his confidence, but if he wished to plunge straight in, then so would she.

"Nay, Majesty, I havenae come solely for the privilege of meeting ye. My father sent me with some rather pressing business. But if I may be so bold, I hope ye'll find the news I bring as enjoyable as the company that comes with it."

He set his eating knife down, which she took as a sign that she'd hooked his interest.

"What pressing business?"

With a deferential tilt of her head, she made a quarter turn on her heels, then snapped her fingers at Artair.

"The missive, Maxwell."

It felt preposterous to treat him thusly, but they each had to play their parts. Artair had straightened from his bow at the same time she'd risen from her curtsy. To his credit, he didn't hesitate to reach for the pouch on his belt. He extracted the folded parchment her father had given them and extended it to her without a word.

He had the wherewithal to keep his gaze lowered, but as she reached for the truce, she saw that there was murder in his downcast green eyes—directed toward Balliol. His fingers had turned white around the outstretched missive, and the parchment trembled ever so slightly, vibrating with the tension held in his body.

He was like a rabid, feral animal who was mere seconds from breaking free of its cage. Though she doubted anyone standing more than a foot away would notice, he looked ready to spring forward and strangle Balliol with his bare hands.

This was the moment he'd been hankering for since Scone—since Dupplin Moor, no doubt. He was in the same room as the Usurper, only a few paces away. And he had to act the part of a mute guard, little more than a servant.

Dinnae snap, she silently prayed. *No' yet.*

She knew her body blocked Balliol's view of Artair. So as she reached for the missive, she let her fingers graze his. It was only a brushing contact, but his gaze flicked up to hers for an instant. *Hold on*, she tried to tell him with her touch, and her eyes.

Though she longed to say so much more, Balliol was watching. Taking the folded parchment, she turned back to the Pretender. He cast a glance at Artair as if noticing him for the first time. Sybil's gut clenched even as she thought fast.

"My father's man," she commented casually. "He was sent to watch over me—and this document." She waved the note, the motion regaining Balliol's attention.

To her relief, she saw no lingering suspicion or recognition in his dark eyes as he refocused on her.

"Bring it here, then," he said, flicking his fingers at her.

She strode forward, halting at the base of the dais. Rather than making the presumptuous move of stepping onto it, she remained below him. As elegantly as she could, she strained across the table so that he wouldn't have to reach far for the missive.

As he casually broke the seal and unfolded the parchment, she stepped back, clasping her hands modestly before her. His eyes scanned the document, his features giving away naught.

"How...interesting," he murmured, lowering the truce offer and fixing Sybil with his gaze once more. "I wonder. Your timing is most fortuitous, Lady Sybil.

Might your arrival, and this offer, have something to do with a certain mutual friend of ours?"

Unease twisted in her belly. Ignorance was far more dangerous than knowledge in such situations. And she had no idea what Balliol was referring to.

"Forgive me, Majesty, but...mutual friend?"

"Aye. He is here, now." Balliol twisted in his throne. "I require the Earl of Carrick," he called over his shoulder to one of the servants. The servant darted behind the dais toward the spiraling stairs that led to the upper floors of the tower keep.

The Earl of...

Her thoughts ground to a halt, even as her head began to spin. Nay. Nay, that couldn't be right. He couldn't be here.

"Mayhap rumors of his presence in my camp reached your father," Balliol was saying. "I wouldn't put it past Douglas to send his daughter as a reminder of the standing arrangement you two have."

Sybil shook her head, which only made the spinning worse. "I...I assure ye, Majesty..."

"Ah, here he is," Balliol cut in, his gaze landing on the man descending the last few steps and striding into the great hall. "Look who has paid a visit, Bruce. It is Lady Sybil Douglas—your fiancée."

CHAPTER 15

I t took every last drop of willpower for Artair to remain rooted where he stood. Not that he knew what he would do if he had moved.

Some instinct told him to step in front of Sybil. The way her voice had hitched as Balliol had spoken of some mutual friend had made his already taut nerves pull impossibly tighter. And at the mention of the Earl of Carrick, they began to fray.

Now he watched, struck dumb as a rock, as Alexander Bruce, Earl of Carrick, strode into the great hall.

The man was of an age with Artair, though his build was more diminutive and his sandy brown head would come up a hand-span shorter than Artair's. He wore a midnight blue doublet threaded with silver, the cut of which was unmistakably expensive. As he entered the great hall, he paused, his blue eyes taking in the unusual scene quickly.

What in the bloody hell was he doing here? He had

fought as a loyalist against Balliol at Dupplin Moor mere months ago. From the way he was dressed and the easy air of calm about him, he was no prisoner.

Did that mean...had Alexander Bruce flipped allegiances? The man was a damned Bruce, nephew to King Robert the Bruce and first cousin to David. Yet here he stood, the apparent guest of the Usurper, blood and justice be damned.

Belatedly, Artair ripped his gaze away. As he suspected, he'd never crossed paths with Bruce—a blessing, for the man wouldn't recognize him, despite the fact that they'd fought in the same battle that very summer.

Bruce did, however, recognize Sybil. When his gaze landed on her, his eyes widened.

"Lady Sybil. What are ye doing here?"

If Artair hadn't been standing so close to her—only a pace away—he likely wouldn't have been able to read the emotions that flashed one after another behind her eyes. Confusion. Fear—at being found out in their scheme. And then calculation as the same realization that had hit him reached her. There was only one good explanation for why Alexander Bruce was here. And it boded naught but ill.

As the stunned silence stretched, they both seemed to remember themselves at the same moment. Bruce sketched her a bow and she gave him a half-curtsy.

"I would ask ye the same question, my lord." She was too skilled to let her tone slide toward accusation. Instead, she managed to sound surprised yet perfectly poised at the same time.

Bruce turned toward where Balliol sat on the dais

and gave him a stiff nod. "I am honored to grace our new liege's presence with my company."

"And delve into a spot of business," Balliol added, undercutting Bruce's vague formality.

Now that wee comment deserved investigation. What business did Alexander Bruce have with Balliol? And how would the pair's apparent newfound alliance affect their efforts to oust the Usurper?

Artair would have no answers now, however. He was forced to stand mutely by, praying that Sybil could navigate this new turn of events for the both of them.

Yet again she proved that he had no cause to worry. After her initial shock, she seemed to have recovered herself.

"It has been several years, my lord, but I am glad to see ye in good health," she said to Bruce.

"Your arrival seemed almost too perfectly timed," Balliol commented to Sybil. "I wouldn't have put it past Douglas to offer a truce if he'd caught wind that Alexander Bruce has ingratiated himself to me."

That confirmed it, then. Bruce had turned traitor against his own family and the loyalist cause to back Balliol. Artair swallowed hard against the hot vitriol climbing up his throat. There was no price in the world that would make him do the same, but it seemed Alexander Bruce was more easily bought. Artair could only wonder at what he'd been promised in the bargain.

Fleetingly, a new realization hit him. Mayhap that explained why Balliol's English soldiers had been crawling all over the Bruce family's ancestral lands surrounding Lochmaben. Aye, it seemed Bruce had not only flipped his allegiance, but also turned the proverbial keys to the Bruce family castle over to Balliol.

"But your surprise appears genuine," Balliol continued, eyeing Sybil.

"Indeed Majesty, I had no idea the Earl of Carrick was paying a visit. I dinnae wish to intrude—"

"Nonsense," Balliol interrupted. "You could never intrude on your own fiancé."

"*Intended* fiancé," she murmured, but Balliol ignored her.

"You have done as you've promised, Lady Sybil," Balliol said, lifting the unfolded parchment once more. "You've brought me a most intriguing bit of information to consider. I find my curiosity is not close to satisfied, but you must be weary from your travels. Allow me to host you for the evening meal, and take your rest in one of the keep's guest chambers in the meantime."

With a wave of his hand, another servant leapt forward, seeming to materialize from naught.

"This way, milady," the older man murmured, then set off for the spiral stairs.

Sybil had no choice but to dip into a hasty curtsy before following.

Artair bowed, but neither Balliol nor Bruce paid him any mind. At Balliol's gesture, Bruce stepped onto the dais and took up one of the chairs beside the Usurper, their voices lowered in murmurs as Artair fell in behind Sybil.

∾

THOUGH SHE LONGED to speak in private with Artair, Sybil wasn't given a moment alone for the next several hours.

Once she was shown to her chamber, Artair, as a dutiful bodyguard, was forced to wait outside while several maidservants attended to her. The trunks containing her gowns were hauled up the stairs and placed in the chamber, and the maids set to work carefully shaking out, brushing, and hanging each fine garment.

While she waited, a wooden tub and dozens of buckets of warm water were delivered as well. Despite all the effort she'd put into bathing before being presented to the Usurper King, it seemed she was to be afforded two baths in one day. At least her hair would not require washing again. Her cheeks heated at the memory of Artair's assistance in the task earlier that morn.

It was hard to believe it was the same day. Though she sat poised on the edge of the chamber's bed while the servants worked, inside she was a storm of anxiety. What on earth was Alexander Bruce doing here? The line she walked with Balliol was narrow enough as it was. Now she had to juggle her traitorous almost-fiancé at the same time.

And all she wanted to do was turn to Artair.

Though she would have liked to send the maids away, they insisted on staying to assist her. She left her hair braided to keep it from getting wet, however. Once she was scrubbed and dried, the maids helped her into an even finer gown than the crimson brocade she'd arrived in.

This was a gold silk that caught the candlelight and made her practically glow. The wide square neckline showed an expanse of creamy skin that was fashionable without being immodest.

Sybil opted to unplait her hair, keeping only the front pieces pulled back with the pearl-studded clasp her mother had gifted her. Because it had been wet when she'd braided it that morn, her locks fell in a wavy cascade of shimmering auburn down her back.

While men of war donned armor before battle, she had this, she mused—silk for chainmail, a smile for a shield, and her wits as her only weapon to wield.

Giving her thanks to the maidservants, she ushered them out, following behind. She found Artair leaning on the wall opposite her chamber door. As the maids scurried past, he straightened, his green gaze sweeping her.

"Am I fit to hold court with a King?" she asked, feeling suddenly nervous and hot under his perusal.

He opened his mouth, but had to clear his throat before any words would come out. "Aye, ye…ye look more than suitable."

For his part, he still wore his travel-worn boots, though somehow he'd managed to change into a fresh pair of trews and a tunic. Despite his simple garb, he looked both mesmerizing and lethal. He was meant to blend in with the other guards and servants who moved in the orbit of nobility, yet his powerful build, coiled strength, and the intensity of his emerald-green gaze were hard to hide.

"I just learned from one of the servants that Balliol and Bruce have already descended for the evening meal," he murmured, stepping aside so she could move into the stairwell beside him. "This may be our only opportunity to talk."

She glanced both directions in the stairwell before nodding and beginning a slow descent. Artair stayed close, offering her his arm, which she gladly took.

"Did ye have any inkling that yer intended had turned traitor?" he demanded in a low whisper.

"Of course no'," she replied. "Nor do I understand why he would hitch his wagon to Balliol. It makes no sense."

"Aye, well, there must be a reason. Find out what ye can, as will I. His presence…complicates things, but the mission isnae compromised. We can still see this through."

"If I can answer Balliol's curiosity satisfactorily," she amended. "He seemed intent on riddling me with questions, and he certainly isnae without suspicion."

"I have every faith in ye."

She paused, her foot hovering over one stone step. Artair now stood a step below her, but they still weren't quite eye to eye. In the flickering light from a wall sconce partway up the stairs, she studied him.

"Ye do?"

"Aye," he answered without hesitation. "And I never should have doubted ye. Ye are smart, capable, and just as yer father told me, ye are a hell of a lot stronger than ye look."

A breath gusted from her lungs even as warmth

suffused her. She hadn't realized until that moment how much she needed to hear that—and from Artair most of all. Though she put on a brave face, inside she was terrified at the responsibility she bore—for the cause, and the lives of the men who would sacrifice everything for it.

But she was not alone. Even if he could not stand beside her, she knew Artair believed in her. That knowledge gave her the strength she needed to face Balliol yet again.

"Thank ye," she breathed, unable to say more around the lump that had suddenly risen in her throat.

"Ye can handle Balliol—and Alexander Bruce," he said, giving her a nod. "All we need is for them to believe in the truce, and to let us leave unscathed."

"What of ye?" she whispered as they began their descent once more.

"I will scout as much as I can tonight, once ye are safely bolted into yer chamber."

"The castle's defenses seem…formidable."

While she didn't wish to cast doubt into his mind, she was sure he'd noticed the same things she had. The multitude of walls, gates, and armed soldiers would make the inner tower keep nigh impossible to penetrate. Though the castle was rather aged, launching a stealth attack against its defenses would be almost impossible.

He muttered a curse. "Aye, but let me sort that out. Ye worry about getting us away from here without drawing more suspicion—hopefully by tomorrow. The sooner we are out of this viper's den, the better." He cast her a sideways glance that brought an involuntary blush to her cheeks. "Just dinnae charm Balliol so much that he doesnae wish to let ye go."

As they approached the bottom of the stairs, Artair released her arm and fell back a few steps to trail her. The great hall, empty last time she'd seen it, was now filled with over two hundred soldiers in crimson tabards. They sat at trestle tables lined before the raised dais, where Balliol once again sat. Alexander Bruce was to his right, and an empty chair she assumed was meant for her sat on his other side.

Straightening her spine, she glided across the space toward the dais. More than a few heads turned and whispers followed in her wake as she went. She paid them no heed, waiting for the moment Balliol caught sight of her.

When he did, she ducked her head modestly, pausing at the base of the dais to give him another deep curtsy.

Alexander Bruce leapt to his feet and extended his hand, helping her up and to her seat. On a whim, he ducked over her knuckles and gave them a kiss before releasing her hand, much to Balliol's amusement.

"Well done, Bruce," he commented, taking a sip from his gilded goblet.

For her part, she had to force herself not to snatch her hand away and wipe it on her gown. Just that morn, Alexander Bruce had been no more than a stranger. He'd been easy enough to look upon in their one and only meeting, though she'd had her misgivings about what sort of man he was. Now that she knew him to be a traitor to not only the cause but his own family, she found him downright revolting.

Like a familiar shadow, she sensed more than saw Artair move into position behind her. His nearness was a comfort, though neither of the men beside her seemed to even notice him. The King, himself, had his own personal guards at each corner of the dais, and despite his lack of red tabard, Artair appeared to be just another in their number.

She darted a quick glance at him. He stood with his hands clasped behind his back, his gaze scanning those gathered in the hall as if looking for any threat to his mistress. With so many servants flitting about between the high table and all the others, he drew no attention, yet she knew he watched and listened with the acuity of a hawk.

"I am struck once again at the remarkable excellence of your timing, Lady Sybil," Balliol commented once she was settled in her seat. "To travel across half of Scotland to deliver a missive, only to find your fiancé, is rather too convenient, do you not think?"

Yet again, she had to suppress her surprise at his blunt directness. It seemed she would be given no quarter to eat in peace before his inquisition was to begin. But a King—even an illegitimate one—was no doubt used to demanding answers whenever he chose.

And she knew just what he was fishing for. Despite his convivial tone, his continued prodding about why she was here at this particular moment revealed his suspicion.

"'Tis an odd twist of happenstance, most certainly,

Majesty," she replied evenly. "But I assure ye, I had no knowledge of the Earl of Carrick's presence here. Nor did my father."

"Please, my lady, call me Alexander," Bruce said, leaning past Balliol to give her a stiff smile. "We are to be wed, after all."

Sybil had to bite down on the correction that rose to her tongue. They were not engaged just yet, despite what he might assert. With Bruce's change in allegiance, she had no idea where their proposed union stood anymore. But given her tenuous position with Balliol, there was no way in hell she would bring that up.

"I had thought mayhap Douglas was offering the truce in light of my new ally," Balliol continued, glancing at her. "And that he sent you to either win Bruce back or join us on our path to victory."

Sybil lifted a morsel of roasted pheasant to her lips, chewing to buy herself time to think. Heaven help her, Balliol clearly had no qualms about stating his accusations. He spoke to her like she was a man, which she would normally appreciate, except that it took away her ability to hide behind charm and manners. Balliol must have had some inkling that she'd served her father in his political maneuverings to speak to her so plainly of strategy.

Though she was caught off-guard by his bluntness, the more he spoke, the more she learned about how his mind worked.

He was clearly a tactical thinker himself, sensing moves and countermoves even when there weren't any. That would be explained by a life spent in royal courts, angling for power and position. He was also profoundly suspicious, which she would have to redirect away from herself if she and Artair were to escape alive.

"Why else would Douglas send you on such a trek?" Balliol added as she swallowed.

"My father would have brought the offer himself," she said smoothly, "but he wished to set to work wrangling parliament straightaway, Majesty. Like herding cats, 'tis."

"I am surprised he would find that task so pressing." Though his voice was still casual, she did not miss the sharpness in his gaze as he continued to stare at her.

She understood what he was really asking. Why the hell would her father wish to force parliament into a decision over who could rightfully claim the throne when one of the two outcomes would mean his ousting from the position of Guardian? *Especially* given the fact that they wanted Balliol to think his claim was the more favored of the two.

She needed to take control of the narrative Balliol was forming about her, her father, the truce—all of it. She chose her next words very carefully. "My father grows older, Majesty. It is a time when many men look to secure their legacies."

"He wishes to be aligned with the victor, ye mean," Bruce murmured. Balliol smiled faintly without removing his gaze from her.

Fighting not to curse Bruce for the slimy snake he was, Sybil tilted her head deferentially. "Ye will have to forgive the blindness of a loving daughter, Majesty, but I dinnae believe my father is driven by pride." Her mind flicked back to her conversation with Artair on pride and power. "At least no' entirely," she added.

"Then why would he offer a truce," Balliol said, patting the chest of his velvet doublet, where she assumed he'd tucked the parchment, "especially if he thinks the mood is with me, as he implies here?"

"The latter part of a man's life is also a time when the larger picture often becomes clearer. Scotland is in turmoil. He sees what this unrest—this uncertainty—is doing to our people. We need a clear path forward, no' all this chaos and in-fighting."

Balliol leaned back in his chair, his mouth compressing ever so slightly under his manicured mustache. "How noble of him."

Though she hadn't meant the implication, she now saw that Balliol had taken her words as a subtle criticism. He was responsible for bringing war back to Scotland after years of relative peace—the country had been united under Robert the Bruce, and had even wrested a multi-year truce from England.

Thinking fast, she brought a troubled frown to her face. "Forgive me, Majesty, but nay, my father doesnae act solely out of the goodness of his heart. I shouldnae speak so plainly, but…"

That piqued his curiosity. His brown eyes flickered with interest even as he gave her a coaxing smile. "Come, Lady Sybil. You can have no secrets from your King."

Now she had him hooked and was nearly in his trust. But she had to make him feel as if he were extracting some dark confidence from her, else his suspicion would continue to simmer.

She gnawed on her lip as if struggling with the decision. At last she nodded to herself. "He would want ye to understand, though he couldnae put it in writing. Let me be blunt, then. It is no secret that my father stood behind David's claim to the throne. The line of succession was obvious. But after Dupplin Moor...things changed."

Both Balliol and Bruce hung on her next words, their trenchers of food and goblets of wine forgotten.

"Yer victory was so decisive—and the loyalists' failure so absolute—that my father realized the peril in David's youth. 'Twould be another decade of waiting for his majority—a decade that would leave Scotland open to attack."

Loathing sat like a hot stone in her throat. It was galling to have to speak such words. The worst part was there was some truth to them. Scotland *was* vulnerable, as proven by Balliol's coup.

But she, like the rest of the loyalists, knew that freedom came with risk. David carried the legacy of his father, Robert the Bruce. He stood for a Scotland free of English tyranny. Balliol, on the other hand, was little more than a puppet of England's King Edward. He cared naught for Scotland, except insofar as he could use it for his own personal gambit for power.

And Alexander Bruce must be no different to have turned away from his family legacy to embrace Balliol. Both men were driven by selfish hunger for more. And she had to convince them that her father was just like them.

"But with ye on the throne, we need no' wait on an uncertain future." Behind her smile, her teeth ground together. "And stability benefits us all, does it no'? Wars are expensive. Men. Supplies. Coin. It is we, the nobility, who feel those costs the greatest."

A floorboard creaked behind her, and she knew Artair had shifted his feet on the dais. It was a miracle he hadn't surged forward by now to stop the flow of filthy lies she spouted.

Speaking the vile words—that lightening the purses of already-wealthy nobles was a greater tragedy than the lives lost among the soldiers who actually did the fighting—left a bitter taste in her mouth. But they had the intended effect.

Bruce's sandy brown eyebrows winged, and Balliol shook his head ruefully.

"You have the right of that, my lady. Even as we speak, these men Edward sent threaten to eat me out of house and home."

It was working. She was earning their trust. A new idea dawned on her—a way to help the loyalists even more. The move would be bold—dangerous—but she needed to cement the progress she'd already made.

"I suppose," she said, pursing her lips in mock thought, "one benefit of the truce my father offers is that ye could send away at least some of yer English reinforcements. At least for the Yuletide season. No need to feed so many men when ye have a cease-fire in hand from the Guardian."

She held her breath as Balliol considered her for a long moment, his features flat. After what felt like an eon, he gave a slow nod.

"I see now why Douglas sent you, Lady Sybil. You may be a woman, but you have the Douglas wit."

"Ye are too kind, Majesty. But sending me was meant more as a gesture of good faith. My father wouldnae send his only daughter into yer camp without trusting we can come to an... understanding. The truce ceases this needless conflict while benefiting both parties."

"I see. So your father buys himself time to bring parliament around." He paused, waiting for her to nod in confirmation. "While also protecting his coffers from a long, drawn-out conflict." She nodded again.

Balliol's eyes wandered out over the sea of soldiers dining in the great hall. She could practically hear him calculating the savings he would reap by sending the men home for a few months.

As far as he knew, the loyalists hadn't pulled themselves together after their defeat at Dupplin Moor. With Bruce at his side and a truce offer in hand, mayhap he thought the tides truly were turning in his favor.

Yet what remained unacknowledged was the fact that Balliol had found no support to speak of among the Scots, not even in the Lowlands. He must have also been considering the precarity of his position—an unwanted, unliked King who had been forced to flee to this ancient keep to regroup. His only backing came from Edward of England, a man singularly reviled across Scotland.

She saw in his keen eyes his suspicion over the unexpected boon of the truce. But it was simply too tanta-lizing an offer to refuse.

"You have represented your father, and your case, well, Lady Sybil."

She was about to release the breath it felt like she'd been holding since the moment she stepped foot inside Annan Castle, when Balliol went on.

"But…"

Heaven help her, what more could she do or say to convince him?

He waited for a server to step forward and refill his wine goblet, seeming to enjoy stretching the moment.

"I have seen too many truces crumble in my life. Some were never meant to hold, while others, even well-intentioned, fell apart over the slightest inconvenience or misunderstanding."

"Majesty, I'm no' sure—"

"Because what is this" –he reached into his doublet and extracted the truce— "but a wee bit of ink on parchment? Nay, I require more than that."

Fear coiled like a snake in the pit of her stomach. "What do ye have in mind?" she heard herself ask.

Balliol smiled, but it didn't reach his brown eyes. "It occurs to me that your arrival has dropped an unusual opportunity in my lap, Lady Sybil. An opportunity to unite as allies in more than mere words."

He turned to Bruce, who was listening with a puzzled look on his face. "I wish for the two of you to be wed. Here and now."

CHAPTER 16

Artair nearly choked on his own tongue at the Usurper's request. Nay, demand, for it seemed he would not accept the truce otherwise.

Which meant that if they hoped to leave Annan Castle alive, they would be forced to acquiesce.

Or rather, *Sybil* would be forced.

Nay! some primal voice inside him screamed. He could not let that happen. She could not marry that traitorous worm. But how the hell could he stop it?

A breath gusted from her lungs. From where he stood behind her, he could only see the side of her face that was turned toward Balliol, but he knew she'd let her calm façade drop and her shock was clearly written on her face.

"What? We cannae…that is, I cannae simply…"

"Bruce here has become a trusted ally these last few months," Balliol said, unperturbed by Sybil's fumbling. "And it seems Douglas would like to become one as well. Still, I cannot put all my faith in his allegiance to me, given his ties to the loyalists. But if his only daughter were wed to one of my closest allies…" He grinned as if he were most pleased with his solution.

Bloody, rotting bastard.

"I…I am sorry for the confusion, Majesty, but ye must understand there is no formal arrangement between us," Sybil said, her gaze darting to Bruce. "We cannae simply be wed. No' on such short notice. Nor without my father's permission."

Ignoring her, Balliol turned to Bruce. "What do you think, Bruce?"

The man looked nearly as shocked as Sybil, yet he was recovering far faster. "Aye, I can see the logic in it, Majesty. A clever bit of alliance-building, that."

The arse-kissing weevil.

"Majesty, please, I must protest…" Artair watched on, helpless, as Sybil's throat bobbed on a hard swallow, and then another.

He knew exactly what raced through her mind now. To defy the King's wishes would destroy all her hard work in gaining his trust. Though she'd been forced to play a precarious game with him, she'd managed to sell the truce, conceal her father's true motives, and ingratiate herself to him all at once. She'd been masterful, subtly guiding Balliol without him ever becoming aware of the lead by which she pulled him.

If she refused to marry Bruce, all her efforts would be for naught.

But if she agreed…

She'd told him once that her life was devoted to the cause as surely as a foot soldier's. Aye, she did not stand on a battlefield or risk being run through, but if she were to marry Alexander Bruce, she'd be sacrificing her body, her very life, all the same.

Their only hope, only the barest of slivers wide, was to delay—and pray to find a way out of this disaster.

It seemed she'd reached the same conclusion Artair had.

"I...I couldnae wed without my father's blessing," she mumbled. "I must insist on his behalf that he be given a chance to stand by my side on my wedding day. As he is all the way in Scone, I dinnae see how—"

"Then let us send him a message via pigeon," Balliol cut in, "Though I did not know how I would use them at the time, I brought several messenger pigeons with me from the palace dovecote after my coronation. It seemed wise to be able to communicate with Scone on short notice."

"Indeed, Majesty," Bruce remarked.

Balliol clapped his palms onto the wooden table's surface. "'Tis decided then. We'll send word to Douglas first thing tomorrow morn."

"He will have no way to reply, Majesty," Sybil offered weakly.

"Nay, but mayhap if he is as determined as you say to see his daughter wed, he will come with all haste. How long did it take you and your party to reach Annan, Lady Sybil?"

"Six days, Majesty," she whispered.

"Then we will give him a sennight. But mark me." Balliol leaned toward Sybil, fixing her with his gaze. "Whether he arrives or not, a wedding will take place."

She nodded mutely, and the group on the dais was distracted for a moment as the servants removed their trenchers.

"Forgive me, Majesty, but I find my travels are catching up with me. I'd ask yer permission to retire for the evening," Sybil said once the table was cleared of all but their wine goblets.

Balliol waved his hand in approval, but before Sybil could rise, Bruce sprang from his chair.

"Allow me to escort ye, my lady," he offered, extending his hand toward her.

Artair nearly stepped forward and snapped the man's wrist in two, but some last thread of sanity stopped him. Sybil hesitated, but then accepted Bruce's proffered hand.

As Bruce guided Sybil off the dais and toward the stairs, Artair fell in behind them, feeling like the prowling hound she'd called him to Lieutenant Harcourt. He caught up with them as they paused at the landing outside Sybil's chamber door.

"I would speak with ye a moment, Lady Sybil," Bruce said, casting his gaze down the spiral stairs at Artair. "Alone."

Artair was about to bark a refusal when Sybil held up one delicate hand to stay him. She pursed her lips, considering Bruce.

"Mayhap we might take some fresh air on the tower's battlements?" Bruce offered, nodding to where the stairs continued to climb upward.

It was the perfect opportunity to extract valuable information from Bruce, of course. They would be away from Balliol's dominant presence and the servants' and soldiers' prying eyes and ears. Mayhap she could learn why Bruce had turned to the Usurper's side, or even find a way out of their looming forced marriage.

But some irrational, overprotective side of him screamed that he shouldn't let her out of his sight.

"Wait for me here, Maxwell," she ordered in that condescending tone nobles so often used with their servants. Yet as she spoke, she fixed Artair with a look that said *Trust me.*

Artair ground his teeth against a sharp rejoinder. To keep up appearances that he was merely her bodyguard, he couldn't go about contradicting her in front of Bruce.

All he could do was give her a curt nod of acquiescence and watch her go as she and Bruce continued up the stairs.

When they reached the top of the stairs, Bruce put his shoulder to an arched wooden door. The door groaned in its frame before popping open, sending cold air swirling through her skirts.

Extending his hand to her once more, Bruce guided her up the last few stone steps to the open battlements atop the tower keep. The night was dark, the moon concealed by clouds, but four torches lit the battlements, one at each corner.

Two guards turned to look at them as they mounted the last stair, one on the eastern wall of the battlements overlooking the little town below the castle, and the other on the west above the river. Sybil tucked away that bit of information to share with Artair later.

"Leave us," Bruce ordered flatly. The guards hesitated, but when Bruce fixed them each with a cold stare, they abandoned their posts.

The hairs stirred on Sybil's nape and arms, and it had naught to do with the sharp early December air. Alexander Bruce had been naught but a well-mannered gentleman since he'd appeared in the great hall earlier that day. Yet mayhap that had all been an act for Balliol's sake.

He guided her to the southeast corner of the battlements, farthest from the door. Then he turned midnight blue eyes on her.

"So, we meet again, Lady Sybil."

"And what an unusual meeting it is, my lord."

He flashed his teeth at her in something that was close to, but not quite, a smile. "I told ye before, my lady. Ye must call me Alexander, for we are to wed—rather soon, it seems."

"Unless my father objects. It appears yer circumstances have…changed since our union was originally proposed."

Though she was careful to keep her voice neutral, his eyes narrowed ever so slightly.

"Aye, I suppose ye are wondering why I am here. Let us speak plainly, Lady Sybil. I know ye are something of an advisor to yer father."

Distantly, she wondered if Bruce had told Balliol as much, which would explain the Usurper's willingness to talk bluntly with her.

"Which means ye understand better than most the inner workings of politics," he continued. "The winds of power change. Old alliances crumble. New ones form."

"And yet," she said, fighting to keep her temper leashed, "the bonds of blood remain."

In the flickering torchlight, his features hardened. "Ah yes, the bonds of blood. 'Tis a funny thing though —I was bastard-born. So despite the Bruce blood running through my veins, I was made to be a half-stranger in my own family."

Sybil blinked. "But clearly now ye are accepted. Ye have inherited yer family's title."

"Only because there were no other heirs," he retorted. "It took years after my father's death to secure my rightful claim to the earldom."

She was now certain that his courtly manners earlier were all a façade. A new picture of her intended was beginning to emerge. He seemed a petty man, and aggrieved despite his powerful position.

Mayhap that was why he had turned on the loyalists to join Balliol. Though they'd lived lives of luxury and influence by dint of birth alone, they both thought they deserved more.

"Ye must have felt passed over," she said carefully. "Much like Balliol."

Bruce scoffed. "I can see what ye are getting at, but nay, I dinnae feel some deep affinity with the man. The Balliol family's claim to the throne is about a solid as a soap bubble. And yet, here we are." He waved his hand as if to take in both Balliol and himself. "Nay, my motives are less ideological and more...practical."

"Why, then?" she murmured, examining his features.

"I told ye, I had to fight for my inheritance—my title and lands. After Dupplin Moor, it was obvious that the loyalists couldnae protect them—protect me and mine."

Instinct told her there was still some bit of information she hadn't grasped. Unease rippled over her like a cold breeze.

"And Balliol could?"

He stared down at her intently. "Ye dinnae know, do ye? I had assumed Douglas had caught wind of what Balliol has planned. That the truce was meant to stay Balliol from his course before Edward of England could accept his offer."

The rapid thud of her pulse echoed in her ears. "What offer?"

Bruce gave a dry chuckle. "For once, I put too much stock in old Archibald." Refocusing on her, he gave her a patronizing look. "I suppose there is no harm in telling ye, as ye'll hear from our new King soon enough. Though Edward of England has sent men, coin, and supplies to Balliol's cause, he hasnae publicly declared his support. He is close, though. Balliol means to give him the final nudge."

"How?" she demanded, not quite managing to check the edge to her tone.

"He intends to cede the shires of Berwick, Roxburgh, Dumfries, Peebles, and Edinburgh—among others—to Edward in exchange for his formal backing."

"W-what?" she breathed. "He cannae—"

"He is King, Lady Sybil," Bruce cut in coldly. "Of course he can."

"But that is nearly the entirety of the Lowlands." In fact, it included the lands and castle upon which she currently stood. And Balliol meant to simply…*give* it to the English. "How… and when?"

"Balliol has already begun drafting his pledge of loyalty," he replied, sounding almost bored. "He means to send it by the start of Yule—a wee Yuletide gift for Edward." He smiled, but it didn't touch his blue eyes. "And he plans to declare his intent publicly as well, so that Edward knows he means it. Edward will surely agree, though he would likely take even more if he could."

In the haze of shock that surrounded her, a new realization sliced through her mind. "He would have taken Bruce lands, ye mean."

Bruce fixed her with a hard look, and she found herself taking an involuntary step back. She bumped into the cold stones of the battlements, cornered.

"Aye, Balliol would have offered up my portions of Galloway and Dumfries if I hadnae…convinced him to make an exception."

"That is why ye are here—why ye've joined him. To protect yer own hide at the expense of the rest of Scotland."

"Careful, my lady." Bruce took a slow set forward. "Ye sound dangerously close to a loyalist. And those arenae welcome here."

In her fear and shock, she had failed to check her tongue. Desperately, she reached for her normal cool composure, but through the maelstrom raging inside, she could not quite grasp it.

"I dinnae know if ye are telling the truth about yer father's motivations in offering the truce, but it doesnae matter now. It plays nicely into Balliol's hand," he said, watching her with cold eyes. "The promise of no further violence from the rebel loyalists will only sweeten the pot for Edward. Our union is an added bonus, as well."

"Oh?" she mumbled.

"Oh aye. Once Edward recognized Balliol as Scotland's King, yer father will be forced to step down as Guardian. I will take charge of forming Balliol's new parliament—with ye by my side. I doubt Douglas would have the stomach to lead a loyalist offensive if it meant putting his only daughter in danger."

A shiver swept over her as her understanding—of Bruce's nature, and Balliol's plans, as well as her own future and that of the cause—was now fully complete.

There had to be some way out, some solution to this disastrous situation, but her mind could not conjure it.

Her only hope was to be away from Alexander Bruce and pray that she and Artair could come up with something.

"I am cold," she said, forcing herself to stare back into his hard gaze. "I am going inside now."

"Mayhap I can warm ye." He took another half-step forward and placed a hand on the stones on either side of her, effectively caging her in. "Ye are a vision tonight, my lady."

Panic shot through her like a flaming arrow. She was cornered between the battlement stones and Bruce's larger form. She could call upon his noble sensibilities to let her go, but he'd already shown her that he had none.

"Nay," she said in a loud, firm voice. "Let me pass, my lord."

"I can see the struggle behind yer eyes," Bruce said, ignoring her command. "Ye are still loyal to yer father— an admirable trait. But soon enough ye will be loyal to me and me alone. I will expect naught less as yer husband." His dark gaze slid over her, making her skin crawl. "Ye might as well get used to that, for in a sennight, ye will belong to me."

With no further warning, his arms closed around her and he clamped his mouth over hers. She tried to scream, but the sound was muffled by Bruce's assailing kiss. Even if she'd been able to cry out, who would have heard her all the way up on the battlements?

He pressed her back into the stones. Their rough surface scratched her hands where they were pinned to her sides, but she hardly felt it, nor the cold seeping through the silk of her gown. She tried to writhe out of his hold, but he only squeezed her tighter, until her lungs burned for want of air.

Distantly, she knew he would not stop until she submitted to his assault, but she never would.

Artair. Her heart screamed out to him, but he was not there.

CHAPTER 17

Artair had given them bloody well enough time alone. Still, she had asked him with her eyes to trust him. If he undercut her at the wrong moment, it could raise Bruce's suspicions about Artair's true role there.

He paced the small landing outside her chamber door for what felt like the thousandth time. It was only a step and a half long, so he likely had walked it a few hundred times already.

Muttering a curse, he took to the stairs, no longer able to hold himself back. Something about the man didn't sit right. And not just because he was a bloody traitor to the cause. His manners were too pretty, his affect toward Balliol too obsequious.

As he neared the top of the tower, he slowed. He was acting like an overbearing brute, not to mention ignoring his "mistress's" orders to stay put. Mayhap he could discreetly check on Sybil without charging onto the battlements like a bull with a bee up its arse.

He passed the tower garrison on the last landing before the top, where soldiers were typically stationed between their shifts on watch. Someone had left the door ajar, and two voices, along with the warm glow of candlelight, seeped out into the stairwell.

"...think he has her skirts up around her ears, yet?" one of the English guards was saying.

"Bloody rutting Scottish savages," the other muttered, then spat.

"You only wish you could take a turn with her," the first shot back, chuckling. "If I were in that Scot lord's shoes, I would already..."

Artair had heard enough. Aye, Sybil needed to get Bruce alone to speak with him, but if those filthy guards thought the two were slipping away for a tryst...then Bruce might, too.

He would have to deal with those foul-mouthed Englishmen later. He shouldn't have left Sybil alone for so long, appearances be damned.

He shot up the last few steps and reached for the door that led to the battlements. When it stuck in its frame, he used the full force of his strength to shove it open. The door flew outward, banging on the stone battlements.

What he saw curdled his stomach even as white-hot rage flared through him.

Bruce had Sybil cornered, his mouth crushing hers. She struggled in his hold, but his arms held her prisoner against the stones.

The sound of the door slamming into the wall made Bruce jump and swivel his head. Artair didn't remember scaling the last few steps onto the flat expanse of the battlements. Nor did he remember crossing to the far corner, where Bruce held Sybil.

The next thing he knew, his hands were closing on Bruce's fine doublet and he was flinging the man off Sybil. Bruce gave a startled yelp, which turned into a grunt as he crumpled to the stones half a dozen paces away.

Sybil staggered as Bruce's hold on her was abruptly torn away. But before she could fall, Artair caught and held her.

"Art—" Despite the chaos of the moment, she stopped herself just in time. "Maxwell," she breathed instead.

Never had he longed so badly to hear his real name spoken. "Are ye well?"

Even as he spoke, he scanned her for signs of injury. The flickering torchlight revealed fear shining in her eyes, and her lips were swollen and unnaturally red. Yet she gave him a shaky nod.

"I am fine—now."

"How *dare* ye lay hands on me?" Bruce demanded from the ground behind him.

Artair turned, using his frame to block Sybil from the sight of the bastard.

Bruce was slowly picking himself up and straightening his rumpled clothing. "I am an Earl and yer better."

Artair squeezed his hands at his sides to prevent from punching the teeth out of Alexander Bruce's head.

"And I am here at the behest of Archibald Douglas, Guardian of Scotland, to ensure that the lady is unharmed," he rasped.

"I wasnae harming her, ye insolent son of a who—"

That was it. The man needed the living shite beat out of him, and Artair was more than happy to oblige, consequences be damned.

He took one step forward before Sybil's small hand on his arm halted him.

"Stop!" she cried, though Artair wasn't sure if the words were meant for him or Bruce.

She sidestepped around Artair, casting him a pleading look before focusing on Bruce.

"Maxwell was only doing his duty," she said, visibly fighting to regain her composure. "A duty which wouldnae have been necessary had ye no' taken…liberties beyond which ye should have," she added quietly.

Through the raging bloodlust pounding in his veins and roaring in his ears, he distantly marveled at her ability to placate Bruce while also subtly chastising him. At least one of them was keeping their head and protecting the larger mission.

"Ye are practically my wife," Bruce hissed. "Mine to do with as I please."

"But no' yet," Artair ground out.

Bruce eyed Artair, taking his measure. They both knew that despite the Earl's higher social standing, Artair would best him in every other contest.

Muttering a curse, Bruce turned his head and spat. Artair was gratified to note that it was tinged with blood.

"Balliol was too lenient in granting a sennight for yer father to give his blessing," he muttered, fixing a hard glare on Sybil. Artair nearly shifted in front of her to shield her from the bastard's vile look, but he knew he ought to be deescalating the situation instead of adding to the tension.

"Even if the old codger could arrive in time—which I doubt he can," Bruce went on, "Douglas would be a fool to deny our union. It would mean crossing Balliol, and with Edward's backing, Douglas might as well run himself through with his own sword than say nay."

"Mayhap," Sybil said, her voice steady now. "But until that time, I am in my father's keeping, no' yers."

With one last dark look at Artair, Bruce muttered another curse and strode to the still-open door leading off the battlements.

Artair hadn't realized he took a step after the man until Sybil caught his arm again.

"Let him go."

He turned to her, Bruce instantly forgotten. "Ye are truly all right?"

She lifted a shaky hand to her lips, which were no doubt tender. Her eyes suddenly clouded as she let her calm, controlled mask slip.

"I-I prayed ye would come."

He was about to gather her into his arms and hold her until she knew she was safe again, but faint footsteps on the battlement stairs had him spinning around. He half-expected Bruce to be back—and he would happily fling him down the stairs if he required assistance—but instead of the Earl, the two guards on watch shuffled onto the battlements to take up their posts.

"We cannae do this here," she whispered behind him.

"Aye, my lady," he said, loud enough for the guards to hear, and gave her a stiff bow.

Christ, he'd nearly just been caught embracing her as a lover would. The rage he'd felt at seeing Bruce pinning Sybil still tinged his blood and clouded his mind.

He stepped aside so she could glide past him toward the stairs. As he followed her, he gave each guard a sharp look. Though they did not know he'd overheard their crude talk, he was pleased to see both shrink back slightly as he passed.

When they reached her chamber door, she turned to him.

"I have much to tell ye."

"Matters of business can wait," he murmured. "Ye dinnae have to put on a brave face now."

Her lower lip wobbled. "Will ye come in with me— just for a little while?"

"Aye." He opened her chamber door for her, scanning the room quickly to ensure no one lurked inside. Satisfied, he moved back onto the landing to let her inside. Soft footsteps echoed up the spiral stairs. A maid climbed toward them, her head down.

"My mistress has a headache," he said once the maid noticed him. "She doesnae wish to be disturbed for the rest of the night."

"Aye, milord," the maid said, bobbing a quick curtsy before continuing on toward the chambers higher abovestairs.

Even after the maid was out of sight, Artair waited, straining for sounds of anyone else's approach. Assured that no one was near, he ducked inside Sybil's chamber.

It was completely improper and downright dangerous to bolt himself into the chamber with her, but he didn't care at the moment.

Once the door was firmly shut and the wooden crossbar lowered, he turned—only to find his arms suddenly full of Sybil. She gripped his shoulders, burying her face against his chest. He stood frozen for a moment, worried he might frighten her with the intensity of his feelings. He still wanted to bash Bruce's skull in, and whisper soothing words to Sybil, and squeeze her so close that there was no space left between them.

Her small, soft body trembled against him, and he belatedly realized she was crying. He'd known her only as an incredibly strong, capable woman, and it only fueled his anger at Bruce that he had made her cry.

"There now," he offered softly. "He willnae touch ye again."

She pulled back a little, gazing up at him with glistening eyes. "But he will. In a sennight's time."

"Nay." The word came out hard as granite, yet he could not modulate his tone. "Ye willnae wed that bastard. I promise."

Her auburn brows pinched together. "Ye need to hear what I learned from him."

To his regret, she stepped out of his arms and

smoothed a hand over her gold silk gown. As she relayed all that Bruce had told her—of the man's cowardly motivations for turning traitor to the cause, and Balliol's plans to gain Edward's backing—a knot of trepidation pulled tighter and tighter in his gut.

When she had finished, he stood in silence as he absorbed the grim picture.

"Balliol was always little more than Edward's puppet," he muttered. "But I didnae believe the man would literally give Scotland away in chunks to England."

"Bruce said Balliol would wish to include both news of my father's truce and Bruce and my union in his missive to Edward," Sybil said. "Which means that we have a sennight before Balliol sends his proclamation of fealty to England—and likely no more. He willnae want to wait any longer to secure Edward's backing."

Artair scrubbed a hand over his stubbled jaw. *Bloody hell.* What a mess this was.

"If ye arenae here, ye cannae be wed to Bruce. We could slip out somehow, head back to Scone and—"

She shook her head slowly. "Fleeing would alert both Balliol and Bruce that something is afoot, that the truce—and my presence here—werenae what they seem."

Breathing a curse, he strode to the hearth, which glowed with a low fire.

"What is more," she continued, "leaving now wouldnae stop Balliol from sending word to Edward. And once he has England's full backing, the loyalist cause willnae stand a chance. Nay, we cannae flee just to save me from having to wed Bruce."

Damn it all, she was right. If they dropped appearances that their visit was friendly and that Douglas was open to working with Balliol, they would likely be drawn and quartered as traitors and spies. Fleeing would have the same effect—it would rouse the Usurper's suspicions, alerting him to the fact that the loyalists were up to something.

Yet waiting about on the hope that not only would Douglas receive Balliol's message, but that he would also be able to reach Annan in a sennight, was a fool's errand. Douglas would be walking into a trap, one in which he would be forced to give his consent for Sybil to wed Bruce or else risk exposing them all.

And even if they could find a way to stop the marriage, it would not stop Balliol from signing away Scotland's lands and freedom to Edward.

"We cannae do naught," he bit out, even as he strained to come up with a single solution.

"There is…one possibility."

He spun to face her. She had her hands clasped before her, her fingers working nervously against each other.

"Or rather, a chance." She huffed a chuckle, but there was no mirth in it. "More like a prayer."

"What?"

She hesitated, and unease rippled over him.

"If we could get word to my father somehow… mayhap he could mobilize the loyalist army and…" She met his gaze, her eyes refractive as cut amber in the low firelight. "And they could launch an attack on Annan Castle."

He couldn't be understanding her correctly. "After we have escaped, ye mean?"

"Nay. With us inside."

"How would... and when..." Full sentences—nay full thoughts—escaped him.

"In the next sennight," she replied. "If the army could move fast enough, they would arrive when Balliol expects my father. Or else..." Her throat bobbed on a hard swallow. "Or else mayhap not until after Bruce and I are wed."

To his utter disbelief, he realized she was serious. "Nay. Absolutely no'. That is the maddest bloody plan—nay, it isnae even a plan, but a fantasy—that ever was. Nay, Sybil. No way in hell."

She hastily strode to him, clasping his hands in a wordless plea. "But think on it, Artair. Balliol is complaisant. He believes he is safe inside Annan's walls, and thinks he has the upper hand. He imagines he is in control. This is our best—and mayhap *only*—chance to oust him before he has the full strength of England behind him."

"Do ye hear yerself, lass?" he demanded. "An army cannae be mobilized across more than a hundred miles in a mere sennight. And even if they could, there is no plan of attack. We cannae simply pound away at Annan's walls. We'd need a strategic approach."

"Which ye can form while we wait for the next sennight."

He pulled his hands away from hers to rake his fingers through his hair. "How would I even communicate a plan to them. There wouldnae be time to—"

"Ye are right, there wouldnae." She gave him a resigned, sad smile. "Somehow we will have to find a way."

"Nay." He shook his head, staring at her. "Nay, Sybil. I willnae let an army lay siege to the castle—no' with ye inside."

"What other choice do we have?" she asked softly. "I'm no' turning tail and running to save my own hide at the expense of the cause, and of Scotland. I'd be no better than Alexander Bruce if I did."

Bloody fecking hell and damnation.

He wasn't sure if he spoke the curses aloud or if they simply rang through his head as loud as church bells.

She touched him again, laying gentle fingertips on his arm and drawing him out of his tumultuous thoughts.

"I know it is mad. I know it is dangerous. But I see no other way."

Desperation clawed at him. He could see no other way either, yet to put her in the middle of danger like that…

His heart hammered hard enough to crack open his ribs. Hot bile filled his throat as the memories rushed back. Of the blood. And his baby brother's rasping last breaths.

"Ye dinnae understand," he heard himself say, as if from a great distance. "I cannae…"

When he forced himself to look at her, she was studying him, her eyes glowing with a new alertness. "What dinnae I understand? What arenae ye telling me, Artair?"

All the air rushed from his lungs, as if he'd taken a punch to the stomach. He needed her to know why he couldn't put her life at risk with this mad scheme of hers.

Which meant he needed to tell her about Ewan.

CHAPTER 18

Sybil watched Artair with mounting trepidation. Aye, her plan—or fantasy, as he'd called it—was far from perfect. What was more, the stakes—for the cause, and their lives—couldn't be higher.

Yet something else seemed to be chewing him up from the inside out. His green eyes had taken on a haunted look. His large, lean frame radiated tension, over which his control seemed to be rapidly unraveling.

With a sharp exhalation, his taut energy suddenly shifted. He closed his eyes for a moment, his throat bobbing on a swallow.

"I never told ye," he began, his eyes still shut. "My brother was with me at Dupplin Moor."

A new wave of apprehension washed over her. "Nay, ye didnae. In fact, I didnae know ye have a brother."

When he opened his eyes at last, they were shadowed with pain. "*Had.*"

The breath stilled in her lungs. "I am sorry."

"He died on the battlefield. And it was my fault."

"Nay," she replied without thinking. Her heart twisted to think of not only the agony of losing a brother, but the blame he apparently carried. "I'm sure it wasnae——"

"Aye, it was," he ground out, his features turning to granite. "For if it hadnae been for me, he wouldnae have even been there."

He scrubbed a hand over his face, breathing an oath. "I shouldnae be snapping at ye," he murmured. "But I need ye to understand."

He looked around the chamber. As there were no chairs, he gestured toward the large wooden chest that sat at the foot of the bed. "Come. Sit."

Once they were both settled, she waited for him to continue.

"He could have been my son, so many years separated us," he began, his emerald eyes going soft and distant. "I was first-born to my ma and da, but they faced only losses after me. Until Ewan."

Ewan. Sybil sent a silent prayer up for his soul.

"I was seventeen when he was born, and already off to fight at Bannockburn. His arrival, though a blessing, took our ma to heaven. Our da went no' long after that, so Ewan was raised by distant relations." He scoffed quietly. "They must have filled his wee head with outsized stories of my exploits in the Bruce's army, for whenever I managed to come home, he would beg me to tell him tales of great battles and play-act all my heroic victories."

The lad must have worshipped Artair. And how could he not, with an older brother like that? Even she had heard the rumors of his preternatural abilities and skills.

"By the time he was twelve, he was begging me at every visit to take him with me, let him join the cause," he continued. "'Twas easy at first to deny him. He was too young, though he vowed that he trained every day with the sword."

He shook his head slowly. "But this spring past... He was a grown lad at last, strong and strapping. And he was seventeen—the same age I'd been when I set off for war. I...I couldnae refuse him any longer."

Artair's gaze drifted back to the low flames in the hearth. "Of course, I knew that no matter how well he'd trained, he wouldnae be ready for the battlefield—no man is. Ye cannae prepare for the chaos of it, the noise and confusion. Nor the bloodlust that surges in yer veins. But I was to be there by his side. I was to look out for him."

The last was spoken in a low, strained murmur. Sybil couldn't help herself. She reached out, placing her hand over the fist he had clenched atop his thigh. Though his fingers eased ever so slightly, his voice still reverberated with taut emotion.

"What was more, Dupplin Moor should have been naught more than a wee skirmish. We had Balliol's English forces outnumbered ten to one. We had the advantageous position on the north bank of the River Earn. But none of that mattered."

Sybil had to swallow hard against the rising lump in her throat. She knew what had happened next. Balliol's men, aided by the traitor Andrew Murray on the loyalist side, crossed the river in the dead of night and set upon the Scots while they slept.

It hadn't been a battle but a slaughter. It was said that in the pandemonium, many Scots had not even had time to lay a hand upon their swords before being slain. The bodies had piled higher than a spear propped up on its end.

"Ewan…" Artair's jaw worked for a long moment before he could go on. "He fell beside me. I held him as his life's blood drained from him. And I lied to him."

His green gaze, still distant on the fire, sheened with unshed tears. "He kept asking if he would be all right. And I told him he would be. But he must have known I was lying, for he had fear in his eyes until the verra end."

Tears now streamed unchecked down Sybil's cheeks, but she would not remove her hands—the other hand joined the first to clasp Artair's clenched fist—to wipe them away.

She thought of her own brother, John, and what it would mean to lose him.

"Och, Artair," she whispered. "It is enough to bear the weight of yer grief for Ewan. Ye neednae add blame and self-recrimination atop it."

"But I *am* to blame," he countered, his voice going hard. "Ewan never would have been there if it wasnae for me."

"Aye, he would have," she countered. When he turned wide eyes on her, she hastily went on. "The way he looked up to ye, he would have gone with or without yer blessing. And if no' Dupplin Moor, he would have found a different battle."

"Then he was cursed to have me as an older brother," he rasped. Before she could reply, he added, "And he wasnae the only one I failed. I should have seen the weaknesses in our strategy. We should never have been caught so unawares. Ewan and so many others paid the price for my failure."

Suddenly Sybil could see the whole of Artair's drive to take Balliol down. She glanced down at his squeezed hands—the same hands she'd washed what felt like a lifetime ago at Scone. Back then, she'd thought him too impatient, full of dangerous haste to launch a counterattack against Balliol.

But he wasn't acting out of personal vengeance, as he'd led her to believe before. Nay, he sought absolution for his perceived sins. Ousting Balliol wouldn't bring Ewan or the others lost at Dupplin Moor back, but mayhap it was the first step in atoning for the wrongs—misplaced though they were—he heaped upon his own shoulders.

There was no use in arguing with him that he wasn't solely responsible for the loyalists' destruction. Nor the fact that Balliol was to blame for Ewan and the other loyalists' deaths, not Artair. Despite that, his drive for justice very well might be what saved Scotland.

Which was why it made no sense to her that he would argue against their chance—albeit slim—to scrape together an attack on Annan.

"What if this is our only chance to make it right?" she asked carefully. "Wouldnae ye regret no' taking it, even though the odds are against us?"

He turned to her, searching her with those incisive

eyes. "I made a vow," he murmured, tracing her features with his gaze. "After Dupplin Moor. Despite all his grand ideas and training, Ewan was an innocent. I should never have brought him into the hell that is warfare. I promised myself I wouldnae involve other innocents in this fight. Dinnae ye see?"

His hand slipped out from under hers to cup her cheek tenderly. "If the loyalist army attacks, ye'd be in the dead center of a battle. I cannae put ye in danger like that. If I were responsible for another innocent life lost…"

He dropped his head, giving it a little shake as if to clear away the dark possibility.

A new realization dawned on her. This was why he'd been so against the idea of her coming along on this mission. He'd alluded to as much before, but now she saw what was at the root of his protectiveness. It wasn't because he thought her incapable. He feared that if aught happened to her, he would bear the blame— another black mark on his very soul.

"Ye arenae responsible for my life," she countered gently. "I am. And I would choose to take this chance for our cause."

He gave a frustrated exhale. "'Tis more complicated now, lass. I cannae risk that. I cannae risk *ye*, Sybil. No' when I've come to—"

She'd been about to form another protest, but the words died on her tongue.

"—to care for ye," he said haltingly. "A great deal."

Everything froze for an instant, including her heart.

Then it began beating madly like the flapping wings of a caged bird, desperate to break free.

"I have come to care for ye, too," she breathed.

Their gazes collided, and the chamber dissolved around them until only they remained. Time slowed, just as it had when they'd kissed by the loch. She needed his kiss again, to feel his strength, his passion. She needed even more.

She leaned toward him, tilting her head up, silently begging for his mouth. He, too, drew in as if pulled by an invisible thread, but then his gaze slid to her lips. He froze, his dark gold brows lowering.

"Ye will be sore from what that bastard Bruce did. We shouldnae—"

Sybil shook her head. "I dinnae wish to ever think of his lips on mine again. Please, Artair, take away the memory. Give where he took."

Something changed in his face then. His hesitance melted away, to be replaced with a raw hunger that would have frightened her if she didn't trust him completely.

Then suddenly his lips connected with hers. Yet despite the desire that had flashed like green fire in his eyes right before he'd closed the distance between them, it was barely more than a feather-soft brush.

That would not do. She knew now what it was to be kissed, thanks to their interlude at the loch. She leaned into him, wordlessly demanding more. Her hands found his shoulders, pulling him closer.

"Easy, lass," he breathed against her lips. "I aim to take my time with ye this night."

Shock at his bold proclamation sent warmth rippling over her skin. Did he mean to… Would they…?

How she loathed her ignorance in these areas. All she knew was that she wasn't supposed to allow—or want—any of this. But all that she'd believed about propriety and virtue had been thrown to the wind upon learning of Alexander Bruce's true character.

How could it be right to give herself, body, mind, and soul, to a man such as Bruce? And how could it be wrong to want Artair MacKinnon, who was brave, honorable, fiercely protective, and who saw and accepted all of her—who knew her very heart?

Yet for all that certainty, she was traveling into uncharted waters now. What would it mean to give herself to Artair when she was to wed Bruce in a mere sennight?

Though Artair insisted it would never come to that, what if the army didn't arrive in time to stop the marriage? Would Bruce be able to tell that she'd betrayed him? She no longer cared what the consequences would be for herself, but would Artair be punished somehow?

As if she'd spoken all her questions aloud, Artair paused and pulled back slightly.

"Ye will still be a maiden after this night, Sybil," he murmured. "Yer virtue is yers to give only when ye are ready. But I need to show ye how I feel. Let me give ye pleasure."

His words chased away all the lingering doubts and uncertainties. Aye, she would need to consider just what it would mean to give herself completely to him—sometime when her senses weren't already clouded with desire. But to share this night with him...to let him show her what lay beyond this white-hot longing she felt...

"Aye," she breathed.

And suddenly he was kissing her again. But now, all hesitancy had fled. He still moved slowly, deliberately, yet there was an intent behind his kiss that sent a thrilling shiver through her.

One of his big, heavy hands came to rest on her knee, the other lifting to cradle her head. She practically melted like warm tallow under his touch. Her initial over-eagerness eased as she let herself sink into the moment, into the slow-building heat of his kiss.

Now that she knew what to expect, she immediately opened to the warm caress of his tongue. He tilted her head, delving deeper. Dimly, she realized this mating of their mouths was an explicit prelude to a more complete joining. That sent her anticipation ratcheting higher, wringing a moan from her throat.

His fingers reflexively curled, bunching her skirts at her knee and tugging gently on the hairs at her nape. Little darts of sensation shot through her, gathering low in her core.

When he broke away, her breaths came in ragged pants. He dragged his mouth down her neck, pausing to kiss the fluttering pulse in the hollow between her collarbones.

"Ye dinnae know how badly I've wanted this," he rasped against her heated skin. He kissed a trail down the square neckline of her gown until his lips grazed the rapidly rising and falling swell of one breast. "But I never let myself hope it would happen."

He released his grip on her hair and her head sagged back. Holding the weight of it up seemed too great a demand when sensation pummeled her in warm waves. He dragged one finger along the same path as his lips, down one side of the gown's neckline, then across her chest to the other side.

Gooseflesh chased after his fingertip, drawing her nipples taut beneath the silk. She ached for his touch there—to find relief from the need, or to send it soaring higher, she did not know.

Once again, he seemed to read her thoughts. Even while he kissed his way back up her neck, his hand slid down to cup her breast. Despite the layers of cloth separating them, his palm felt hot as a brand. He moved slowly over her, creating a delicious friction against her nipple.

She arched shamelessly into his touch, hungry for more of the rapidly blossoming heat coursing through her. She nearly jumped from her skin when he dipped below the gown's neckline and brushed her pearled nipple with his fingertips. A gasp stole from her lips just before he claimed her in another deep kiss.

Warm need gathered between her clenched thighs as his skillful onslaught continued. Vaguely, she registered him tugging at the laces running down her back. The laces loosened and the silk sagged from around her shoulders, giving Artair more room to work.

He slipped his whole hand inside her gown, his callused palm rasping deliciously against her overheated skin. She moaned into his mouth, the mounting sensation making her feel bold and reckless.

Then he was kissing his way back down her neck again, this time tugging down her gown as he went. She'd thought she could not feel more than she already did, but when his warm, wet mouth closed over one of the peaked tips, she realized just how wrong she was.

She would have flopped back onto the bed if she hadn't caught herself on her arms. Even still, she let her head loll back, luxuriating in the sensation. He lingered over each breast, laving, kissing, caressing, before sliding lower still.

He came down onto his haunches before the chest on which she sat. Inexperienced as she was, she had no idea what he planned to do until he began slowly rucking up her skirts.

"Open for me," he demanded softly.

Though modesty told her not to, she was too far gone. Molten need pulsed through her, demanding relief. So she eased her knees apart. Satisfaction flashed in Artair's eyes as he moved into the space between them.

He pushed the silk higher, baring her stockings. Then cool air tickled her exposed thighs. His hands skimmed higher still, until he brushed against her most private place. Sybil jerked involuntarily. She'd never been so sensitive there as she was now.

And Artair gave her no quarter. One thumb slid along her sex, wrenching another shudder and a moan from her. She was shockingly wet, but then again, Artair didn't seem perturbed by it. In fact, he murmured something low and appreciative as he parted her and dragged his thumb thought the moisture.

Just as he had with her breasts, he played with her. Teased her. Slowly explored her while she panted and squirmed. She should have been horrified at her wanton abandon, but all she could feel was a need that slowly spiraled higher and higher.

He shocked her yet again when he abruptly gripped her hips and gave her a sharp tug forward on the chest. She now sat perched on the edge—with his face right between her legs.

Before she could discern his intent, he leaned forward and closed his mouth on her. If her arms hadn't been propping her up, she would have collapsed backward. So *this* was the pleasure he'd spoken of. If she'd known she was capable of experiencing this with him, she never would have hesitated out of shyness or decorum.

Soon it was all too much, as if her body could not contain all the sensations. She began to tremble as she felt herself reaching a crest. Then all at once the wave broke over her. She bit down on a cry as she swirled through ecstasy. He rode it out with her, his mouth wringing every last drop of pleasure from her until at last the tremors subsided.

She was vaguely aware of him rising and straightening out her skirts. Then he scooped her up like a ragdoll and lowered them both onto the bed. Instinctively, she curled into him, practically purring like a cat as he ran a hand up and down her back.

"That was…" For once, a pretty turn of phrase

failed her, so she simply made a noise that was part-sigh, part-satiated groan. Her half-lidded gaze slid over him, snagging on the prominent bulge straining against his trews.

Though she was sheltered and innocent when it came to such matters, she knew what it meant when a man...grew.

"Can I...?" Tentatively, she laid her hand on the thick column. He flinched and hissed as if she'd dealt him a blow.

Startled, she snatched her hand back. "Have I done something wrong?"

"Nay," he breathed. "No' in the least. But dinnae ye fash over that." He shot a glance down at himself. "This night was for ye."

She fell into a satiated lull as he continued to stroke her back and hair, but all too soon, he stiffened and shifted out from under her.

"I know I said I meant to take my time," he said, easing up from the bed, "but it isnae wise for me to stay here. Even with my warning to leave ye be, if one of the maids came knocking..."

Reluctantly, she nodded. He was right. If they were caught, even their slim hope of making it out of this alive would be dashed.

"And tomorrow?" she said, sitting up and holding his gaze. "If Balliol stays true to his word, he'll send a messenger pigeon to Scone. What are we to do?"

She watched a war wage on his features. The pleasure he'd given her was like a dream, heady and perfect, yet it changed naught of their predicament.

The harsh reality outside this chamber still awaited them.

Artair scrubbed a hand over his chin, muttering a curse.

"The missives I gave yer father just before we left Scone."

"Aye?"

"In them, I told each Horseman to be ready for a strike against Balliol. Scattered as they are across Scotland, I wrote that they ought to begin gathering more centrally in case we needed to attack soon."

He looked heavenward, releasing a breath.

"I thought by 'soon' I meant no' long after ye and I returned to Scone with a scouting report on Annan—in the early new year, or mayhap even just after Hogmanay, if we could mobilize quickly. No' in a bloody sennight."

Cautious hope budded within her. "I know it isnae ideal—"

He snorted at the understatement.

"—But there is at least a chance the Highland army has already begun moving south, then, isnae there?"

"*If* the missives reached them," he amended, "and *if* yer father does indeed receive Balliol's summons to Annan. And *if* we can somehow alert him to our new scheme. And *if* he can get word to the other Horsemen about it. And *if* they can mobilize across half of Scotland in a sennight's time. And *if* we can form a plan of attack against the castle. Then aye, there is at least a chance."

It was so preposterous to hope that a half-wild

chuckle rose in her throat. "When ye put it like that, ye make it sound almost too easy." Just as quickly, she sobered. "Still, it is our best chance."

Artair sank to his knees beside the bed so that they were eye to eye. "Ye must promise me something, Sybil. I will do everything in my power to keep ye safe, but ye must keep yerself safe as well. Whether from Balliol or Bruce or the English soldiers or, hell, from the loyalist attack if it ever comes."

His eyes were dark with intensity as he scanned her face. "Naught can happen to ye," he murmured, almost more to himself than to her. "I couldnae lose ye."

Suddenly her throat was too clogged with emotion to speak, so all she could do was nod.

CHAPTER 19

Artair squinted into the sharp winter sun as he descended the stairs that led from the tower keep to the lower bailey. Balliol had insisted on taking them to the castle dovecote himself, so Artair was forced to play Sybil's shadow once again.

It was its own form of torture to be so close to her, yet not be permitted to touch her. After giving her pleasure last night, he felt half-crazed with the memory of the feel of her, the taste of her.

The way she'd responded to his touch, he'd nearly ripped his clothing off and tumbled her back into the bed, his promise to leave her a virgin be damned. And when she'd laid her delicate hand over his aching cock, he'd nearly come in his trews like a green lad.

As it was, he'd had to give himself relief from the pent need after he'd slipped from her chamber and made a quick sweep to ensure that all was quiet in the tower keep. If he hadn't, his raging lust would have kept him up all night where he'd slept on the stone landing outside her door. He hadn't wanted to impose upon her, especially after what she'd endured with Alexander Bruce, but he'd be lying if he didn't admit that he'd longed for her touch rather than his own.

The more he got of her, the more he needed. Yet in the light of day, before the others, he could only act as her bodyguard, a hired hound following at her heels.

Not that he minded watching over her—especially because Bruce was among their rather odd little party. The man's presence was a forceful reminder that Artair needed to keep his wits sharp and his senses alert. Fantasies about Sybil would have to wait until later that night, when she was safely bolted into her chamber.

Balliol had taken the lead, flanked by a few of his personal guards. Artair thought that ridiculous. Why would the man need protection while sealed inside his own fortress, surrounded by his own soldiers? Spending time with Balliol face to face, Artair was coming to learn that he was all too self-important, believing it was his birthright to claim both the crown and the privileges that came with it.

Which was likely why Balliol wore an ermine-trimmed velvet robe of deep royal purple, the train of which dragged behind him for several feet. The scribe, whom Balliol had ordered to accompany them, trailed after him, careful not to step on the Usurper's robe.

After the scribe came Sybil and Bruce, who'd greeted her with stiff formality that morn in the great hall. Artair moved close behind them, ever watchful, yet Bruce made no move toward Sybil, nor even spoke to her.

Their odd procession had the soldiers in the bailey yard parting before them like water around a ship's prow. As they passed, Artair once again attempted to make a rough count of the soldiers' numbers, the location and size of the armory, the positioning of guards along the outer wall—aught that would give him even a slight edge. If they were to have any chance of success against the solid old castle, he would need every scrap of information he could gather.

Past the stables, their party came to a halt. A small dovecote had been built against the inside of the curtain wall. A man—presumably the pigeon fancier who bred and looked after the birds—was just stepping through the low wooden door built into the conical brick structure.

Catching sight of the King, the fancier hastily bowed. It seemed he had already been alerted to their purpose, for he held a small grey dappled bird in his hands.

"Majesty," the fancier said, straightening. "The pigeon ye requested."

"First we need the missive," Balliol said, shooting a look at the scribe.

With a flourish, the scribe, a short, balding man who squinted even now that they were out of the cold winter sun, opened the handled box he carried. He extracted an ink pot, feathered quill, and a rectangular piece of parchment not much bigger than Artair's palm. The man handed all his supplies to Bruce, then with a few maneuvers, the box itself turned into a small writing surface with legs.

The scribe arranged his materials with care, then dipped his quill and lifted his head to Balliol, giving him a nod of readiness.

"To Archibald Douglas, Guardian of Scotland, Parliamentarian, and leader of the distinguished and powerful Douglas family and clan," he began, assessing Sybil and Bruce with keen brown eyes. "Your truce is benevolently received and your daughter is safe in my keeping. In recompense of your gesture of good faith, I have one of my own."

It seemed the Usurper had no interest in being short-winded, despite the limited space on the parchment. The man not only liked to hear himself talk, but apparently he liked to be read at length as well. Artair glanced down at the scribe, whose bald pate was bent to his task, but the man was unperturbed. In fact, his writing was so tight and small that there was still plenty of room for Balliol's musings.

"Lady Sybil's intended, Alexander Bruce, Earl of Carrick, is currently in residence with me at Annan. To build the newfound will of friendship between us, they will marry in one sennight's time, here at the castle. You are cordially invited to grant your blessing and present your daughter on her wedding day."

Artair couldn't help but note Balliol's choice of words, which were certainly intentional. Douglas was invited, but not required for the marriage to go forward. Of course, the invitation was more a loyalty test than aught else, to see if Douglas was truly willing to be in league with Balliol—and Edward of England, by extension—for his own personal gain.

"Safe passage, and may this be the beginning of a fruitful union." Balliol chuckled softly at his double-entendre—he could mean the union between he and Douglas, or Sybil and Bruce. Artair had to clench his hands behind his back to avoid doing something foolish with them.

The scribe passed Balliol the quill, and he signed his name, followed by a large 'R' to denote his status as King.

"Majesty, if I may be so bold?" Sybil interjected.

Before Artair had left her chamber last night, they'd discussed how to handle this moment in careful detail. She needed to add her own message to Balliol's, one that would make their scheme clear to her father without raising the Usurper's suspicion.

Balliol looked at her, one brow lifted.

"I believe my father's mind would be put at ease to have a brief word from me, as well," she said, giving Balliol a demure smile. She glanced at the scribe. "Written in my own hand. That way, he will know I am hale and that I have agreed to this."

"What does your agreement have to do with aught?" Balliol said, his mouth turning down slightly behind his russet mustache.

Careful, lass. It was torture to be forced to watch without being able to speak or intercede. All he could do was trust that she could handle herself—and Balliol.

Her smile turned bashful, and she lowered her eyes, fluttering her lashes. "Och, I only meant that I, too, wish for him to be here. Mayhap hearing from me will help him take yer invitation for what it truly means—a chance for a new alliance, and a new future. I would ask for yer approval of every word, of course," she added.

Balliol simply looked at her for a moment. When at last he waved his hand at the scribe, Artair silently released a breath.

The scribe passed Sybil the quill and stepped aside. She turned the scrap of parchment over, then touched the feathered end of the quill to her lips as if considering what to say. It was an act, of course, for they'd selected her exact wording the night before. Still, Sybil carried the ruse perfectly.

After a few seconds, she leaned over the makeshift table and began scratching out a neat, tidy string of letters. Once she was done, she gently blew on the ink, then handed the scrap of parchment to Balliol.

The Usurper held the parchment up to his face. "*Dearest Papa,*" he began reading aloud, "*Heed your King and come to Annan with all haste. The time is right to make good on our pledge to the Bruce family, and I would not want you to miss this special moment. As I have already brought one of my four best horses with me, please bring the other three, to be wedding gifts to the Earl and King Balliol. I will eagerly await your arrival. Your loyal and devoted daughter, Sybil.*"

Though the message would sound innocuous enough, Sybil had assured Artair that her father would glean the hidden meaning buried in the words.

The pledge she spoke of could be read as the intended engagement between she and Bruce, or the vow of fealty Douglas had given to Robert the Bruce's son and rightful heir to the throne, David II. She was alerting him to the rapidly closing window for the loyalists to strike, and telling him to gather the other Horsemen and the army. The use of the word 'loyal' was intentional as well, a reminder of the cause they both served.

Now all they could do was pray Douglas not only received the message, but understood its urgency and instructions as well.

Balliol nodded absently and passed the parchment to the scribe. "Very fine sentiments," he said to Sybil, who ducked her head in modesty. The scribe rolled the missive into a little cylinder, then wrapped it in an outer layer of waxed cloth to protect it from moisture. The pigeon fancier held the bird out while the small packet was tied to one of its legs with a ribbon. Then with a murmured word to the pigeon, the fancier tossed the bird into the air.

The pigeon gained its wings and took a half-turn above the dovecote before angling toward the northeast, rising in the clear blue sky as it went. In just a moment, it was blocked from view by the bailey's outer curtain wall.

"Should be there in a matter of hours, Majesty," the fancier said with a deferential nod.

"Excellent," Balliol replied. "Bloody hell, 'tis cold out this morn. Elgan, run ahead and tell Cook to prepare mulled wine to be served while we break our fast."

The scribe, Elgan, bobbed his head. "Aye, milord." He hastily reconfigured his makeshift table, folding the legs back in and flipping panels until it was a box once more. Then he hied off to do Balliol's bidding.

As the Usurper swanned away, his guards falling in around him, Sybil followed a respectful distance behind his trailing robe. Artair was about to follow when Bruce's hand closed around his arm, halting him.

"A word, if ye please, Maxwell."

Artair fought back the desire to pound the look of cool superiority from Bruce's face.

"Aye, milord?"

"Regarding last eve…"

For some foolish reason, Artair wondered fleetingly if the man was going to apologize for his base behavior, but when Bruce went on, that notion was snuffed faster than a candle in high wind.

Bruce took a step forward, yet Artair remained rooted, forcing the shorter man to look up at him. "I will have ye pilloried for yer interference," Bruce hissed, narrowing his blue eyes on Artair. "And then I will have ye publicly flogged until the blood flows in one wide river from yer back for yer insolence in laying hands on me."

"I serve Douglas, no' ye," Artair countered through clenched teeth. "Only he can order one of his own punished. Mayhap when he hears how roughly ye treated his daughter, ye will be the one put to the flog."

Bruce sneered. "Once I marry Sybil, whom do ye think Douglas will listen to—his son-in-law, or his hound? And whom do ye think he will be more eager to please?"

"Mayhap ye are right. But until that time," Artair practically growled, "I will follow my lord's orders to keep his daughter safe from *any* harm. If ye fancy yer hands—and yer cock—ye'll keep them to yerself."

A new light crept into Bruce's eyes as he stared Artair down. "Ye have spent a good deal of time with Lady Sybil on the journey from Scone, have ye no'?" he said, his voice unnaturally casual. "Mayhap the two of ye grew…close."

"My mistress is a lady of unimpeachable character," Artair snarled. "If ye think to impugn her honor, I'll take that as a threat just as surely as a blade wielded against her."

Bruce's lips peeled back from his teeth in a half-smile, half-sneer. "Nay, no' a threat. Just a reminder that I'll be keeping my eye on ye, Maxwell. Dinnae think to sample what is promised to me. And know that once Sybil is mine, I'll have my recompense for yer disrespect. If her father willnae see ye punished…well, mayhap *she* can pay yer debts."

Artair saw red then, but before he could do something mad, Bruce stepped around him and headed back toward the tower keep.

Though he hated to let Sybil out of his eyesight for so long, Artair stood there for another several moments, until the roar of bloodlust in his ears had calmed to a dull thud.

He didn't know how, but he would not let Bruce touch Sybil ever again. If the loyalist army didn't arrive in time, or their attack was unsuccessful, Artair would rather murder Bruce with his bare hands and take a hanging, drawing, and quartering for it than let Sybil fall into the man's clutches.

As it was, he already faced a traitor's death several times over. And not only if their scheme was discovered. Though he had no proof, Bruce must have intuited something about Artair's true feelings for Sybil.

He could not lie to himself any longer. He loved her, damn it all.

Which could cost them both everything.

CHAPTER 20

S ybil paced the length of her chamber for what felt like the hundredth time. She'd long ago given up sitting placidly before the fire, drying her hair. And she'd sent away the hovering maids who'd sought to help her bathe, hoping to capture a bit of peace in solitude.

Instead, her insides churned like a roiling sea in a mounting storm.

Six days had passed since the messenger pigeon had been sent to Scone. Six long, tense days with naught to do but wait and pray for a miracle.

Artair had kept himself busy by covertly scouring their surroundings for any tidbit of information that could aid the loyalists' attack. He kept close account of the guards' rotating watches, the blind spots from the curtain wall, even the drinking habits of the soldiers.

The castle staff were beginning to prepare for the start of the twelve-day long Yule celebration. Extra deliveries flowed more frequently now from the village— sacks of grain, casks of ale, and livestock for the slaughter were regularly carted in through the lower bailey's gates.

And Artair came and went, too. He paid a discreet visit to the village inn and alehouse every day to meet with the Douglas guards who'd escorted them to Annan.

After a lengthy discussion, she and Artair had agreed that the ten men should be brought in on their plan. Artair had been hesitant, for breathing even a hint of what they were about risked being found out—and given a traitor's death for it. If one of the men was careless with his words after a few ales, or worse, intentionally sought to thwart them…

But Sybil had insisted that the guards' loyalty was unquestionable. Their devotion to both her father and her meant that they would do everything in their power to serve them—including join a treasonous attack against the Usurper King. Besides, as she'd pointed out, they needed all the help they could get.

Eventually, Artair had relented. Once he'd briefed them on the situation, Artair had set the Douglas guards to their tasks.

If the loyalist army arrived in time to stop Balliol from sending his pledge of fealty to Edward—or to declare it publicly—Artair needed to be the first to know. But given the army's imperative to avoid detection, they couldn't simply march to Annan's gates and knock politely for Artair to come out and tell them the plan of attack.

So Artair had ordered the Douglas guards to fan out to the north of the castle, in anticipation that the army rode from that direction. Each man was tasked with scouting for signs of the army's approach, and to send a man back to the village each day to give Artair a report.

And each night after gathering the news, Artair returned to the castle and shared what he'd learned with Sybil. Which so far was all but naught. Of course, they hadn't expected word of the army's arrival in the early days after the missive was sent to Scone. But as the days stretched, it became ever more difficult to wait with no word of hope.

For her part, Sybil had spent increasingly more time in her chamber, claiming fantom headaches or simply requesting to be left alone. She would have welcomed Artair's company, but he'd kept their interactions brief and focused on their mission since that night he'd given her pleasure. He'd warned her of Bruce's suspicions about them, and his threat to keep a close eye out. It was dangerous enough to meet even briefly to discuss their secret operation, let alone linger together for another intimate dalliance.

Which meant she was left to find company with the two men she loathed most in the world. She found Balliol—who mostly spent his time either dining in the great hall or swanning about enjoying the sound of his own voice while ordering about servants and soldiers alike—to be intolerable.

And Alexander Bruce was even worse. Though he'd made no moves toward her since the incident on the tower battlements, she felt his eyes following her like a snake watching a mouse. Aye, she was to be his next meal, and the only thing that stood between them was time.

Time which had almost run out.

Tomorrow was to be her wedding day. The priest had arrived earlier that evening, and was presently enjoying the bounty of the castle kitchens with Bruce and Balliol belowstairs.

Sybil had gotten out of it with an excuse about needing to prepare herself for the wedding. That had led the servants to hastily transport the wooden bathing tub and a dozen buckets of warm water to her room, interrupting her solitude. While the bath had helped somewhat to ease the knots in her neck and shoulders, it did little to untangle the snarls of worry in her belly.

But her impending marriage was only half the reason she paced her chamber now. Artair was late in returning from the village with a report. If the loyalist army was to arrive in time to stop the wedding, tonight was their last chance.

A quiet rap on her door had her spinning on her heels.

"Sybil, 'tis me," came Artair's low voice on the other side of the thick wood.

Uncaring that her hair was still unbound and damp, and that she wore naught more than a thin chemise, she hastened to the door and lifted the bolt. When she eased the door open a crack, Artair was carefully scanning the stairwell to be sure he wasn't seen entering her chamber.

The instant he slipped inside and the bolt was lowered once more, she could not wait another moment.

"Any word?"

He turned to her, and even before he could speak, his grim-set features told her all.

"Nay."

A breath gusted from her. On legs that felt like water, she stumbled to the chair that had been set before the fire. She sank down into it, her gaze on the flames but seeing naught.

"Dermid spoke with each man, but none had aught to report," Artair added softly behind her.

Dermid had become the runner of sorts among the Douglas guards. Mayhap he'd drawn the short straw again, as he had with the fire watch on their journey, or mayhap it was because of his youth, as the task meant riding all night between each guard in the deep woods to the north, then back and forth to the village.

Either way, the lad had performed admirably according to Artair. Sybil thought distantly that she would have to recommend his promotion to her father —assuming any of them lived through Yule. Or that she would ever be able to speak to her father again, after her wedding. Alexander Bruce could forbid it once he effectively owned her.

"The last of Balliol's English regiments cleared out this morn," he offered.

That was the one bright spot of the past sennight. Balliol had taken up Sybil's delicate suggestion to release most of his English forces from service for the Yule season. Though the castle still remained well-manned with over five hundred guards and soldiers, the bailey and village below no longer crawled with men-at-arms on loan from Edward.

Besides the obvious savings on coin and food, sending the men away was a sign of just how confident

Balliol was in his position. He had a truce in hand from the Guardian, the loyalists hadn't made a peep since their defeat at Dupplin Moor, and his newfound support from Alexander Bruce was about to yield a marriage alliance with the Douglases. Not to mention he was on the cusp of securing formal support from England for his claim to the Scottish throne.

Without realizing it, Balliol had created the perfect conditions for a loyalist counterstrike. Yet no matter how advantageous an opportunity it was, none of it mattered if the loyalist army never arrived. Their window for a stealth attack was rapidly closing, for once Balliol publicly announced his fealty to Edward, they would not simply be facing a well-fortified and fully garrisoned castle, but the entire might of England.

It was maddening to be trapped inside, holding the vital information necessary to take Balliol down once and for all, yet not be able to get word to the rest of the cause. It felt as though God himself was toying with them.

Artair's warm, gentle hand swept her unbound hair over one shoulder, then came to rest there, drawing her from her dark musings. "Dermid said they willnae rest this night," he murmured. "They'll keep scouting, and mayhap push even farther northward. There is still a chance…"

She shook her head, still gazing at the fire. The low flames blurred and wavered through the tears gathering in her eyes. She could not cry. Could not fall apart now.

It had always been mad to hope that this scheme would work. That her father would receive the messenger pigeon, and be able to act on the veiled instructions in her note. That he would be able to mobilize a thousand-man army across half of Scotland in just a sennight's time. But some small, selfish part of her had hoped against hope that she could be saved from having to wed Alexander Bruce.

She blinked hard against the tears, forcing them back. This was bigger than her. This was about Scotland's fate, not the life of one woman. She could not give up now, just because her own path was sealed.

It had always been the most likely possibility that no aid would come, at least not in time to save her from Bruce. But she still had agency over her choices. And she knew what she wanted now.

She stood abruptly, turning to Artair. He took in her emotion-sheened eyes, and his already-tense frown drew deeper.

"Sybil, we will find a way, I prom—"

"Nay." Impulsively, she pressed her fingers over his lips to halt him. "Dinnae make promises ye cannae keep. Besides, I dinnae want yer promises. I want something else."

His emerald gaze held her. "Ye can have aught in my power to give."

Nervous flutters began low in her belly. She'd already decided what to do. But standing here, on the precipice of the unknown, her bravery wavered.

"Make love to me."

Artair's golden brows winged fractionally with surprise. "Ye would give me yer innocence?"

Before he could think to deny her, she hurried on.

"After the other night…when ye showed me what it could be like to experience such intimacies…" She swallowed hard. Never had she felt so naïve before, yet also so certain. "I cannae share that with Bruce. I dinnae want him to be the first."

A shadow descended over his face. "I vowed I wouldnae let him touch ye ever again."

She lifted one of his clenched fists in both of her hands. Tenderly, she kissed his whitened knuckles. "Ye cannae stop this any more than I can. But ye can show me what it means to love and be loved—if only for tonight."

"Nay, no' only for tonight." He caught her chin in his free hand and tilted her face up to his. "I love ye, Sybil Douglas. Every night, and every day, for the rest of my life."

Bittersweet tears sprang to her eyes yet again. "I love ye too, Artair MacKinnon."

Suddenly he was kissing her, and it wasn't the slow, careful exploration he'd showed her before. Nay, he ravished her with his mouth, wordlessly demonstrating to her just how deep and powerful his love was.

His hands were everywhere, in her hair, skimming her back, cupping her arse and pulling her flush against him. She matched his eagerness if not his skill. She clutched his shoulders, feeling his strength clenched just beneath his tunic. There was so much of him she hadn't yet explored.

Impatient, she tugged on his tunic until he broke their kiss to hastily assist her in removing it. She only got one glimpse of the broad, muscular expanse of his chest before he fused their mouths once more, but her hands could explore what her eyes could not.

He was lean and hard everywhere, his warm skin stretched over the powerful planes of his back. She skimmed upward to the taut column of his neck, the knotted muscles of his shoulders and the rock-hard swell of his chest.

Such strength was hard-won, she knew. He was battle-honed and scarred, not just on his flesh, but in his heart as well. Yet somehow he'd let her in, given her his love. Naught they would face in the light of day tomorrow could ever take that away.

He broke away for an instant to ruck her chemise up and over her head. It passed over her heated skin like a whisper, and suddenly she stood before him naked. Though she was innocent, she was not ashamed—not with Artair. His eyes feasted upon her, sliding from her breasts to her waist, over her hips and down her legs.

He breathed a pained curse, then abruptly, he scooped her off her feet and strode to the bed. They tumbled down together, a tangle of mouths and hands and bare skin.

"Now, Artair," she murmured as he rolled on top of her. "Dinnae make me wait."

He gave a shaky exhale, pinning her with hungry eyes. "Patience, princess. I mean for ye to enjoy this, and ye arenae ready."

She began to protest, but he cut her off. "For once, ye arenae the most knowledgeable person in the room. Let me lead."

He was right about that, but still she found it difficult

to bite her tongue. Her body already hummed with need and she felt restless in her own skin. Now that she knew what bodily pleasure felt like, she was all too eager for more.

Yet to surrender to Artair was no struggle. He already had her trust—and her heart. Giving herself in this way felt as right as the sun rising in the east every morn. To let him lead…well, that might take some getting used to, but she was willing to try.

Any further coherent thought fled in the next instant, for he lowered his head and captured one of her nipples in his mouth. She was coming to learn she was sensitive there. His touch shot arrows of sensation directly to her core.

Her back arched off the bed as she sought more of his mouth. But to her shock, instead of obliging her, he drew back, his warm breath teasing the taut peak. When she reached to tug him closer, he snatched up her wrists in one hand and pressed them into the mattress above her head.

She made a noise that was half affronted huff and half pleading moan. He only gave a low chuckle before lowering his head, his tongue moving over her in torturously slow teases. With naught else to do, she squirmed beneath him, an aching need building deep within.

He gave her other breast the same languorous attention until she was writhing and moaning incoherent pleas. Only then did his free hand skim down her stomach to the crux of her legs. Instinctively, she parted for him. At his first grazing touch, her hips bucked of their own accord. Her flesh felt over-sensitized already and he'd barely made contact.

He dragged a finger through her wet heat, teasing and caressing as he had before with his mouth. Yet this time, he moved to her opening. She automatically stiffened, yet as he circled slowly, she eased into the sensation. When he pressed inside, he paused, giving her a moment to adjust to the invasion. Once she'd relaxed around him once more, he began to move in and out.

Distantly, she realized it was an imitation of the act they were about to share. This was already more intimate than aught she'd ever experienced. To take Artair into her body, to be joined as one... Aye, this was why she'd wanted him to be her first. *And only*, some desperate voice inside called. *Only Artair, forever.*

"Please," she moaned, her head tossing from side to side.

Suddenly, he withdrew and was gone. She blinked lust-hazed eyes open to find him looming over her, working himself free of his trews.

She let herself indulge in the sight of him. His lion-gold hair, normally held back in a tidy queue, hung loose and slightly tousled from her fingers just above his wide shoulders. The firelight danced across his chiseled torso, casting shadows between the swells of muscle.

When his manhood sprang free of his trews, she couldn't help but gape. It jutted, stiff and thick straight toward her. How would *that*...

"'Twill only hurt at first," he said, his voice surprisingly gentle. "Then the pain will be replaced with pleasure—I promise."

She decided to trust him, for he'd never misled her before.

He leaned down and kissed the inside of her knee, then worked his way higher until he was *there*, just as he'd been the other night. Yet this time, he did not linger. He moved higher, kissing a path upward even as he lowered himself between her thighs. By the time he reached her breasts, she could feel the pressure of his manhood at her entrance.

"Open for me," he ground out, nuzzling her neck.

She didn't know what to do besides ease her clenched muscles.

"Aye, that's it, lass." He pressed forward, and suddenly they were joined.

As he moved deeper, the pressure turned to pain. She winced, holding her breath, until his lips found her ear. Whispered endearments blurred with soft nips and flicks of his tongue, making her gasp. Then his hand found her breast and the ache mingled with need until one became the other.

He began rocking in and out, kindling the sensation until she was meeting him, moving with him. Pleasure built deep within as he drove harder, faster.

When his hand slipped between them, finding that spot where she needed him most, she shattered. Ecstasy broke over her in great waves, wringing the breath from her lungs. She rode the crest until it began to ebb.

Only then did she become aware of the tension radiating from Artair's body. He was drawn taut as a drumhead, his arms trembling where he held himself up, yet he'd kept himself at bay until she'd found her release.

"Hold on, lass," he hissed through gritted teeth. He gripped her thighs, his fingers digging into her soft flesh, then unleashed his pent need. He thrust hard once, twice, thrice, before a groan ripped from him. He held himself deep, his body shuddering as his own release took him.

Spent, he sagged above her, resting his forehead on hers as their ragged breaths mingled. After a long moment, he eased himself to the mattress beside her, tucking her into his arms. She nuzzled into his chest, floating in a heady afterglow.

"Bloody hell, we didnae even make it under the covers," he said sometime later, picking up his head to look down at them where they lay atop the coverlet.

She breathed a chuckle. "Is...is that how it normally is between a man and a woman?"

"Nay," he said, his voice sobering. "That was... something special."

"But that is how it would be for us," she murmured. "If..." *If we could have had a life together.*

Unbidden, a lump of emotion rose in her throat. Aye, it had been a glimpse of something beautiful—a union full of love and passion. A life that could not be theirs.

He must have sensed her rising sadness, for he stilled beneath her.

"If things were different," he began, low and soft. "If it were another time and place... I'd be the one marrying ye on the morrow."

The breath caught in her lungs, tears yet again burning behind her eyes.

"I'd swear myself to ye as yer husband," he went on into the hush, "and ye to me as my wife. We'd raise red-headed bairns who were stubborn as mules yet silver-tongued and sharp-witted as their mother."

A wobbly laugh escaped her. "Dinnae forget the golden-haired ones who'd be twice as bullheaded but equally as braw."

"Aye, verra well," he replied warmly.

The tears flowed freely now, pooling on Artair's chest where she lay her head. "'Tis a beautiful dream," she whispered. "One I dinnae wish to wake from."

Beneath her, he stiffened. "We could still run," he murmured.

Reluctantly, she pushed herself up to sitting. Gazing down at him, she found his eyes drawn with anguished desperation.

"But we willnae," she said for him. "Duty demands more of us."

His brows crashed down. "Sybil, if ye wed Bruce and he takes ye to the marriage bed, he may realize ye arenae a virgin. And if by some miracle my seed takes root and ye carry our bairn..." He hissed a pained breath. "He will take it out on ye. I know ye've pledged yer loyalty to our cause, but ye cannae sacrifice yerself in this way."

Sybil had to swallow hard before she trusted her voice to be steady. "Aye, I can. There is no other way."

Artair sat up, his mouth pulling into a frustrated snarl. "Then mayhap I should simply kill Bruce with my own two hands. And Balliol, while I'm at it."

"Ye know verra well that willnae work," she countered. "This is bigger than either man's life. We need to send a message to Edward that he cannae hold Scotland through a puppet. Killing one man, even the Usurper himself, isnae enough. We need to rout him, just as he routed the loyalists—show him we cannae be yoked, no' under Balliol, and no' under England."

His colorful curses told her he knew she was right.

"Well what the hell am I supposed to do then?" he demanded. "Once ye are wed, I willnae be able to protect ye from him. Christ, he's already drooling over the chance to order my flogging."

"I-I dinnae know," she said honestly. "I cannae think on it, or else I'll...I'll..."

Just as a great heaving sob broke from her, he caught her up in his arms. He squeezed her so tight she could barely draw a breath, but she didn't care. Crushed against him, she felt safe. It would likely be the last time.

Once the tears had ebbed away, he sat rocking her for a long while. Eventually, though, he peeled himself away.

"I cannae stay," he said, his green eyes haunted.

"I know."

Still, it took all her strength to let him go. She sat on the bed and watched as he dressed, the firelight dancing over his lean, powerful frame.

Once he was done, he turned to her, his features now shuttered behind a stony mask. She knew he had to pull away, to protect himself from what was to come on the morrow, yet it still hurt to see him walled off from her.

"Bolt the door behind me," he ordered. "I intend to

wait in the village in case Dermid comes with news. But I promise ye, I'll be outside yer door come morn. I willnae let ye face Bruce alone."

With one more lingering look, he turned and strode to the door. After cracking it to check the stairwell, he slipped out, closing it softly behind him.

Leaving Sybil alone with her slowly crumbling heart.

CHAPTER 21

T he faces of the guards and servants filling the great hall were a blur as Artair pushed his way through.

He had enough wherewithal to skirt the stone walls, avoiding the attention of Balliol, Bruce, and the priest. Despite the late hour, the three sat at the high table, drinking wine and making merry, likely in anticipation of tomorrow's wedding.

Once he was outside, he drew a shaky breath. The air was thick with fog and bitingly cold, but he hardly felt it. The memories of what he'd just shared with Sybil burned like a bonfire inside him. Her skin. Her scent. Her soft, delicate body taking him in, claiming him forever.

After what they'd shared—the words of love and promise, the union of heart, body, and soul—he was simply supposed to turn her over to that bastard Alexander Bruce?

Bloody hell, if he didn't get away from there, he just

might turn around and kill the man with his bare hands, despite the fact that it would change little, just as Sybil had said.

He descended to the lower bailey, his head spinning and his gut churning. Though the fog blocked the moon, lit torches lined the bailey's outer wall, casting a muted orange glow over everything.

To his relief, the gates were already open. A late delivery of what looked—and smelled—like baskets of fresh fish were being trundled through the gates on a mule-drawn wagon.

Though he wasn't exactly friendly with the castle guards, Artair had at least become a familiar sight to them for his once-daily visit to the village. However, this would be his second time passing out of the castle that evening. He didn't want to have to explain himself, so he simply gave the guards a nod as he slipped around the wagon.

"Gates are closing soon," one of the guards commented, eyeing him as he passed. "Willnae open again until dawn."

Artair hesitated. Despite saying earlier that he'd wait for further word from Dermid, any hope that the army would arrive in time to stop Sybil's wedding to Bruce had dwindled to naught now. Yet if he remained inside the castle walls this night, he just might do something mad like strangle Bruce—or Balliol.

Or worse, he'd find it impossible to stay away from Sybil and risk exposing them both.

He'd promised to be waiting for her in the morn. If he returned at dawn when the gates were opened again, he could still keep that promise, and likely save both their necks by staying away until he could think straight.

Once he was through the gates and across the drawbridge over the moat, his feet carried him toward the village. He didn't know where else to go. Mayhap an ale or three at the local alehouse would settle his thoughts—or at least dull the throbbing pain in his chest.

He turned down one of the village's winding alleyways, wishing now he'd thought to bring his cloak. The frigid mist had a way of sinking into one's bones, and—

"MacKinnon," a low voice hissed behind him.

He spun, reaching for his sword, but cursed to remember it was still locked away in the castle's armory.

From the dense fog stepped…

"Dermid? What the hell are ye—"

The lad shot forward and grabbed Artair by the front of his tunic, then hauled him around the corner of a building into a smaller passageway.

"The army," the lad breathed, his eyes wide in the low light. "They are here."

Artair's heart froze in his chest before lurching into a wild gallop. "What?"

Dermid glanced around. The streets were empty at this late hour, but the fog cast an eerie sense of presence around them, as if they were surrounded by spirits.

"Nevin spotted them no' long ago in the woods to the northeast. He hasnae made contact, but—"

"Take me there," Artair ordered.

Dermid nodded soberly, then turned to lead Artair presumably to where he'd left his horse.

Artair's own mount, along with his sword and cloak, were now sealed behind the castle gates.

Along with Sybil.

Bloody fecking hell and damnation.

Sybil.

There would be no way to get word to her until the morn that the army had arrived. Aye, he could beg and plead with the castle guards to let him in, but that would draw attention he couldn't afford.

What was more, any time he wasted bickering with the guards was time stolen from advancing the loyalists' attack on the castle.

And they needed to strike tonight. The longer the army lingered nearby, the greater the risk of detection. Despite the fact that the sun had set hours ago, this close to the winter solstice, they had several hours left of darkness in which to make their move.

If Artair could reach them in time, he could brief them on the castle's defenses and the plan of attack he'd been hatching these past few days. They just might stand a chance of stopping not only Balliol's alliance with England, but Sybil's wedding.

But if they failed…

He couldn't let himself think of that. Nor of Sybil trapped inside the castle as they laid siege. He didn't know how, but he'd find a way to keep her safe. What had happened to Ewan could not happen to her.

At the edge of the village, Dermid untethered his horse, then waited for Artair to mount before vaulting up behind him to ride pillion. He pointed off to the north.

"There, mayhap two leagues away," he said.

As Artair spurred the horse into motion, he couldn't help but stare over his shoulder at the castle rising to his left. The fog made it an indistinct mound, its outline limned with the orange glow of torchlight.

Sybil. I willnae fail, I swear it.

As the mist swallowed the castle from view, he turned to face the nigh-impossible task that lay ahead.

LONG BEFORE THEY'D traveled two leagues, Artair took up a low whistle that imitated an owl's hoot. The signal was something they'd used in Robert the Bruce's army on many occasions. He could only pray that before they stumbled upon an overeager scout, or worse, the whole of the loyalist army, someone would recognize the call before putting an arrow through them both.

The woods were dense, and the heavy fog only made the traverse more perilous. Without the moon or any landmarks, their direction was a loose guess at best. Just when Artair was about to bellow in desperation, he heard a noise that made him freeze.

Sound bounced around the mist as if through water, making it almost impossible to tell where the noise had come from. He reined the horse to a halt and held up a hand to silence Dermid. Then he gave the owl's call again, softly.

When an answering hoot came back, he nearly sagged out of the saddle.

"Artair MacKinnon approaching," he said into the

trees. It was a risk to declare himself, but he didn't have time to faff about anymore.

"MacKinnon?" came a voice off to the right. "Bloody hell, man."

Out of the mist stepped none other than Gregor the Black MacLeod. He pursed his lips and set up a trilling whistle different from the call Artair had used. Two dozen echoing whistles filtered through the fog-shrouded woods. The calls continued, moving farther back from where they stood until the sounds grew so distant as to be swallowed by the night.

MacLeod, a giant of a man even compared to other Highland warriors, approached.

"I wasnae expecting to find ye wandering through—"

"Where are the others?" Artair cut in. "Is the army with ye?"

Gregor blinked. "Aye."

"I'll explain aught, I swear. But I dinnae have time to repeat myself. We attack Annan Castle tonight."

Gregor's dark brows shot up, but he was a man forged by war, used to plain speak and decisive action. He gave Artair a quick nod, then motioned for him to follow deeper into the woods.

In a short time, the forest fell away and opened onto a massive clearing. Though the fog filled the wide glen, Artair could make out rows upon rows of tents. It was a veritable sea of them, enough to make an entire village.

The tents were interspersed with low-burning cook fires, with men gathered around for warmth and light.

He could only imagine how many more loyalist fighters were hunkered down inside their tents for the night.

"Bloody hell," he murmured as Gregor led him farther into the camp. "I thought ye said the army only numbered one thousand."

"It did when we left the Highlands," Gregor commented over his shoulder. "But everywhere we went, men wanted to join our cause. It seems every farmer, shepherd, and tradesman wants to personally kick Balliol's arse out of Scotland."

"How large is the force now?"

"At least two thousand by my guess, though I lost count just south of Glasgow."

Artair would have whistled in amazement, but just then, Gregor halted before a tent larger than the others. Sliding from the horse's back, Artair turned to Dermid. The lad sat wide-eyed and gaping at the massive army camp.

"Go, lad," Artair ordered. "Find the others and bring them here."

Gregor quickly showed Dermid how to make the signal used by the loyalist scouts, then the lad was off to collect the other Douglas guards.

Pulling back the canvas flap on the tent, Gregor stepped inside. "Back already from my turn on watch," he said as Artair ducked in behind him. "And ye willnae believe what I found."

CHAPTER 22

T he three men sitting at the table inside the tent all surged to their feet as Artair stepped around Gregor.

"MacKinnon." Laird Domnall MacAyre was the first to reach him, gripping his forearm in a crushing shake.

"Glad to see ye alive," Tavish MacNeal murmured, clasping forearms with him next.

"Where is Sybil?" Archibald Douglas demanded from behind the wall of Highlanders.

"She is safe—for the moment," Artair said, giving Douglas a reassuring nod. "But we cannae delay."

"He means to attack this verra night," Gregor said to the others.

To their credit, none of them gainsaid him, but a few brows lifted.

"Ye obviously got Sybil's message along with Balliol's," Artair said to Douglas. "Otherwise ye wouldnae all be here."

"That was...quite a feat in itself," Domnall murmured. Glancing at Artair, he added, "which is a tale for another time."

Nodding his thanks, Artair turned back to Douglas. "Ye'll know that Balliol intends to wed Sybil to his newfound friend—Alexander Bruce." As Artair quickly explained how Bruce had come to be a turncoat, the murmurs of the others turned to curses. Gregor spat on the hardpacked ground.

"Bloody traitorous, cowardly—"

"The wedding is to take place tomorrow morn," Artair interjected. "But that isnae all."

The four men's faces grew increasingly grim as Artair detailed Balliol's plan to declare Scotland a fief of England, and to pledge his fealty—along with half of the Lowlands—to Edward in the coming days.

"If we dinnae stop him..." Artair murmured.

The silence filling the tent was deafening until Domnall spoke up. "Then all hope of a free Scotland is lost."

Tavish, who was a man of few words even by Highland standards, glanced at each of them in turn. Then he gave Artair a steady nod. "Tonight it is, then."

At the grim yet determined looks on their faces, Artair felt the first spark of hope in a long while.

"Verra well, then. Listen up, lads. I have a plan."

FOR A BAND TWO THOUSAND STRONG, the loyalists mobilized surprisingly quickly. Campfires were hastily doused and weapons donned, though they left the camp intact. If they succeeded, they could return once the castle was secured. And if they failed, their discarded tents and bedrolls would be the least of their worries.

Though most of the foot soldiers were armed with swords, they had a fair contingent of bowmen. A few of the less experienced men carried scythes, axes, and even walking sticks carved into spears. Besides a select few, their cavalry was limited, but as this was to be a siege and not pitched warfare, Artair could not let himself worry over that.

Artair was given a horse of his own, as well as a sword. He and the other Horsemen, along with Douglas, led the army out of the forest and onto the open, rolling hills that lay to the north of the castle.

Even under cover of night, it made Artair itchy to lead such a large force into the open. Yet the fog provided more than enough cover for their approach. Still, they sent several scouts ahead in case they stumbled upon an unforeseen threat.

Though Artair longed to charge straight to the castle, the mist held them to a walk. When he stood in his stirrups for the third time, straining to see through the murky darkness, Domnall muttered a curse.

"Ye are making Fern twitchy," he said, patting his speckled white horse's neck. "Calm yerself, man. It will be more than an hour until we reach the castle."

Artair breathed an oath of his own. Damn it all, Domnall was right. He'd drive himself mad if he kept himself drawn this taut until…

Until Sybil is safe.

He needed to be at his sharpest when they reached Annan. Which meant he had to get his mind on something—anything—other than her.

"How the hell did ye lot manage to reach the Lowlands in a mere sennight, then?"

On his other side, Gregor snorted. "By sheer luck—and mayhap a wee bit of foresight on my part. Even before I received yer missive about moving into position, I had a sense that we were close to striking. I'd already begun to mobilize the army south when Douglas's man delivered yer note advising the same. Luckily we were almost to Scone by then."

"'Twas only a few days after yer missive arrived that we each got word from Douglas about attacking Annan before Yule," Domnall added, nodding toward Tavish. "We rode like hell from the west and south, and managed to catch the army just past Stirling."

It was a credit to the people of Scotland that not a peep about a sizable force of men moving rapidly across the countryside had reached Balliol. Normally, word spread faster than thistle down on the wind among Scots. But to keep Balliol in the dark, none had breathed a whisper. The will of the people truly was with them.

Artair looked at each of them in turn. "I wasnae sure it was even possible."

Domnall flashed him a wolfish smile. "Ye should know better than to doubt a Highlander, MacKinnon."

"We havenae won yet," Artair replied dryly. "'Twill take another miracle—and I've lost count how many that is now—to take the castle, and Balliol along with it."

261

"'Tis a bold plan," Domnall said, sobering. "But one just mad enough to work."

"It has to," Artair murmured under his breath. "If aught happens to her…"

"To Lady Sybil?" Gregor commented from Artair's other side. He cast Artair a knowing look. "I noted how ye referred to her rather familiarly as just Sybil."

Artair glanced in Douglas's direction, but the man was far enough down the line that he hadn't overheard Gregor's observation.

"'Tis all right, MacKinnon," Domnall murmured, his pale blue eyes dancing. "It seems we are all…similarly afflicted now."

"Syb—Lady Sybil told me ye are wed," Artair said with a scowl, internally kicking himself for the slip.

"Aye—to Andrew Murray's sister, of all lasses."

"And I've married the Morgan Laird's daughter," Gregor added.

Artair blinked, but he was not prepared for Tavish to pipe up next. "My wife waits for me in the Lowlands— where I'll be calling home."

Gregor snorted. "Christ, 'tis a miracle we've had time to lead a loyalist coup against Balliol with all this wooing and wedding and bedding."

Tavish gave a low chuckle and Domnall barked a laugh. But they all sobered when Artair spoke.

"Sybil isnae mine to call wife," he ground out. "If she falls into that bastard Bruce's hands—"

"We willnae let that happen," Domnall interjected. "For we'll fight like any one of our lasses was inside that castle. This is about more than revenge against Balliol."

"Aye," Tavish murmured.

"For Scotland," Gregor added. "And for a better future for our bairns."

They rode in a grim silence until one of the scouts sent up a whistle, then emerged from the fog in front of them.

"Only a furlong to the castle," the man breathed.

Domnall gave him a nod, and he fell back into the sea of men behind them. "Ye are up, Douglas."

The older man gave them each a solemn look. "Godspeed to ye. Give them hell, lads."

Just as the four Highlanders reined to the west, Douglas called out, "And MacKinnon!" When Artair turned in the saddle, Douglas fixed him with a fierce stare. "I'm trusting ye to get my daughter out of this alive."

With a sharp nod, Artair spurred after the others as they peeled away from the rest of the army.

Domnall was right—this scheme was bold, but just mad enough to work.

The entirety of the loyalist army, with Douglas in the lead, was to attack the castle from the front. Since sending his English soldiers away for the Yuletide season, the castle only boasted five hundred men. Yet the fortress itself would prove the greatest obstacle.

In truth, attacking head-on gave those inside the castle much advantage. There was no weakness to exploit in the moat, the curtain wall, the outer bailey— though old, Annan was solid.

Except for the earthen mound that supported the tower keep. Where the River Annan cut its course around the back of the motte, some of the ground had been washed away, likely from a flood years or decades ago.

A great force of men could not attack from that side. The river provided a natural defense. Yet for a few select warriors who could get close enough...

Artair and the other three Highlanders rode in silence, each man drawing inward as they prepared for battle. The hope was that the army's attack would provide a diversion, pulling enough attention that they'd be able to slip into the tower keep without notice. But they'd all been in enough battles to know that it never went how one expected.

Blood would be spilt this night.

Mayhap their own.

When the glow of the castle torches warmed the fog ahead, they guided their horses across the river. The water was ice-cold and deep as the horses' bellies, but fortunately slow-moving.

They had to cross again once they reached the back-side of the castle's motte, this time without the horses. They dismounted and began wading in, holding their swords above their heads to keep the blades dry. The cold stole Artair's breath, yet with hot anticipation pumping through him, he hardly noticed.

They scrambled onto the eroding bank, only the sounds of their breathing and the soft whisper of the river filling their ears.

Artair stared up at the soaring expanse of stone before them. The top of the tower was high enough above them that it disappeared into the frosty fog.

The curtain wall that surrounded the tower keep did not make a complete ring. Instead, it joined the tower at the back, the keep's western-most wall serving as the connector. With both the river and the high earthen mound of the motte as added defenses, it must have made sense to save the additional stone required to fully circle the keep. Yet with the motte crumbling away, they were able to crawl right to the base of the tower without having to scale the wall.

As they stood catching their breaths and belting on their swords once more, shouts began filtering to them.

"Douglas has arrived at the gates," Gregor murmured.

Artair gave the others a nod. "Then it is time."

CHAPTER 23

S ybil had tried to crawl under the covers and get some rest after Artair had left. But after tossing and turning for what felt like hours, she finally rose, resigned to the fact that she could not sleep knowing what awaited her in the morn.

With naught else to do, she slowly moved through her ablutions, then braided her hair away from her face. As she always did, she reached for the pearl-studded clasp to secure the plaits. Though she'd done it a thousand times before, her fingers fumbled to secure the three-inch-long pin into its hook behind the bed of pearls.

The clasp had been a gift from her mother, who in turn had been gifted it on her wedding day by Sybil's father. Theirs had been a political union, yet it had quickly turned into a love match.

Her mother had hoped to give it to Sybil for her own wedding, but as she'd grown increasingly ill with a wasting of the lungs, she'd known she wouldn't make it to that day. So she'd called Sybil to her sickbed and pressed the clasp into her hand. She'd died only two days later.

Wearing it had always kept the memory of her mother close, but it had also reminded her of the tender, loving bond between her parents. Only now did Sybil realize she'd been holding onto a secret, naïve hope to find the same in her own marriage someday.

A bitter lump rose in her throat to think of the cruel irony of wearing the beautiful clasp on what was to be the worst day of her life—her wedding day.

She dressed in a lustrous emerald-green gown with delicate gold threading in the pattern of flowers across the bodice. It would be the dress she wore to wed Alexander Bruce, yet the color was the exact same as Artair's keen, penetrating eyes.

Then all that remained to do was wait. From the chamber's narrow window—little more than an arrow slit—she could tell that dawn was still hours away. She wasn't sure if she should feel grateful for winter's long nights, which bought her a little more freedom, or if she should curse the cruel torture of having to wait.

Was Artair on the landing outside her door, sleeping? Or mayhap he, too, could not find rest as the moments ticked by, bringing them both closer to their versions of hell. He'd said he would stay away in hopes of some desperate last chance of salvation. Dare she crack open her door to see if he waited for her?

Of their own volition, her feet carried her to the door, but when her hand landed on the crossbar, she hesitated. He'd made her promise to leave it lowered unless he expressly knocked and identified himself. No matter how much she longed to see him one more time before being carted off to marry Bruce, she wouldn't break her word to him.

A firm pound on the other side of the door, just inches from where she stood, had her jumping back. She clamped a hand over her mouth to catch her startled gasp.

"Lady Sybil, open the door. 'Tis me, Alexander."

Unease coiled in the pit of her stomach like a snake. Before she could reply, distant shouts from outside filtered through the arrow slit. Scuffing boots echoed in the stairwell beyond the door.

"Where is Maxwell?" she called, backing away slowly.

"I dinnae know. Now open the door, my lady." His tone was testier now, more impatient.

Artair wasn't nearby? The shouts grew, turning into a sustained cry that must have contained hundreds of voices. Then a low, rhythmic thud began in the distance.

"What goes on out there?"

"The castle is under attack. Come now, Lady Sybil, open the door and let me in."

Attack. Could it be…?

She hadn't realized she was still pacing backward until the backs of her knees bumped into the bed. She sat down hard with a whoosh of breath, her thoughts racing. Had the army arrived after all? But where was Artair? Had he somehow managed to reach them, direct their assault against the castle?

One thing was certain—there was no way in hell she was opening the door to Alexander Bruce.

"If we are under siege, wouldnae it be safer for me to remain bolted inside my chamber?" she called.

He pounded harder on the other side of the door, likely using his entire fist.

"I said open the door, ye insolent woman." Now he threw his shoulder against the oak, making the door vibrate and rattle on its hinges. But the wood was solid and the crossbeam secure.

"Nay, I willnae," she said, standing. Hope made her bold. His rising desperation was unnerving, but he couldn't break down the door even if he flung his whole body against it for hours on end. If she could just wait out the siege—

"Ye mule-headed, meddlesome bitch," Bruce hissed outside. Suddenly something new impacted the door, something that made a sharp thunking sound. "Ye are coming with me, even if I have to cut ye out of there." The thunk sounded again, as if he were taking an ax to the wood.

Or a sword.

Cold fear shot through her, her momentary confidence evaporating. Her gaze darted around the chamber, but there was nowhere to go. The arrow slit was too narrow to crawl out of. She could hide, but the chamber was small enough that it would only take him a moment to find her once he broke inside.

She didn't even have an eating knife to use as a weapon. Crossing to the armoire, she frantically rummaged through her hanging clothes for aught she could wield against Bruce. But all she found were fine silk and brocade gowns.

Silently, she cursed Bruce, and then herself. This was exactly why Artair had fought against bringing her on this mission. Aye, her beautiful gowns and charming manners had gotten her this far, but now that she faced true danger, she was helpless to stop it.

Blinking back the frightened tears, she forced herself to look over every inch of the chamber again. She could not give up. Somehow, she had to stay alive—for herself, and for Artair. She couldn't—

At the next sickening thunk against the door, the tip of a sword pierced the wood. As Bruce withdrew for another strike, a few splinters came out with the sword. He hacked again, widening the small opening.

It was only a matter of time now before he cut a hole big enough to pass through. She could only pray the loyalists succeeded in time to stop him. Or that she could stop him herself.

As Bruce chopped away at the door, she hastily darted over to the small table where the washing bowl and pitcher sat.

"Ye'll pay for costing me so much time, ye harridan." Bruce's voice now came clearly through the jagged opening.

Sybil's head snapped around. To her horror, he reached inside through the hole, his hand fumbling with the crossbar.

Snatching up the earthenware pitcher, she rushed toward the door. But before she could smash his hand, he'd already lifted the crossbar and dropped it onto the floor.

She darted behind the door just as he swung it open. The point of his sword appeared first as he stepped inside. The hammer of her heartbeat roared in her ears, but she forced herself to remain still, holding her breath.

"Where are ye?" he demanded, clearing the door. His hard gaze scanned the chamber. "Dinnae make me waste more time searching for ye. Ye are coming with m—"

She lifted the pitcher and lurched forward, bringing it down with all her might on Bruce's head.

He staggered back, cursing loudly. A stream of blood immediately coursed from his scalp over his brow and down his cheek. Yet he remained on his feet, still conscious.

Bruce lifted a hand to his head, swiping the little rivulet of blood out of his eye. He looked down at his fingers, which were stained deep crimson. "Ye bitch."

Defeat threatened to make her crumble, but as long as she was alive, there was still a chance for escape. With Bruce momentarily distracted, she had a chance to dart around him to the open door. Who knew what dangers lurked in the rest of the tower keep, but she doubted any could be worse than being in Alexander Bruce's clutches.

As he wiped irritably at the blood again, she shot past him. But just as she passed through the doorway, he yanked her back from behind.

"Och, nay ye dinnae," he growled, hauling her backward by her fine emerald gown. She collided with his chest, knocking the wind from her lungs.

He wasted no time, wrenching her arm behind her with one hand and lifting his sword to her neck. "I willnae let ye go so easily," he rasped in her ear. "For ye are my assurance of safe passage out of this hellhole. When the siege began, I ran to the bailey wall along with all the others. I saw yer father leading the charge. Which means ye are coming with me."

She cried out as he gave her pinned arm a tweak. The small movement made it feel as though her shoulder was being ripped from her torso. With a nudge from behind, she was forced to step through the doorway.

"Where are ye taking me?"

He huffed behind her, steering her down the stairs, but did not bother to answer.

Her mind spiraling with fresh terror, she could do naught but go where he willed her.

CHAPTER 24

Artair was the last to scale the tower keep's wall.
Domnall had brought the rope, assuring them
that he had some experience with such things. "'Tis how
I infiltrated Stalcaire Tower when I was hunting
Murray," he said, making a loop at one end of the rope.
Then he swung it at his side to build momentum before
giving it a great heave upward.

The looped end disappeared into the mist, but with
a few tugs, Domnall confirmed that he'd managed to
catch one of the stone crenelations. He ascended first,
followed by Gregor and Tavish, each climbing hand
over hand up the rope.

By the time Artair reached the battlements, the
others had already made quick work of the two guards
stationed on watch. They'd raised no alarm, which
meant that they hadn't even had time to shout before
the Highlanders emerged from the mist and set upon
them.

The air now rang with battle cries and the distant

thud of a battering ram against the bailey's gates. With any luck, the majority of the castle guards had already rushed to the bailey's wall, leaving the tower largely unprotected.

"Balliol's private chambers are on the first floor above the great hall," Artair told them. "Remember, the aim is to capture, no' kill."

Though it had been a bitter draught for them to swallow, the other Highlanders had eventually agreed to leaving Balliol alive.

As Artair had pointed out, though parading the Usurper's head on a pike would satisfy their lust for vengeance, marching him to Scone in shackles, to be dumped in the same dungeon the four of them had sat in for a fortnight before their hanging, would send a more powerful message. Parliament could do what they saw fit to him, but in the meantime, it would show Edward of England that his puppet now belonged to Scotland.

With a look between them, they drew their swords in unison. Artair took the lead, as he knew the castle like the back of his hand after a sennight of scouting.

He led them through the door to the stairs, pausing just outside the garrison. He lifted his sword in preparation to encounter more guards, but the garrison was empty, the door partway ajar.

Just as they'd intended, the army's siege must have drawn the guards to the bailey. Artair continued down the stairs, hesitating at each landing in case of a surprise attack. Like a fish on a hook, he hastened his pace.

Sybil's chamber was close. It was still well before dawn. She should be safely ensconced inside.

To hesitate, to stop his advance toward Balliol's chamber to check on her, could mean losing valuable seconds in their mission. Yet he could not pass without at least warning her to stay inside—and reassuring himself that she was well and safe.

As he took the last curving steps to her landing, some instinct pricked his senses. He held up a fist to halt the three behind him. When his gaze landed on her chamber door, he froze.

The oak was a splintered ruin, a ragged hole hacked into the middle of the door.

"*Sybil.*" Her name ripped from his throat on a rough exhale. "*Nay.*"

He reached for the door. It swung open easily. Someone had lifted the crossbar from the inside. He charged into the room, but naught met him but the low-flickering fire in the hearth.

"Sybil!"

The others rushed in behind him, quickly scanning the chamber. But there was naught to attack, naught to do. She was gone.

"I'd wager my life that bastard Bruce had something to do with this," Artair ground out.

His gaze landed on her still-made bed. The bed they'd made love upon mere hours before.

Tavish's hand squeezed Artair's shoulder. "We'll find her," he said, his features grim.

"They cannae have gotten far," Gregor added.

"None will be able to leave the castle with the army outside the walls."

Some rational part of him knew they were right, yet he couldn't think straight knowing that Sybil very well might be in Bruce's clutches.

No' again, he howled inside his chest. This could not be happening again. First Ewan, and now Sybil. *I cannae lose her.*

With a surge of feral determination, he charged back out the door and down the spiral stairs.

"Sybil!" he bellowed, his voice bouncing off the stones as he went. He didn't care that he alerted all in earshot to his presence. The time for stealth was over. He had to get her back. *Now.*

"Artair!"

Relief and panic collided like two sharpened steel blades within him. *Sybil.* She was alive. But her voice, which had echoed faintly up the stairwell from somewhere deeper in the tower keep, was filled with fear.

He practically flung himself down the steps after her distant call. Remotely, he registered the other Horsemen rushing after him.

"Sybil!"

When she gave another wordless cry in response, he knew he was closer. As he leapt the rest of the way to the next landing, he skidded to a halt. The door to Balliol's personal chambers was slightly ajar.

Even before he could form a guess as to what he'd find inside, instinct had him charging through the door.

The sight that greeted him shot ice through his veins.

Alexander Bruce held Sybil in his grasp. Though she was struggling mightily, he was in the process of shoving her into an enormous fireplace at the far end of Balliol's chamber.

Except it wasn't a fireplace. Instead of stone, the back of the hearth was a gaping black hole. The slab of rock that should have backed the fireplace had been slid aside to reveal a secret passageway.

At his abrupt arrival, Bruce spun around to face Artair. He twisted Sybil's arm so that she came in front of him, using her like a shield to protect himself.

"Artair," she breathed, her wide, frightened eyes finding and fixing on him. Fear and hope mingled in their amber depths.

Though she was in one piece, her hair hung loose in disheveled waves, and her green silk gown was marred with blood stains. He couldn't tell if it was her blood or Bruce's, for a trickle of red ran down the man's forehead.

He wasn't about to wait to find out. Without thought, Artair charged toward her. But Bruce jerked up his sword, angling it across Sybil's body so that the end of the blade rested against her neck.

"No' so fast, Maxwell," Bruce snapped. His midnight blue eyes narrowed. "Or was it Artair?"

Artair skidded to a halt at the sight of the sharpened sword touching Sybil's exposed skin.

"Ye are a dead man, Bruce," he hissed. "For laying yer filthy hands on her, I'll kill ye myself. But if ye hurt her now, I vow I will make it slow and painful."

Ignoring the threat, Bruce glared at Artair. "What is yer name? Yer real name."

When Artair remained silent, Bruce pushed the sword more firmly against Sybil's neck. She inhaled sharply.

"MacKinnon," he blurted, his gaze riveted on the spot where the steel pressed into her flesh.

Bruce's light brown eyebrows dropped and he blinked. "MacKinnon." His gaze flicked over Artair's shoulder. He hadn't noticed, but the three others had plowed into the chamber behind him, only to halt just inside the doorway at the sight of Bruce holding Sybil.

"And the rest of ye are..."

The Highlanders remained silent for a long beat, but then each grudgingly gave his name.

"Domnall MacAyre, Gregor MacLeod, Tavish MacNeal, and..." Bruce fixed his gaze on Artair again. "And Artair MacKinnon. I know those names. Ye lot are the ones they call the Four Horsemen, hell-bent on bringing Balliol down."

Domnall took a cautious step forward. "And where is the Usurper now?"

Belatedly, Artair realized he hadn't even contemplated Balliol's whereabouts, so focused on Sybil had he been. Without turning his head from Bruce, his gaze quickly scanned the chamber.

The silk-upholstered chairs and finely hewn and polished table on the other side of the hearth spoke to the Usurper's expensive tastes and elevated sense of himself. As did the rich purple draperies around the four-poster bed. Though the luxurious down-stuffed silk coverlet was thrown back, revealing a recent occupant, Balliol was nowhere to be seen.

"He is long gone," Bruce said with a sneer. "Just as we will be." He gave Sybil a little shake, jostling a gasp from her.

"Gone where?" Gregor demanded. "And how? The castle gates are under siege."

"See for yerself," Bruce taunted, jerking his head toward the covered arrow slit on the far wall.

Never taking his gaze from Bruce and Sybil, Artair slowly sidestepped toward the narrow window. It was shuttered to keep the cold night air out. With his sword still lifted and pointed at Bruce, Artair fumbled with one hand to pull the shutter back. At last tearing his eyes away, he looked out.

Balliol's chamber faced northwest, overlooking the night-black curl of the river. Mist still hung heavy in the pre-dawn air, blocking the moon, though the light from the torches atop the tower cast a muted, ambient orange glow overhead.

A flicker of movement below snagged Artair's gaze. At the edge of the river, a figure was staggering out of the water.

Balliol.

He wore only a nightshirt, which was soaking wet and clinging around his bare thighs. As he crawled onto the far riverbank, Artair also noted he had on only one boot, which streamed with water as he lurched to his feet. The other must have been sucked away by the river.

Balliol stumbled toward where their four horses

stood waiting. He first reached for Domnall's speckled stallion, but the beast reared back and nearly took Balliol's fingers off with his teeth. The Usurper hastily moved on to Artair's steed, the comparatively calm gelding he'd been given back at the loyalist camp.

Hauling himself up into the saddle, Balliol kicked the horse into motion.

"Damn him," Artair growled. "He's getting away."

Tavish moved to his side, staring out the arrow slit at Balliol. Then without explanation, he bolted from the chamber.

"My ancestors built this passageway when Annan was converted from wood to stone," Bruce said, snagging Artair's attention once more. He tilted his head toward the tunnel behind the fireplace. "The master of the keep needed an escape route should an army lay siege—just the situation we find ourselves in now. When my great-grandfather gifted the castle to the Balliols, he let them in on the wee secret. Balliol was wise to use it."

"And ye think we'll let ye do the same?" Artair ground out.

A cold smile played on his lips where he peeked around Sybil. "Ye cannae stop me. No' unless ye wish to see the lady's blood soak the rushes at yer feet."

Though he tried to fight it, Artair's mind flashed back to Dupplin Moor. To holding Ewan as his life's blood leeched from him. *Nay. No' again. No' to Sybil.*

He took an involuntary step forward. Desperation clawed at his insides like a rabid wolf. "Dinnae," he snarled, though his threat was hollow. Bruce could slit Sybil's throat long before Artair could reach him.

A light of realization shone in Bruce's eyes. "I knew it. There is something between the two of ye. Did she spread her legs for ye, Maxwell—or rather, MacKinnon?" He torqued Sybil's arm even higher up her back, making her cry out. "Did ye whore yerself out to him, ye filthy cu—"

A wordless bellow tore from Artair's chest. Distantly, he could recognize that his control was slipping like grains of sand through his fingers. Yet he couldn't seem to care—not when Sybil's bonny face contorted in pain.

"MacKinnon." Domnall's voice behind him held a warning, but he hardly registered it.

"He willnae kill me—no' yet anyway," Sybil blurted in a strained voice. She held Artair's gaze, her eyes silently pleading with him. "He means to use me as leverage to save his own skin—yet again."

"Silence!" Bruce roared, giving Sybil another shake.

Artair realized what she was doing. She was drawing Bruce's attention back to herself to allow Artair to regain some semblance of control.

But in buying him time, she risked snapping whatever was left of Bruce's restraint.

"Easy, now." Artair held up a hand, praying he could stop Bruce from doing something mad.

"Dinnae test me, woman," Bruce said to Sybil, ignoring Artair. "Ye only live because ye are still of use to me. Yer father willnae hurt his own daughter, even if it means letting me escape." His cold blue gaze fixed on Artair. "Nor will ye."

Just then, Tavish dashed back into the chamber, breathing hard. "By the time I made it to the battlements, Balliol had already crossed back over the river and was cutting an arc to the southeast. Toward England. He is gone."

A slow smile broke across Bruce's face. "As will I be." He began backing into the massive hearth, pulling Sybil along with him.

Artair moved to stop him, but Bruce halted him with another press of the blade to Sybil's neck.

"Ah, dinnae even think of it, MacKinnon. The lot of ye will stay where ye are."

Artair stood rooted, his eyes locked with Sybil's. Aye, Bruce needed Sybil alive in case he required leverage over Douglas. But he wouldn't put it past the man to panic if Artair and the others were to attack. He might maim or even kill Sybil if pressed.

Helplessness washed over him in a great wave, eroding the last of his sanity.

"Sybil, I..."

As Bruce forced her back toward the passage opening, she began struggling with renewed urgency.

"Do ye remember that first night when we danced in Scone Palace's great hall?" she said, her gaze fused with his.

"Shut yer trap, I say," Bruce ordered, stepping beneath the hearth's wooden mantel and into the open mouth of the passageway.

Sybil winced again, and Artair could only imagine the agony Bruce was inflicting on her pinned arm as he pulled her backward.

"Sybil, dinnae," Artair pleaded. To be helpless to stop Bruce from taking her was enough to rend his heart to sunders. But to see him hurt her was more than he could bear.

"We spoke of the advantages of a woman's approach," she went on undeterred, speaking solely to Artair as if only the two of them existed.

Just then, a flash of something shiny caught the light of the chamber's wall sconces. She held a small object enclosed in her free hand and tucked in the folds of her emerald gown. It was the pearl-studded hair clasp she wore so often, he realized.

That night rushed back with sudden clarity. She'd stomped on his foot to prove a point—that women can hide much behind their skirts, their schemes going unnoticed by men thanks to a bit of brocade or silk.

An eon seemed to stretch between one heartbeat and the next. His eyes darted up to hers, and he knew what she meant to do.

Nay! He screamed at her silently. It was too dangerous. If Bruce lurched back, or even if his sword-hand slipped, the blade would be slicing across her throat in an instant.

But from the glint in her glowing amber eyes, he knew she'd already made up her mind.

In one swift motion, she jerked her hand from her skirts and drove the pointed end of the clasp into Bruce's wrist. He roared in surprise and pain, his hand reflexively opening and his sword clattering to the ground.

At the same instant, Artair surged forward. In a single heartbeat, he reached them. Grabbing Sybil with his free hand, he yanked her out of Bruce's grasp. Still fighting to hold on to her, Bruce staggered forward—straight onto the end of Artair's sword.

Bruce's momentum carried him up the length of the blade, fully impaling him. He half-fell into Artair, and for a moment they stood like that, almost embracing.

Bruce blinked up in stunned comprehension at Artair, the light already beginning to fade from his blue eyes. Then he slowly crumpled to the ground, sliding off the sword as he went. He fell halfway into the passageway, his life's blood pooling in the ashes at the bottom of the fireplace.

Only when the traitorous coward's eyes glazed in death did Artair look away.

"Sybil, are ye—"

He turned to find himself facing a wall of Highlanders. The other three Horsemen had tucked Sybil behind them, using their bodies to shield her. All three had their swords raised and ready to attack had Artair failed to eliminate Bruce.

"I am all right," she said somewhere behind them.

The Horsemen parted, and suddenly the sword was falling from his hand and he was striding toward her. She rushed forward too, and they met in a hard embrace that stole his breath.

"Ye headstrong, reckless lass," he murmured into her hair. "Ye could have been killed for that bit with the hair clasp."

"Aye, but it worked," she countered.

"Ye willnae ever be told what to do, will ye, princess?"

"Nay," she said simply, which drew muffled snorts from the others.

Artair drew back to look her in the eyes. "No' even when I make ye my wife?"

She gave him a dazzling, teary grin and a half-sob, half-laugh escaped her. "Nay, *especially* no' then."

He kissed her, deep and long, thanking every saint and lucky star that she was safe. And she was his.

He would not have stopped, but someone discreetly cleared a throat, drawing him reluctantly back.

"If the castle isnae already ours, it will be soon enough," Domnall said. "Well done, MacKinnon."

Artair instantly sobered, recalling their larger mission. He turned to the other three, but he kept Sybil tucked close to his side, unwilling to permit even a hair's breadth of space between them.

"We could use the passageway to get word to Douglas," Tavish suggested in a low voice.

"Shouldnae we give chase to Balliol?" Gregor demanded, scowling. "Gather a few men and set out after him?"

Though it clearly irked him, Domnall shook his head. "We are only a few miles from the border. Balliol has likely already crossed into England, and we cannae go charging off onto English soil to give chase."

"What of our pledge? We vowed we wouldnae stop until we got justice—and vengeance—for all Balliol has done?" Gregor insisted.

"Aye," Domnall murmured, glancing at each man in turn. "We vowed to rain hellfire down on Balliol and those who aided him. The traitor Andrew Murray has been hanged for his crimes."

"Balliol ordered my village burned to the ground," Tavish said tightly. "The man who lit the fire is now dead."

"Along with Alexander Bruce, who would have handed half of Scotland over to Edward of England to save his own arse," Artair added, not bothering to spare the man's corpse a glance.

"But most importantly," Domnall went on, "we aimed to oust Balliol from the throne and reinstate the loyalists to protect David's claim. Balliol may have survived the night, but he cannae pretend to be the King of Scotland anymore."

Domnall clapped a hand on Gregor's massive shoulder. "Let the Usurper crawl his way across England with his tail between his legs. Let him cry to Edward about his many failures. The fact is, now he knows he cannae hold the crown, nor rally support in any corner of Scotland. And he knows if he tries to return, we'll be here waiting for him."

A chorus of murmured ayes rippled through them at that.

Artair released a long breath. It didn't bring his brother back. Naught would. But for the first time since Ewan's death and the disaster at Dupplin Moor, the knot of pain that lived in his chest loosened ever so slightly.

They'd done it. Less than three months after Balliol had declared himself King of Scotland, they'd raised an army, delivered a surprise attack, and driven the Usurper off Scottish soil.

Aye, Balliol might still find support with Edward, despite his utter failure as a Pretender King. Mayhap he would even try again to yoke Scotland under him. But if they could throw him off once, under seemingly impossible odds, they could do it again. They'd be more than ready to answer the call to defend Scotland once more.

And this time, they'd be even stronger, for they weren't alone anymore.

He looked down at Sybil, who leaned her head on his shoulder as she listened to the others as they spoke of securing the castle.

Aye, having her by his side was his greatest strength of all.

EPILOGUE

Scottish Highlands
Three weeks later

Sybil let contentment wash over her as she took in the Yuletide cheer surrounding her.

The MacAyre clan keep's great hall was decked in holly and evergreen boughs, which filled the hall with the sweet, sharp scent of pine. The massive hearth on the far side, along with the lit torches lining the walls, cast a merry glow that was reflected on the faces of all those gathered.

The keep was filled to bursting with MacAyre clanspeople. They sat at the trestle tables eating, drinking, and toasting their good fortune. There was much to celebrate. Not only had the Usurper King Balliol been ousted, but their Laird had at last returned home—with a lady-wife by his side.

Lady Ailsa MacAyre, née Murray, had only arrived at her new home a fortnight before, but it was obvious to

Sybil that not only had Ailsa taken to her new role like a duck to water, but the clanspeople adored and welcomed her as well.

Sybil looked on as Ailsa exchanged a quiet word with Laird Domnall MacAyre across the high table from where she and Artair sat. Something the warrior-laird said to her made her blush prettily before she swatted his arm.

On Laird MacAyre's other side, Gregor MacLeod lifted his ale mug in salute. "My compliments again, Mistress Lorraine. This is the finest ale I've ever had—and believe me, I've sampled my fair share."

Echoes of hearty agreement circled around the high table where the four Highland warriors and their wives —along with Sybil's father, who was deep in an animated conversation with Birdie MacLeod about clan relations in the Highlands—sat savoring their drinks after the evening's feast.

Next to Sybil, Lorraine, Tavish MacNeal's bonny bride and brew-master, flushed and tipped her head modestly. "'Tis my pleasure to share it with ye all."

That was met with more ayes. Tavish, who wasn't a man of many words but who was clearly smitten with his wife, slipped an arm around her and scooted her chair closer to his.

"How fortunate we are to end Yule together," Tavish murmured, his hazel gaze flicking to each person at the high table in turn.

Fortunate was a wee bit of an understatement, Sybil thought with an inward smile.

Firstly, it was a miracle that the four Highlanders,

who were still called the Four Horsemen in awed whispers all across Scotland, were alive today. Surviving the loyalists' devastating defeat at Dupplin Moor was a feat in itself. Then they'd escaped Balliol's noose—either by an act of God or the Devil, the men jested darkly among themselves—only to lead a rebellion that booted Balliol from Scotland in no more than his nightshirt.

And now here they all sat, closing the Yuletide season together with their wives by their sides, their bellies full and their ale mugs brimming. Thanks to them, Robert the Bruce's heir had been restored, and Scotland was free once again of Edward of England's would-be puppet reign.

Even after their resounding victory at Annan, reaching MacAyre lands in this remote corner of the Highlands in time for the final days of Yule had been its own adventure for each of them.

Once the loyalists had secured the castle, the three other Horsemen had departed with all haste. Laird MacAyre had traveled to the Western Isles to collect Ailsa, then continued on straight to MacAyre lands. Tavish had headed east across the Lowlands to rejoin Lorraine, then the two of them had set out on the long trek to the Highlands for this gathering.

And after appointing Lamond, his trusted right-hand man, to lead the loyalist army on its slower trek north, Gregor had ridden ahead to the Highlands, where he and his new wife, Birdie, had made their home with her family on Morgan lands.

For their part, Sybil and Artair had journeyed back

to Scone with her father before setting out for the Highlands.

There was much to do back at the palace. Parliament was set to formally strip Balliol of his title and crown, though it was more for ceremony's sake, for no one expected the Usurper to show himself in Scotland again for a long while.

And her father was leading an effort to codify David II's claim to the throne in writing, and working with parliament to ensure the Kingship couldn't be stolen again.

Both Sybil and Artair had been helping him with the finer points of diplomacy and politics, which left them little time to celebrate their new marriage.

Practically the moment Annan Castle was brought under the loyalists' control and the last of Balliol's guards had surrendered, Artair had declared that he meant for them to be wed as soon as possible. She'd protested that as the daughter of the Guardian, the occasion was of political import and therefore would require planning and preparation. That had only given him cause to call her princess and tease her for wanting a grand celebration.

She'd relented—after a lengthy debate—and had agreed to wed just as soon as they returned to Scone. But apparently when he'd said "as soon as possible," he'd meant that very day.

After scouring the castle, they found the priest Balliol had brought in to wed Sybil and Bruce cowering in one of the tower keep's garderobes. With her father and the three other Horsemen as witnesses, the priest had conducted a hasty wedding ceremony in the great hall, after which they'd all departed, going their separate ways.

With an escort from Nevin, Dermid, and the other Douglas guards, the journey to Scone had been uneventful, though rather different than she'd pictured their honeymoon. The political goings-on at the palace had kept them busy for a sennight, then they'd hastened to the Highlands for this celebration.

Only now, sitting beside Artair, their hands clasped and resting on his powerful thigh beneath the table, did Sybil feel as though she had a moment to catch her breath and enjoy this moment with her husband.

She looked around the table at the warm smiles of the women and the relaxed ease of the men. Her family had shrunk over the years. First John had gone to foster in France, and then her mother had passed on to heaven. It had been only her and her father for some years now.

But in this moment, as the hour grew late and the Yule log burned low, she knew she'd gained a whole new family. The Horsemen were blood brothers for life now. And she liked to think that their wives would grow to be like sisters to her.

And then there was the family she and Artair would build. It was far too early to know, but she wouldn't be surprised if she came to be with child in the coming months. Artair made love to her with a fierce determination that stole her breath, showing her with each kiss and touch just how deep his love ran. And as in all areas between them, she met him with equal resolve to do the same.

"I dinnae wish to spoil this eve with talk of business," Laird MacAyre said, "but I have a bit of news."

The three other Highlanders, along with Sybil's father, straightened in their chairs.

"Balliol is apparently spending Yule at Carlisle Castle," Domnall went on. "He's already pleading his case with Edward from there, making it known far and wide that if reinstalled to power, he'd carry out his promise to pledge fealty to England and cede much of Scotland to Edward."

"Bloody rotting bastard," Gregor muttered under his breath. Birdie placed a soothing hand over her husband's balled fist, which worked surprisingly well to calm the giant warrior.

"My sentiments exactly," Domnall commented dryly.

"Any word on Edward's willingness to prop Balliol up again?" Sybil's father asked, leaning over the table.

"Nay, none," Domnall replied. "I cannae imagine he'll be in a great hurry to lend Balliol more support given the Usurper's utter failure thus far."

"But if he does," Artair murmured, "we'll be ready for him."

"Aye," the others said in unison.

"Enough of such matters," Domnall said, his features easing into a smile. "And let us have more of Mistress Lorraine's ale." He motioned to a nearby servant, but Artair held up his hand to stay more from being poured into his mug.

"I'll beg yer pardon, but I believe my wife and I will be retiring early this eve," he said, flashing Sybil a warm look.

A rumble of mock displeasure went around the table.

"The night is young, man."

"There is still *uisge beatha* to drink, MacKinnon."

"Come now," Ailsa pipped up over the men, flashing a grin. "They are newlyweds. They must be given some leeway to sneak off early."

Birdie gave a chortle. "Come to think of it, arenae we all newlyweds?"

"In that case—" Tavish shot to his feet, extending his hand to Lorraine. "Let us be off, my new-wed bride."

Lorraine took his hand, and without another word, the two scampered off toward the stairs that led to the guest chambers.

Gregor didn't even wait for Birdie to rise. He simply lifted her out of her chair and flung her over his shoulder. She laughed as he carried her to the stairs.

With a bit more dignity, as befitted their title of Laird and Lady, Domnall rose and offered his arm to Ailsa. Blushing, she took it and allowed him to escort her away, to the cheers of those gathered in the hall.

"Come on, then," Artair whispered to her. Taking her hand, he pulled her after him toward their own chamber.

"Bloody young people," her father muttered as they hurried from the raised dais. Though he hid it behind his mug of ale, she caught a glimpse of his wry grin before she lost sight of him.

Once they reached their chamber and Artair had firmly shut the door behind them, she expected him to haul her straight to the plush bed. But he surprised her by moving to the armoire instead.

"What are ye about?" she said, watching him.

"I have something to give ye," he said over his shoulder as he rummaged through their hanging clothes.

He returned with a wooden box the size of his palm.

"A belated wedding gift, ye could call it."

Sybil felt an excited smile spread on her face. "Ye didnae have to."

"Aye, of course I did. Go on, then."

She eased open the box's lid. Inside sat a hair clasp of delicately woven gold inset with a dozen pearls. A gasp stole from her throat.

"It isnae the same as the one ye lost," he hastened to say. "It cannae take its place, but——"

She flung herself into his arms, nearly knocking the box and the clasp from his hold.

"How did ye…"

"Yer father told me," he said into her hair. "Do ye remember that he and I disappeared for a moment before the priest wed us?"

At her nod, he went on.

"'Twas a bit late, I admit, but I asked his permission to marry ye. I promised him I'd love ye, protect ye, and cherish ye all my days if he would bless our union. I also spoke of yer bravery, and yer cleverness, and yer strength of heart—all of which he knew already, of course. When I told him of yer courage in incapacitating Bruce, he explained what that clasp meant to ye—and him."

His rugged features darkened for a moment. "Though it was yer mother's, I didnae believe ye'd wish to wear it again after…"

Sybil shook her head decisively. "Nay, I wouldnae have ever been able to look at it again without thinking of *him.*"

Artair's frown eased at that. "Good, then I didnae err in no' retrieving it. But I still owed ye a wedding gift. I would have given this to ye sooner, but the palace jeweler needed a full sennight to make it."

She breathed a laugh. "It was rather short notice for him, after all."

"Indeed." He pulled out of their embrace and removed the clasp from its box. Then he turned her by the shoulders so that her back was to him. "This doesnae replace the one yer father gave yer mother, and that she gave ye," he murmured, removing the simple pins holding the plaits back from her face. "But mayhap it will become the one ye give *our* daughter someday."

With the clasp fastened, he turned her back to face him. He was little more than a blur through the tears that suddenly filled her eyes.

"Aye, I'd like that," she whispered around the lump in her throat. She blinked hard to clear the tears. "And of our sons, the first shall be named Ewan."

Now it was his turn to fight against a sudden surge of emotion. He gazed down at her, his misted green eyes cutting straight to her heart. "I cannae wait to meet our bairns, lass. Which means we'd better get to work."

Abruptly, he scooped her off her feet and carried her to the bed. She only had time to shriek in surprised delight before he sealed her mouth with a kiss.

The End

AUTHOR'S NOTE

As always, it is one of my great joys in writing historical romance to combine a fictional romantic storyline with real historical details. Plus, it's such a treat to share not only a thrilling, passionate, and emotional love story with you, lovely readers, but to give you a glimpse at my research into the history surrounding this book as well.

And from a research and history perspective, this one is a doozy! Like all the main heroes and heroines of my stories, Artair and Sybil are fictitious characters. But they are surrounded by real people, places, and events that are too fascinating not to mention.

The entire Four Horsemen of the Highlands series was based on a relatively narrow window of time, from August to December of 1332. It was a tumultuous time in which Edward Balliol (son of John Balliol, one-time King of Scotland and puppet of England) made a grab for the Scottish throne while Robert the Bruce's heir, David II, was only eight years old. The country was being run by various Guardians and parliament at the time.

In the summer of 1332, Edward Balliol sailed from England to Scotland with a sizable force of mainly English soldiers, along with some disgruntled Scottish nobles. He was met by a loyalist army that vastly outnumbered his, but thanks to a bit of help (the traitor Andrew Murray of Tullibardine placed a stake in the River Earn, where the two armies were camped, to mark a spot for Balliol's men to cross undetected), he secured a surprise victory over the loyalists. He then marched to Scone and crowned himself King, despite not having parliament's approval.

Not long after that, he left Scone and bounced around through the Lowlands to gather support. Though Edward III of England had supplied Balliol with men, he hadn't formally announced his support. It was during this time, around October, that Balliol publicly declared that Scotland was and always had been a fief of England, pledged his fealty to Edward, and promised to cede five Lowland shires, along with several other significant towns, to Edward in exchange for his official backing.

At the same time, Archibald Douglas, Guardian of Scotland (a real historical figure) offered Balliol a truce, presumably to buy parliament time to decide how to proceed—either recognize Balliol's new claim to the throne, or continue to support David. For the purposes of my story, I played with this timeline a bit, but both Balliol's public declaration of loyalty to Edward of England and Douglas's offered truce did in fact happen.

While he waited for Edward's formal backing, Balliol retired to Annan Castle for the holiday season. The castle had indeed once belonged to the Bruce family, but had been gifted to the Balliols when the Bruces moved their family seat to Lochmaben Castle. Annan Castle had originally been built in the early twelfth century as a wooden motte-and-bailey-style castle, but had been converted to stone somewhere along the way. A flood sometime in the mid-twelfth century disrupted the course of the River Annan, which partially eroded the back of the castle mound or "motte."

In general, while it had once been considered the ultimate defensive design, the motte-and-bailey style of castle had fallen out of favor by the turn of the fourteenth century. War machines had become more powerful, and wooden structures were being replaced with larger stone fortifications with thick walls and multiple towers. By the time Balliol took refuge there, Annan Castle was no longer a modern military fortress, yet with a truce in hand from the Guardian of Scotland, he likely felt confident in his position.

So confident, in fact, that he dismissed almost all of his troops for Yule. Perhaps this was done to save the cost of housing and feeding so many men-at-arms. Or maybe he really was so sure of his position that he saw no risk in sending his troops away. Whatever the case, it would prove to be a disastrous decision, for in the wee hours of the morning on December 16, 1332, a loyalist army led by none other than Archibald Douglas attacked Annan.

While the loyalist victory was swift and decisive,

Balliol managed to escape. He was said to have fled "through a hole in the wall" according to some accounts, and either "half-dressed," in only a nightshirt, or completely naked, depending on which historical record you ask. Some even say he wore only boots (or one boot) as he flung himself onto the back of a horse that hadn't even been bridled and fled for the English border a few miles away. He took refuge at Carlisle Castle for Yule, all the while publicly pleading his case to Edward III for his support.

Alexander Bruce—another real historical figure—was also present at Annan Castle when it was sieged by loyalists. He had indeed fought at the Battle of Dupplin Moor for the loyalist cause. Though his legitimacy is a bit fuzzy, he was eventually recognized as the son of Edward Bruce, younger brother to King Robert the Bruce, and inherited his father's title of Earl of Carrick.

Despite the fact that David, his first cousin, was in line for the throne, Alexander Bruce flipped allegiances after Dupplin Moor, joining Balliol's side. It wasn't entirely unheard of for nobles at this time to be rather... flexible with their loyalties, especially if changing sides meant living to fight another day, but Bruce is an unusual case given his family ties.

During the siege on Annan Castle, Bruce was nearly killed before he was recognized. The loyalists opted to take him prisoner rather than kill him, though for the sake of my story, he wasn't quite so lucky. Oddly enough, he later changed back to the loyalist side again. He fought against Balliol and Edward of England in their renewed attempt to take Scotland at the Battle of

Halidon Hill less than a year later. Bruce died on the battlefield.

And here is where, as a writer, I have to marvel that history is wilder than any fiction I could come up with. In researching for this book, I'd been searching for a Scottish noble to be Sybil's fiancé—one who had switched from the loyalist cause to Balliol's side. I could have made up a fictional noble, but Alexander Bruce fit the bill perfectly, so I "cast" him in the story. It was only after I'd selected him as Sybil's fiancé that I learned the real Alexander Bruce had actually been married...to Archibald Douglas's only daughter!

Douglas, who was indeed brother to James the Black Douglas, feared warrior, leader, and right-hand man to Robert the Bruce, became Guardian of Scotland at one of the most turbulent moments in Scottish history. Unfortunately, he, too, died at the Battle of Halidon Hill along with Bruce and many others.

His one (known) daughter was named Eleonor, and she was indeed married to Alexander Bruce. After her marriage to Bruce ended with his death, she was married four more times. Little else is known of her, sadly. Interestingly, Douglas also had two sons—William, who became the first Earl of Douglas, and John, who served in none other than David II's retinue in France! Can't make this stuff up!

Regarding my depiction of Scone Palace—the medieval-era palace, along with Scone Abbey, where Scottish kings were traditionally crowned, was sacked during the Reformation. Little remains of the original structure besides a few sketches of the foundation. The palace was rebuilt in 1580 and remodeled in the 19th century, but archeologists and historians still aren't exactly sure what the original building looked like.

So, what is a historical romance author to do? Scone Palace is featured as a main setting in one of my previous books (*Surrender to the Scot*: Highland Bodyguards, Book 7 – and no, I didn't mean to make this new book's title so similar to that one. Total coincidence!). So I re-read all my descriptions of the palace from that book and used it as source material for my depiction of Scone Palace in the new book. Who knows how historically accurate my version of the palace is, but at least in my writing world they will be consistent.

And one more little note—as a nod to my original depiction of Edward Balliol in *Surrender to the Scot*, in which he sits alone in a great hall, eating, that was also how Sybil and Artair first meet him in this story. I also matched his physical description from that book to this one.

Thank you for journeying back to medieval Scotland with me, and here's to many more stories to share!

THANK YOU!

Thank you for taking the time to read *Sworn to the Scot* (Four Horsemen of the Highlands, Book 4)!

And thank you in advance for sharing your enjoyment of this book (or my other books) with fellow readers by leaving a review on Amazon. Long or short, detailed or to the point, I read all reviews and greatly appreciate you for writing one!

Want another historical romance story for FREE? Sign up for my newsletter and have "Aegir's Daughter" (A Viking Lore Short Story) sent directly to you. Sign up at www.EmmaPrinceBooks.com. Happy reading!

TEASERS FOR EMMA PRINCE'S BOOKS

The Sinclair Brothers Trilogy:

Go back to where it all began—with Robert and Alwin's story in *Highlander's Ransom*, Book One of the Sinclair Brothers Trilogy. Available now on Amazon.

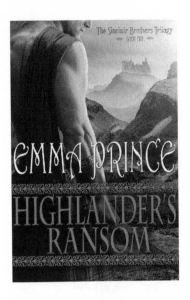

He was out for revenge...

Laird Robert Sinclair will stop at nothing to exact revenge on Lord Raef Warren, the English scoundrel who brought war to his doorstep and razed his lands and people. Leaving his clan in the Highlands to conduct covert attacks in the Borderlands, Robert lives to be a thorn in Warren's side. So when he finds a beautiful English lass on her way to marry Warren, he whisks her away to the Highlands with a plan to ransom her back to her dastardly fiancé.

She would not be controlled...

Lady Alwin Hewett had no idea when she left her father's manor to marry a man she'd never met that she would instead be kidnapped by a Highland rogue out for vengeance. But she refuses to be a pawn in any man's game. So when she learns that Robert has had them secretly wed, she will stop at nothing to regain her freedom. But her heart may have other plans...

Highland Bodyguards Series:

The Lady's Protector, the thrilling start to the Highland Bodyguards series, is available now on Amazon!

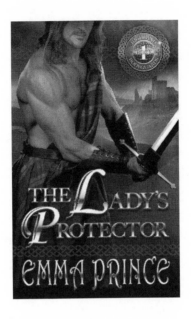

The Battle of Bannockburn may be over, but the war is far from won.

Her Protector...

Ansel Sutherland is charged with a mission from King Robert the Bruce to protect the illegitimate son of a powerful English Earl. Though Ansel bristles at aiding an Englishman, the nature of the war for Scottish independence is changing, and he is honor-bound to serve as a bodyguard. He arrives in England to fulfill his assign-ment, only to meet the beautiful but secretive Lady Isolda, who refuses to tell him where his ward is. When a mysterious attacker threatens Isolda's life, Ansel realizes he is the only thing standing between her and deadly peril.

His Lady...

Lady Isolda harbors dark secrets—secrets she refuses to reveal to the rugged Highland rogue who arrives at her castle demanding answers. But Ansel's dark eyes cut through all her defenses, threatening to undo her resolve. To protect her past, she cannot submit to the white-hot desire that burns between them. As the threat to her life spirals out of control, she has no choice but to trust Ansel to whisk her to safety deep in the heart of the Highlands...

Viking Lore Series:

Love brave, bold Vikings as much as Highlanders? Step into the lush, daring world of the Vikings with **Enthralled** (Viking Lore, Book 1)!

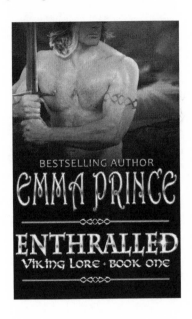

He is bound by honor...

Eirik is eager to plunder the treasures of the fabled lands to the west in order to secure the future of his village. The one thing he swears never to do is claim possession over another human being. But when he journeys across the North Sea to raid the holy houses of Northumbria, he encounters a dark-haired beauty, Laurel, who stirs him like no other. When his cruel cousin tries to take Laurel for himself, Eirik breaks his oath in an attempt to protect her. He claims her as his thrall. But can he claim her heart, or will Laurel fall prey to the devious schemes of his enemies?

She has the heart of a warrior...

Life as an orphan at Whitby Abbey hasn't been easy, but Laurel refuses to be bested by the backbreaking work and lecherous advances she must endure. When Viking raiders storm the abbey and take her captive, her strength may finally fail her—especially when she must face her fear of water at every turn. But under Eirik's gentle protection, she discovers a deeper bravery within herself—and a yearning for her golden-haired captor that she shouldn't harbor. Torn between securing her freedom or giving herself to her Viking master, will fate decide for her—and rip them apart forever?

ABOUT THE AUTHOR

USA Today bestselling author Emma Prince whisks readers away to another time and place with her steamy historical romances—where the passion is legendary, the adventure never ends, and the happily ever afters are guaranteed!

After several years as a college English instructor (where she savored her "fun books"—usually historical romances—on the side), Emma turned her love of page-turning, richly historical stories into a career. She lives in drizzly Seattle with her husband, their daughter (the wee lass) and a crazy cat named Oban (after the town in Scotland or the whisky made there, depending on who you ask).

Emma loves connecting with readers! Sign up for her newsletter and be the first to hear about the latest book news, flash sales, giveaways, and more—signing up is free and easy at www.EmmaPrinceBooks.com.

Follow Emma on Amazon and BookBub for alerts on sales and new releases. Or join her on Facebook for loads of fun at: www.facebook.com/EmmaPrinceBooks.